ORIGO

SON OF DARKNESS

BOOK ONE OF THE ORIGO SERIES

by

KERI BROWN

Illustrated by:

Phil Eads
Austin Blockson
Keri Brown

Seven Brownies Pub

Origo
Son of Darkness
by Keri Brown

First Printing – February 2021
ISBN: 978-1-7340241-0-4

Printed in the U.S.A.

FOR JIM

CONTENTS

Contents

PROLOGUE

In the beginning, the Great Mistress of the Stars was dancing along the cosmos when she discovered the young Earth. Inspired by its beauty, she decided to create a little world of her own. She took a pinch of soil, a drop of water, a gust of wind, and a flicker of fire from Earth, pulled them into space, rolled them together, and sprinkled stardust on them. A unique and powerful scale called a 'Qi' formed on each of them, and they became the first dragons—elemental, immortal, and perfect.

The Mistress pulled a dead star from the heavens, rubbed it against the sun, and then gave it a kiss of life, creating the Magma Heart. She put it between the dragons, and they covered it with soil, water, wind, and lava. The Magma Heart gave life to the lands, creating a diversity of creatures and vegetation in four continents arranged by compass. And thus, Origo was born, an unseen planet that follows closely behind Earth's orbit.

She doted on her creations with pride and love but knew something was amiss. Four powerful dragons ruled over a world of lesser creatures with little to no special powers. Something needed to bridge the gap. After several days of consideration, she came to one conclusion. Only dragons could relate to dragons, and creatures of lesser power could only relate to their own kind. So, she merged the two.

From that point forward, all dragons hatched as creatures of the lands. This would be their Dú. As such, they would grow shoulder to shoulder with other humans, elves, wolves, or whatever their Dú was. Upon maturity, an emerald Qi would appear on their chest, releasing their dragon form to represent and rule their communities as viceroys. Before long, DúHumans, DúElves, DúWolves, and many other types of dragons filled the lands. Origo became a harmonious society of mythical creatures and viceroys under dragon rulers called Qings.

Despite the Mistress's best efforts to create a utopia, evil found its way into the heart of one of her Qings. He was overpowered but still managed to take half the planet with him and set a path for the Son of Darkness.

CHAPTER 1

Whistling and roaring, the strong autumn winds rushed through the trees. Leaves of red, yellow, and brown danced in swirling spectacles, then descended to create a brittle blanket over the bare soil.

A sharp burst of air shot from the ground, giving a few leaves one last dance. A pair of eyes blinked open from the leafy forest floor. Dark green scales multiplied around the eyes while a large groaning yawn poured thick grey smoke over the ground.

Incognito, known as 'Inco,' was a young-adult DúHuman named for his ability to mimic his surroundings by reflecting them and appearing as an undulating apparition. He rolled his massive, jaguar-like body to an upright position. The rough bark of a fallen tree shifted in appearance, revealing scutes that trailed to the spade-shaped tip of the tree.

But it wasn't a tree. It continued to transform until his entire tail was visible. He rose to his feet, stretching his muscular arms and wiggling the five talon-tipped fingers of each paw. He curled his feet, cracking the knuckles of all eight toes.

Finally, the creature stood and shook his body free of the forest debris that had settled on him in his slumber. His majestic, lion-like mane waved back and forth through the air, giving contest to the elegant dance of the surrounding leaves. When he stopped, his dark brown hair fell perfectly into place between the three curved horns on either side of his head and hugged the back of his neck. He pulled a small twig from the hair along his jaw and used it to scratch his scaly chest. His attention turned to the soft, snoring sounds beside him.

There, napping in the leaves, was Gray, who was solid grey from snoot to spade, save his emerald green Qi. The dark smoke from Inco's yawn rolled along the ground toward Gray. It crept over his head like a fluffy black pillow. He let out a cackling cough and quickly pulled his head up and out of the dark smog.

"Which end did that cloud of death come from?"

Inco flashed a grin, then cleared his expression as he stretched out on the ground. As his face passed Gray's, he puffed another small dark cloud right at him.

"Aw, come on," Gray complained.

Inco chuckled and used his tail to poke him, waited for him to turn, then tapped him on the back of the head.

Gray winced as he rubbed the spot on his head, not from pain, but a subconscious reflex.

"Challenge accepted," he declared in a low voice. "When you least expect it. Fear the wrath."

The wind picked up, lifting the smoke and pulling in the fresh air. The two dragons closed their eyes and raised their chins toward the treetops. They breathed deep, enjoying the coolness against the hot, stuffy autumn air.

The wind carried more than a cool reprieve. It also moved aromas from all around. Grass, flowers, and cattle smells mixed to form enticing scents. Deep breaths turned into sniffing. Inco suddenly had a taste for some beef.

"Stay here. I'm going to get us something to eat. I'll be right back."

Gray licked his lips. "A second supper sounds great."

"You're always hungry, aren't you?"

"There's so much more to choose from here on Earth. I want to try it all."

"Eat up. We return to Origo tonight."

He walked away, his nose still up, following the scent of meat. Cow, sheep, and a hint of rabbit all floated on the breeze. Inco's feet left the ground as he hovered high in the trees, following the strongest scents carried by the breeze. Not having wings, their flight was like all other dragon abilities: drawn from their Qi. The single scale lent them grace over a winged dragon thrashing about with their large leathery wings.

Inco's nose led him to a grassy field hugging the tree line. It flowed to a small Anglo-Saxon village with grubhouses lining each side of a wide dirt road. The road tapered to a narrow path, leading to an offset dwelling, facing the rest of the village. A tall rickety fence around it penned three horses and several pigs.

"I suppose pork is out of the question," Inco muttered. "Beef it is." He turned to follow the scent of cow when sounds of terror and pain echoed from the village.

Inco returned to the tree line and stood on his hind legs. A violent invasion of the tiny village unfolded before his eyes.

***

Women and children scurried into their homes at the command of their husbands and fathers just as fourscore of

Teulu men merged onto the road that led into the village, stopping just before the first home. There they stood, separated into four groups, waiting for orders.

"Ymosod," a man yelled from horseback at the back of the last group.

The first set of men set forth, carrying their swords and axes. They spread out, making their way through the village, slaughtering everyone in their path. There was no pattern to their savagery as they killed the village men without explanation. They murdered the elderly who were too slow to escape, and the women and children in the street.

A family of five dropped to their knees, the woman and three children huddled behind the husband, who begged for mercy. The assailant hesitated and looked to his fellow marauders, one of whom came to stand at his side. The villager redirected his plea to the second assailant, but before he could say anything, the savage thrust his sword through the kneeling man's chest.

The second group of invaders followed the first, carrying daggers on their hips. Each man had a large coil of rope hanging from his shoulder and a dog at his side. They went into the dwellings one by one, coming out with women and children bound with the rope.

Two horses, each with two guard dogs, stood at the edge of the village facing in. A man led a third horse away, pulling women and children by a rope fastened to the saddle. Another line of women and children screamed while being dragged to the edge of the village. They saw the departing horse and cried louder.

Despite their pleas, many of them followed without a struggle. They feared for the lives of their families if they didn't comply. A few women, bold enough to struggle, were beaten and whipped.

One woman fought the hardest, refusing to comply with any command. After manhandling her, the attacker threw her to the ground and whistled. His dog jumped onto the woman, and viciously tore into her. Her children sobbed while their mother kicked and screamed, but with her hands bound, she couldn't stop the dog. It continued to bite and tear at her flesh. She died within moments. The man untied the rope from her hands and yanked her sobbing children away.

A particular member of the Teulu stood out as he was far larger than all the others. He paced up and down the village road on the back of a massive, long-haired horse. Steering the beast with one hand, he cradled a loaded crossbow tailored to match his enormous size in the other. A strap crossed his chest down to his hip, where it held a quiver of extra-large bolts. Not only was he the biggest man among the Teulu, but he was also the only one armed with a crossbow.

The third group of pillagers led three horses to each end of the village road. They fanned out to search the houses and re-emerged with their arms full of valuables—blankets, clothing, tools, weapons, and anything they could find. They loaded their spoils on the horses, running in and out until nothing useful remained. With so many raiders, none had to search more than one house.

The last group of six marauders carrying torches split into two groups as they moved down each side of the village road. After the loaded horses cleared, the first invader set fire to the roofs at the front of each grubhouse. The second walked behind, setting fire to the rooftops at the back. The third followed at a distance, placing his torch in various places to ensure the flames didn't go out.

Most of the men from the other groups had gone back to the laden horses, while a small group headed to the last home offset from the rest. Armed with swords, daggers, and rope, they joked among themselves as they reached the head of the path that led to it.

Inside, a woman huddled in a corner with her newborn. Her mussed light brown hair stuck with sweat to her forehead. Blood of childbirth spattered her plain blue dress. A few paces away, her husband peeked through a narrow gap between the door and its frame. When he saw the men approaching, he ran to his wife. He helped her to her feet and rushed her toward the door.

"Are you ready?" The man asked in a hushed panic.

She didn't answer.

"Æmma."

"No," she whispered through heavy breathing.

"Come, there's no time."

He paused to admire his newborn son, his fingertips hovering over the baby's coal-black hair. Holding a memory of the wide-set blue eyes, flat nose, and dimpled chin, he pulled his hand away. He kissed his newborn's frail, reddish-brown forehead as Æmma looked on lovingly. She put her hand on his cheek and rubbed her thumb over his short facial hair.

"Ælwulf…" she faltered, but in her loss of words, her eyes spoke for her. They radiated with love and fear; her light blue irises seemed to float in the glistening tears that welled below them. She took her hand off his cheek to wipe a tear before it fell.

He opened the door enough to peer out, then pulled the door open wide.

"Now. On the horse."

She held her infant close and ran to the horse. He followed and took the baby while his exhausted, aching wife climbed onto the horse. Once his tiny family was secure, Ælwulf lifted himself behind them.

The approaching raiders were talking and joking among themselves and, at first, didn't notice the running couple. As they ascended the hill, coming into the line of sight, one noticed and alerted the others.

"Stop," they shouted as they ran up the path.

"Hold on," Ælwulf yelled.

He smacked the horse's rear, and it ran, bursting through the rickety fence.

***

In the woods, Gray caught sight of a plump deer, munching some greenery. It was an excellent opportunity to practice hunting and show his accomplishment to Inco. He crept forward, close to the ground until he could taste it in the air. As he prepared to strike, a scream echoed from the village, snapping his attention toward where Inco was standing. His sudden movement startled the deer, and it ran off, but he barely noticed. He made his way to Inco's side and watched the couple escape the village with a mounted bowman charging toward them.

Ælwulf steered the horse in a zig-zag pattern through the field. Crossbow bolts hissed around them. He didn't know it, but he was headed straight toward Inco and Gray, concealed in the tree line.

The baby screamed in protest at the vigorous handling. Æmma yearned to soothe him but needed to hold on for balance. She tightened her arm around the baby, hoping to make him feel more secure.

A bolt struck the horse. It reared and twisted with a screaming neigh. The momentum of running caused it to fly through the air before landing on its side.

Æmma and Ælwulf hit the ground and rolled several times. Æmma lost her grip, and the infant flew from her arms, landing nearby. It let out a bloodcurdling, high-pitched scream. She struggled to crawl toward the infant, but the impact of the fall had rendered her breathless. She rolled in anguish, her mouth agape, unable to breathe.

Ælwulf scrambled toward her on his hands and knees. As he rose to his feet, a bolt shot through his neck. It pierced just under the jawline and protruded from the other side below the ear. He jerked up and fell backward.

Æmma finally drew in a deep breath and screamed. "No, no, no, no, no!" She cupped his cheeks in her palms, rubbing her thumbs gently under his eyes.

"Run," he choked.

Ignoring the risk, she leaned in for a kiss. In her mind, she knew it would be the last time their eyes would meet, the last time their lips would touch, and the last time she would feel his facial hair against her cheeks. In her heart, however, she knew nothing of the sort.

"My love," she cried as she pulled herself away.

Frantic with fear for her child, she followed the sounds of her screaming baby through the tall grass, scooped him up, and ran. Exhaustion of childbirth slowed her. The attackers gained ground with every laborious stride she took.

She pressed on, stumbling. A stream of blood rushed down her leg. She slowed her pace to look. A sudden, sharp pain consumed her upper body.

***

The dragons watched in horror as a bolt shot through the woman's back and emerged above her left breast. It barely missed the baby's head. She fell to the ground and crawled on her knees with one hand, holding her baby in the other.

Inco usually avoided getting involved in anything human, ignoring even the most horrible deeds of man. This senseless slaughter, however, was more than he could stand to watch. He'd had enough. Anger boiled. His face grew hot. His lungs quivered. He stepped out from the shelter of the trees and into the field, his eyes fixed on the men. In his peripheral vision, he watched Æmma.

***

She gasped in shock at the sight of Inco. She tried to scream, but the sheer force of terror held it in her throat. As she stared in horrified awe, she noticed that his attention was directed elsewhere. Death seemed to be coming from every direction, but the Teulu had shown aggression. The dragon had not. She slowly crawled out of his way and moved behind him, intending to continue into the woods. As she did, she found herself face-to-face with Gray.

"It's all right," he whispered. "We won't hurt you. Come, get behind me."

Æmma sensed no danger from Gray and was instantly compliant. She watched from behind his tail as Inco released a burst of flames over her assailants, scorching their hair.

***

Only singed, the men turned and ran. Inco assumed that would be the end. He sighed in relief as the men ran toward the village. It had worked better than he thought it would, but he didn't take time to wonder why. He turned to check on Æmma. From the corner of his eye, he noticed the Teulu regroup. His relief now short-lived, he braced himself for the men charging toward him, now thirty strong. The bowman kicked his horse and galloped through the crowd, taking the lead.

"I'm Gray. He's Inco." He lowered his body to be closer to Æmma.

She looked up at him, pain and astonishment pulling her expression in different directions. "Ah…" She choked. "Ah-ma."

"Whoa, whoa. Don't speak. Here, Æmma, is it? Rest over here." He guided her to a hollowed log with one paw behind her in case she fell.

A bolt flew in, headed directly at Inco's face. He saw it and sidestepped the impact. Time seemed to slow as the bolt drifted past his face towards Gray, then sped up before he could react. The broadhead wedged into the scales of Gray's leg.

He let out a pain-filled grunt and looked at Inco, who sighed in relief that the injury was minor. The two dragons shared silent expressions of anger, then turned their sights back to the attackers.

Gray was furious. His leg hurt, Æmma was injured, and the baby was now fatherless. He set his sights on the men who were fast approaching. His face twisted with anger as he rose to his feet.

Inco stepped aside, nodding in reverence. Gray took in a deep breath and released a massive, rolling cloud of dark and heavy smoke into the meadow. A charcoal fog engulfed the bright yellow grass, rising as its reach spread over the field.

Three men in front of the Teulu merged with the cloud. The others slowed to a stop and shuffled backward. The bowman's horse reared and let out a panicked whinny before turning and slamming back down to all fours. Struggling to stay mounted, the bowman unintentionally released a bolt from his crossbow. It zipped through the smoke and shattered through a branch near Inco's head.

An attacker hurtled from within the cloud and plummeted to the ground behind his brothers. Another screamed as he flew from the smoke in a different direction. He silenced with a crunch as he landed on his head. The attackers huddled together. Blood sprayed them from one side to the other, then doused them from the opposite direction. They wiped their eyes and gawped at the smoke, recoiling in shock. A limp, tattered body spun through the air over them.

Gray emerged from the smoke. Blood covered his snarling mouth and dripped from his mane onto his chest. He scanned the enemy and took in another deep breath, his mouth wide, displaying a bright grey glow within his throat. He released the breath: a thundering roar of smoke. Orange and red flecks danced in the cloud. He took another quick breath and freed it with another roar.

The smoke burst into grey flames that covered the advancing enemy, incinerating everything and everyone it touched. The blaze cut a wide swath through the grass, taking on a life of its own, spreading in all directions before thinning to a snuff.

Gray ended his fiery breath and glared at the bowman, who stared back through the aim of his crossbow. The rest of the men seemed to be following his lead. Gray realized that if he took out the bowman, perhaps the others would flee, but as another deep breath filled his lungs, the bowman released the bolt. It pierced Gray's neck, and he fell.

***

Inco felt a thud echo shake the ground. Knowing it could only have come from something the size of a dragon, he looked at the cloud of smoke that was dissolving in the light breeze. Panic and rage shook him to the core as the fog gave way to the shape of a collapsed dragon. He shot from the forest and used all four limbs to scoop Gray from the ground, then turned back into the cloud to place him behind the hollowed log. He would be safe there.

The remaining attackers gathered around the bowman and howled in victory, believing the dragons to be in retreat.

"Cadfael! Cadfael! Cadfael!" They chanted, waving their weapons in celebration. The horseman spread his arms, welcoming the praise of his fellow men. His celebration was brief as he saw a dragon-shaped apparition move through the waning smoke cloud.

"Ysbryd," he shouted, yanking on the reins of his horse to turn and run. A few attackers followed while the others huddled in fear and confusion, watching the haziness above.

Inco descended over their heads and crushed them with his feet. A bolt shot into the bony flail at the end of his tail. He pressed a scaly finger against one nostril and shot a melon-sized ball of fire from the other. It landed at the feet of the horse, causing it to rear up.

The bowman fell to the ground and tried to get back on the horse. It protested with a groaning neigh and galloped away. The rider crouched and scurried to a patch of extra tall grass. It failed to conceal him. He reached for a bolt, only to find an empty quiver.

Inco carefully blew a circle of fire around the patch of tall grass.

"You there. You have nowhere to run. Tell me, why are you terrorizing this village?"

"The land," he answered timidly. "It's rightfully ours. They took it from us, and we're here to take it back."

"And the prisoners?"

"We were going to let them go."

"The truth," Inco snapped.

"Slaves… a-and workers for the fields. We would've treated them well, I swear. Please," he choked, "let me go."

"Very well." He walked away. "You may go."

The man rose to his feet, the grass at chest height. He swatted at the air, trying to clear the smoke, only to see the flames drawing closer. A breeze lightened the density of the smoke, and he looked around in a panic. Flames grew closer from every direction.

"Wait," the bowman screamed, "help me!"

Inco stared straight ahead with glazed eyes as he headed toward the village. He listened with indifference as the man screamed for help, then screamed for mercy until he could scream no more.

A man just outside of town kicked his horse to a gallop. The rope attached to the saddle jerked the line of women and children off their feet, dragging them by their bound hands.

Inco rushed to their aid, landing in front of the horse. It reared, then stomped its front legs nervously. The rider jumped down and ran into a field of crops. Inco used his claw to cut the saddle's mounting straps. The now bareback horse ran free, and the prisoners worked themselves loose.

Inco returned to the village to set the remaining prisoners free. They screamed in fear at the sight of the dragon.

"I won't hurt you."

He broke the rope just behind the horse, then used a nail to loosen the knot on the first woman's wrist. "You can untie the others. I can't fix your village, but you're free." He lifted off the ground and turned back toward the woods.

***

Gray opened his eyes to find himself beside a hollowed log in the forest. Æmma lay against the other end of the log. He shuffled toward her, grimacing at the pain until his nose was a breath away from the newborn, which lay silent and still in its cloth wrappings. Unsure if it was dead or sleeping, he nudged it with his nose. It squirmed and cried.

Æmma opened her eyes to a sliver. The dragon no longer alarmed her. Her only concern was for her baby's comfort.

She tried weakly to adjust the baby in her arms but lacked the strength. She embraced him, and the crying calmed to a quiet whimper. She tried to sit up, gasping with every movement, crying with every exhale. Her hopeless eyes found his.

A single tear rolled from his eye as he rested his head near her arms. She empathized with his despair. Knowing he wouldn't hurt her or the baby, she felt an emotional connection to him. She glanced at each of his wounds—wounds received in his attempt to protect her. She couldn't summon enough air to speak, so her eyes spoke for her. She rested a hand on his scaly nose. Her eyes locked with his, expressing her gratitude for the pain he suffered on her behalf.

Inco approached. His gaze swept over the woman and baby, taking in their poor condition. Gray had bolts in his neck, leg, and chest. Both of them were near death.

"My people." Æmma struggled. "They'll never be safe. Please—" She heaved several times, trying to speak. She stopped and took a deep, deliberate breath. "My baby." The words came more clearly. "Make sure he knows we loved him. His father was Ælwulf, son of Rædwald, and I—I am Æmma, daughter of Æthelric. Find someone to take—take care—of—" she faltered in her pain and inability to draw breath.

She lowered her head, holding her infant close, and gently sang to him. Gray, in great pain himself, moved closer to the sound of her voice, pressing lightly against the arm that held the baby. She caressed his face between his nose and mouth. Her words were cracked and broken, but her tone was soothing.

"*Slæp slæp, Lýtla bera, þū eart ġesund mid mē.*"

Her melody softened until it stopped. The life in her eyes faded, and her body sank in submission to death, but death would not yet take her. She'd merely lost consciousness, as had Gray.

Inco pulled Gray's Qi from his chest. He removed the bolts in his leg and neck and squeezed the Qi over each wound. A single green drop of xenum fell from the Qi and instantly healed the leg. Another droplet repaired the neck. He pulled the last bolt from Gray's chest, and blood rushed from the open wound. Inco pulled him away from Æmma and rolled him onto his back. He placed two green drops into the chest wound, watched it congeal and close up, and then returned the Qi to Gray's chest.

He nudged Æmma gently to loosen her grasp on the infant. The arm fell back lifelessly, but her fingers twitched. He stared at the shallow rise-and-fall of her chest until her heartbeat echoed faintly in his ears. His male xenum would be toxic to her female blood. There was no way to save her here, but he hoped to find someone who could, with speed and a little luck.

Picking up the infant carefully with his rough, scaly paw, it looked at him, cooing. He gently closed his fingers around the baby and lifted Æmma with his other paw. He stood tall with the baby to his chest and rose to hover just above the ground. Wrapping both of his back legs around Gray, he rose higher in the air as he flew over the trees. The baby was quiet as Inco soared over the woods and meadows. Soaring higher to cross the Sud Sæ, he made for the dragon cave at the highest peak of the Alpes Penninae.

CHAPTER 2

To avoid crushing his precious cargo, Inco rolled to his back as he landed in the cave. His eyes adjusting, he looked around, glancing at each of the flat stone slabs scattered along the walls. They were of various heights and shapes, and one was just right for Æmma.

He gently placed her on the stone slab, moving her arm to put the baby between it and her side. He adjusted Gray's body to lie flat on another slab, then retrieved the baby just as he cried again.

Inco hushed and bounced him in his massive paw as he made his way to the rounded corner of the cave near Gray. He stepped into the area, noting the accumulation of dust and debris. With his free paw, he wiped the area to clear a spot to sit, then brushed some dried bones from the pedestal that stood in the center.

He placed the baby on the pedestal and sat in the cleared dip, pausing to admire the outermost layer of fabric wrapped around it. Unlike the ratty, blood-stained layers beneath, the blanket spoke of elegance. It was made of a heavy, deep-green material and grey glyphs embroidered in exquisite detail.

The baby's fussing intensified, pulling Inco's attention back from the blanket. He removed his Qi and tipped it over the baby, releasing a single drop of xenum into the baby's mouth. The baby calmed as it made suckling sounds.

"You probably won't eat for months, now," Inco cooed.

As he put the Qi back on his chest, a magnetic force pulled it from his paw. It hovered over the baby and spun slowly before dropping onto the infant's chest, adhering to his skin.

Inco tried to remove the Qi from the infant's chest, but it had sealed on all sides. His scaly fingers slid over it. Panic set in. He pressed his thumb and forefinger into the skin on either side, making the Qi rise. He pinched his fingers underneath it but released when the baby whimpered. He tried again, but this time the baby squealed, startling him and causing his clumsy paw to scratch the baby across his chest. It screamed in pain, sending chills up his spine.

Taking a deep breath, he shook his frustration and panic away and looked at the baby with uncertainty. As with all dragons, his entire identity rested in his Qi… which had now found a new home on the baby's chest. His powers, strengths, abilities, and everything else he'd gained with his DúKrue, now belonged to this floppy, fleshy newborn.

His front paws were already starting to transform into hands. Before long, he would lose all of his abilities and features, retaining only his life span and the chest lines around the area where his Qi belonged. Soon he would be as meek and vulnerable as any human and wouldn't be able to take dragon form until he retrieved his Qi.

Frustration swelled within him once again. He reluctantly decided it best to take his Dú so he wouldn't slowly and awkwardly change. It would be easier to care for the baby in human form anyway, and there was no point in delaying the inevitable. He stepped away from the infant, took a deep breath, and let it out.

His body shrank. The black hair of his dragon mane came together as his head shifted to human form. His eyes grew smaller and closer together. His pupils rounded, and the yellow around his blue irises faded to white. The black whiskers on the sides of his face shortened and multiplied around his cheeks and jawline.

His long body shortened and straightened. The tail coiled into his lower back and disappeared. His back legs straightened and thinned. Paws shrank. Dragon toes moved closer together and shrank, with a fifth toe emerging on each foot. Arms thinned, and his front paws finished their transition into hands.

Inco stretched his human body, standing taller than an average man, with a lean muscular build. He approached the pedestal again, stared at the baby, and tried to think. His thoughts, however, were disturbed by the arrival of another dragon.

Boris stood on the ledge, took a deep breath, and let it out as he changed to his DúElf form. Even as an elf, he had faint scale lines in his fleshy skin, illuminating with the slightest touch of light.

"Hey, Inco, what do you have th—*Sweet mother of Drake*. Is that a human child?"

"Yes." Inco quickly adjusted the baby's cloth to conceal the Qi. "His mother was injured when her village was attacked. She ran into the woods where we were, but she passed out from her injuries." He pointed to Æmma, then turned the baby to be chest-to-chest and held him tight. "Her wounds are serious. She needs female xenum."

"Where's Gray?" Boris avoided looking at Æmma. Seeing her would set reality into what Inco had just said, and he wanted to avoid reflecting on the sadness. "I'm sure he's getting a kick out of this one, something smaller than him."

Inco glanced at Gray instead of answering. Boris followed his glance.

"Oh my."

"He should be fine in a day or two—he's just sleeping it off."

Gray's wounds had healed, and he would wake to feel fully rejuvenated. Inco no longer worried about him. What had happened with his Qi was far more threatening, but he hadn't even had time to ponder the significance, let alone solve the problem.

A light thump echoed from the entrance. Inco perked with excitement when Misty, another dragon, entered the cave. Misty blew smoke as she changed to her DúElf form. Her smoke, which was uniquely white instead of the typical grey or black, came out heavy and dense but covered very little distance.

"Hello, boys," she greeted, looking from Boris to Inco, then to the infant. "Oh my, is that a human infant?"

"Yes, it is. I found him in the woods. His mother needs your xenum." He gestured towards the slab.

Misty approached Æmma and gasped. "She's in bad shape."

She pulled her Qi from her chest and dripped xenum into Æmma's chest wound. It healed slower than expected, but when it did, her breathing normalized. Misty put her palms on Æmma's large rounded belly and pressed with her fingers. It was soft and fluid-filled. She lifted her dress and noticed blood on her ankles. She continued to roll up the dress, noting as much blood on the fabric as on her legs. As she uncovered her knees, the bloodstains grew larger and redder with fresh blood. When she reached the groin area, she discovered the source of all the blood.

"This woman just gave birth. That baby is but hours old—if that. The poor child will grow many years without her."

Misty dripped xenum onto the swollen abdomen, which immediately shrank in size.

"She was bleeding out. Even without the wounds, she would've died before morning. Now, you know about xenum sleep, right?"

"Sure I do," Inco replied. "If they're unconscious when they're healed, it takes a few days to wake up."

"In dragons, yes. Humans and other creatures are much more sensitive. Healing so many serious wounds on an unconscious human—" Her somber gaze fell to the ground. "Inco, this woman won't be able to raise that baby."

"But you healed her. Surely she won't sleep that long."

"I'm afraid she will. I don't foresee her waking before that child is ten years old, maybe older. Her wounds were quite serious." She looked at him, her mouth a grim line. "Are you sure you're up for raising another child? You won't have my help this time around."

"Well…" He looked down at the infant. His mind reeled, dizzy with all the recent problems he faced. He needed to care for the infant long enough to figure out how to get his Qi, but another seventeen-year commitment wasn't in his plans.

The dizziness faded, and he realized things were falling into place, though he wasn't sure he liked where they landed. If the child were a dragon, he would have his DúKrue at around seventeen, taking dragon form for the first time and receiving his very own Qi. This situation was different because the child was not a dragon. If he had to guess a time for the Qi to come loose, that would be it. It was the only thing that made sense. He looked down at the baby and sighed. Mixed emotions tumbled within him. He suddenly felt nauseous.

"The xenum will continue to nourish her body through the years. But, if she doesn't wake when the xenum wears off, her body will starve. I'll check on her periodically, but if you notice her thinning, turning pale, or any other signs of hunger or thirst, you must let me know."

"I will," he replied without taking his eyes off the baby.

"It's an enormous commitment, Inco. I'm sure we can find him a home in Origo until his mother wakes," she said. "You have authority as third on the council to make an exception to the rules. I'd be glad to back you up. Just like old times."

He looked up from the infant to meet Misty's gaze. Her kind, brown eyes filled with pity while her face showed gentle determination.

"Just like old times," he pondered aloud, a small grin creeping up one side of his mouth.

"Almost. I'll have your back with the council, but you're on your own with this baby. I had my fun raising Gray. I'm happy to be child-free now."

"I'll be fine. The human life is a blink to us dragons. He'll be off on his own before I know it."

"Not if he learns anything from Gray. That boy is twenty-three years old. Don't you think it's about time to cut him loose? He needs to put his future together. It will not happen on its own."

"He's fine, Misty. I enjoy having him around. I'd be lonely without him. And he has great prospects for his future. He has the possibility of joining the council."

She hmphed. "He doesn't have the backbone for it. Now, you know I love him like my own, but the boy is soft."

"You'd be surprised what he's capable of. He made me proud today, the way he took care of those attackers. I think he even blew fire."

"Really?" She perked. "Wait, what do you mean, you *think?*"

"I didn't see it, but something left that field pretty crispy, and it wasn't me."

"Praise be." She waved both hands in the air.

Inco cast a sideways glance at Boris and chose his words carefully. "He's far more normal than you think. He'll find his calling in his own time and on his own terms. We can't push him."

She shifted her weight with her hands on her hips, staring thoughtfully at the baby. "You're a good father."

"Thank y—"

"It's time you tried your skills at being a husband."

"Your proposal is tempting, but I think I'm a little too old for you," he joked, being five-hundred, eighty-eight years her junior.

Misty snorted. "Oh, never mind, you." She opened Æmma's dress laces to expose one of her breasts. "Bring him over. He can drink from his mother before her milk dries."

"Uhm… I don't think he'll drink." He lowered his head and looked at his own feet, avoiding eye contact. He wanted to tell her the truth but couldn't find the right words. "He's very sleepy. I think she fed him recently," he lied, still avoiding eye contact.

"Hmm." She tucked the exposed breast back into the dress. "I suppose it'd be easier to give him xenum, so long as it's not his first drink."

Inco didn't respond. He enjoyed Misty's company and conversation, but the longer she stuck around, the higher the chances of her noticing the Qi. He let the conversation fizzle in hopes of her leaving, which she did. She stepped through the portal, then peeked her head back into the cave. Boris, who had been quietly listening the whole time, followed her cue.

Misty's reference to the baby's first drink echoed in Inco's head. Self-scorn crashed through his thoughts. He knew better than to give xenum to a newborn. It can never be the first drink of a human. There's never been a proven case, but it had been told through the centuries that such an event would turn the human's internal Qi dark, leading to a life of negativity, misfortune, and gloom. A pang of incredible guilt weighed on him at the thought of having ruined this baby's life before it had even begun.

Guilt shifted to confusion and doubt. This baby didn't have a dark Qi. He had *his* Qi. The tales said nothing about the newborn taking the Qi of the dragon who fed it.

CHAPTER 3

Inco stayed in the cave to be present when Gray woke up—or at least, that was what he told himself. The truth was, he didn't have a choice in the matter. The cave was much too high for him to attempt climbing down in his vulnerable human form. This was especially true, considering he'd also have the baby in tow.

The very thing that put him in this mess also made it more tolerable, for he wouldn't have to worry about feeding the baby while they waited. The xenum he'd received the first day would nourish him for months. Inco didn't understand how such a small amount of xenum could produce so many bowel movements. Luckily, the baby had been wrapped in so many cloths, a few could be sacrificed.

Inco, however, had nothing nearby to eat. He reluctantly did the only thing he could; he took Gray's Qi from his chest and drank a drop of xenum. It would be enough to keep him satisfied for a few days.

On the first day in the cave, Inco felt obligated to his new charge. He cared for the infant because he wanted his Qi back. Day and night passed, chopped into many pieces by irregular sleep patterns. The baby only slept a few hours at a time, then woke up crying. Inco knew the most natural way to soothe him would have been to feed him, but the infant wasn't hungry, and Inco lacked teats.

By the second day, he felt trapped as efforts to calm a fussy baby caused his logic to falter. He hadn't realized how easily the human body weakened without dragon abilities, and that made the future seem even bleaker.

That evening, as cold winds blew through the cave with vicious strength, the baby's trembling lips turned a faint shade of blue, and he cried endlessly. Unwrapping the swaddling, Inco put the infant inside his shirt to warm him with body heat. He layered the cloth wrappings over his shirt to provide extra warmth. The extra effort paid off as the baby slept through the night. Inco felt a budding bond with the tiny being that took such comfort against his skin.

By the third day, Inco felt privileged. It takes nearly a century for a dragon to have a natural baby, and here he was with a baby to call his own without the long wait. Inco's newfound feeling of fatherly love was overwhelming.

As the fourth day dawned, an unbreakable bond had developed. Even if the Qi fell off the baby at that moment, Inco would never be separated from him. He looked forward to raising him as his own and couldn't wait to share the news.

Gray stirred as they entered day five. Inco sat nearby and stared at him, letting his mind drift. He recalled the day the boy had hatched—the imagery in his head as fresh as if it were happening at that very moment.

He remembered looking into the egg, his gaze meeting a pair of solid grey eyes, which matched the small tuft of grey hair atop the infant's head. The bond was instant, and Inco had already agreed that he would raise him as his own instead of letting him bounce from one council member to another as other orphaned dragons had in the past. He'd enjoyed one-hundred, eighty-six years of freedom without responsibility and looked forward to caring for someone other than himself. He could think of none more worthy of love than an orphan.

Inco snapped out of his reverie, realizing he was repeating history with another orphan who had also won his love.

"How long was I asleep?" A voice shattered the silence of the cave.

Inco jumped, causing the infant to throw its arms out in reflex and start to fuss. He soothed him, holding him to his chest, and shushing him softly as he swayed near Gray.

"Shh, shh, shh, five days, shh, shh, shh. How do you feel?"

"Like I've been sleeping on a rock," Gray said with a smirk. He lifted his head off the boulder. "Is that the baby?"

Inco pulled back a bit of fabric, exposing the baby's head and face, and turned him. Gray stared at the baby with a subtle look of enchantment on his face.

"What about Æmma?" He spotted her lying on a slab and moved toward her. Inco followed, searching for the right words.

"She's alive, but…"

"But what?" He rested on his belly at her side and put his chin against her hand. Her skin was warm and soft to the touch. A sensation flooded his chest with the warmth of fresh coffee on a winter morning. He stared intently at her, unsure of what to make of the feeling that stirred within him.

Inco sighed. "She won't wake in time to raise the baby."

Gray turned toward him with a solemn expression and brought his nose near the baby. Inco looked down at the baby as well, as if to share a moment of thought, then noticed Gray wasn't looking at the baby.

"He's all alone, just like me." He locked eyes with Inco.

"He's not alone, and neither are you. You both have me, and now you'll have each other."

"You mean we can keep him?"

The deep sadness he felt for Æmma was true and heavy. However, the prospect of having a little brother gave him the perfect reason to tuck his other feelings away.

"I think he's the one keeping us." Inco chuckled, then turned to the baby and continued, "Aren't you? You're keeping us. We're the pets." He chuckled again, then sobered as he wondered how to tell Gray about the Qi. Now wasn't the time, especially after a xenum sleep, but he would have to explain why he needed to be carried off the mountain. There was no other way down.

"What'll we call him?" Gray gently used his claw to pull back Inco's collar a little more to see the baby's face better. "Is there anything about him that stands out? Anything special we can base a name on?"

"No," Inco fibbed. "He's just a kid."

"Just a kid," He repeated. "Just a kid… being raised by dragons," He added with a smirk. "That makes this 'just a kid' pretty unique if you ask me."

"Yes, but I want him to have as normal a life as possible. There's much to discuss, but for now, he's just a kid."

"It's settled then. It's just you and me, raising 'just a kid,' as normal as possible."

"I don't think 'just a kid' is a proper name."

Gray exhaled and took his Dú. As a human, he looked around eighteen years old. He had silvery-grey hair, grey eyes, and dimples, standing nose-high to Inco, but was of a heartier build.

"Of course not." He reached for the baby, but Inco pulled away.

"He needs to be wrapped."

Inco tossed the pieces of cloth onto the stone slab and leaned to place the baby on them. He kept his back to Gray to block him from seeing the Qi. Once wrapped, he handed him over.

Smiling from ear to ear, Gray took the baby. He leaned in close and gently bounced him in his arms.

"We should call him… Jak."

"Jak," Inco repeated. "I like it." He leaned in and brushed a finger across the baby's cheek. "Welcome to the family, Jak."

The wrappings on Jak unfolded as Gray swayed with him, exposing the Qi on his chest. He looked to Inco for an answer.

"I messed up," he sighed with frustration and paced the floor while nervously running the fingers of one hand through his hair. "I don't think this child ever nursed from his mother. The xenum I gave him—I believe it was his first drink."

"Isn't that supposed to give him a dark human Qi? Why does he have a dragon Qi? It isn't even dark."

"It's my Qi." He stopped pacing and paused, his hand half-way through his hair, staring aimlessly at the cave floor, then dropped his arm at his side. "It flew from my hand and attached to him after the drink. Hopefully, it'll detach when he reaches maturity since that's when dragons usually *get* their Qi. It's all I can think of."

"Are we only keeping him to get your Qi?"

"At first, yes, but he's grown on me. I want to raise him regardless of the Qi."

"Good," Gray scolded, upset at the thought. He turned away, refocused his attention on Jak, and smiled again.

Inco approached his side. They glanced at each other as if to communicate their shared feelings before returning their attention to Jak.

Inco broke the silence. "It's best we raise him amongst his own kind, here on Earth, but he's going to differ from other humans."

"That's for sure."

"And he won't be like any dragons either."

"I can relate."

"Exactly. He's going to need your help the way Misty helped you."

"You both helped me."

"Yes, but Misty did the heavy lifting when it came to emotional support. When you were seven and found out about your mother—"

"When I learned how I'd lost what I never truly had," Gray reminisced.

"And when the other children called you 'old guy' for having grey hair."

"I liked that nickname. It was funny, but they stopped when I had my DúKrue, and my dragon body matched my hair."

"Maybe so, but if it weren't for Misty, you might have never come out of that depression when you couldn't blow fire after your DúKrue."

"Hey, I did. I blew fire at those guys back there." Grey suddenly glowed with excitement.

"I thought so. I saw the burnt grass."

"It was grey."

Inco furrowed his brow, unsure how to respond.

"Have you ever heard of grey fire? What do you think it means?"

"I don't know. Everything else about you is grey, so I guess it makes sense."

"I guess." He smiled and touched his nose to the baby's, then gasped and playfully pulled his head back. As he humored the baby, he lowered his free arm to his side and reached behind Inco. With a quick flip of his wrist, he slapped the back of Inco's head.

"What was that for?"

"Sweet revenge."

"Wha—from five days ago?"

"Yep," Gray said, still looking down at Jak, "when you least expected it. Can't get me back, I'm holding a baby."

"I guess I taught you well." Inco rolled his eyes with a smirk.

"And now we can teach him." He leaned his face closer to Jak. "It's ok to be different, little guy. I'll always be here for you. Welcome to the family, little brother."

CHAPTER 4

Procerus surveyed the room and rose to his feet, towering near the ceiling in his frail, elderly, DúElf form. One by one, he nodded to each of his fellow council members.

In turn, they each dipped their heads in reverence. Attending were Misty, the motherly DúElf, Zebulan, the introverted but respectful DúHuman, Grace, the graceful DúHuman, Chance, the cheerful DúHuman, Boris, the nervous DúElf, Percy, the melancholy DúFairy, and Roe, the lickspittle DúHuman. Being in their Dú was necessary for the meeting since the council chambers weren't built to accommodate nine dragons.

They each sat in a wooden high-back chair with beautiful red velvet upholstery. Each chair was custom made to the size and shape of the member using it. A matching table sat next to each chair where a single candle cast dancing shadows onto the notepad beside it.

Sconces lined the walls with lit candles, illuminating the cabin with a warm, wavering light. Between them hung portraits of dragons in their Dú and a few in their dragon form. Old policies of the dragons were on display on tables below the portraits.

Procerus came to the empty chair between Misty and Zebulan.

"Where's Inco?"

Boris squirmed in his seat. He looked at Misty, and she returned his gaze. She opened her mouth to speak but was cut off by Boris.

"He's raising a human child on Earth with Gray. He saved him… and his mother… but not his father. Misty helped. I was ther—"

Procerus raised a hand for silence.

"Inco's on Earth?"

Boris nodded.

"In his Dú?"

Boris nodded.

"With a human child?"

Boris nodded.

Everyone fell quiet. All eyes rested on Procerus, who made brief eye contact with everyone in the room as if he were reading their thoughts.

"So be it." He broke the silence and turned to Misty. "What's first on the agenda for today?"

"That's it?" Zebulan slammed his hands on the table.

"What do you wish me to do?" Procerus snapped. "Ban him from the council? Drag him back to Origo against his will? He knows we meet today."

"When did the council start raising random orphans? Isn't it enough that we raise all the orphaned dragons? He reared the last one practically on his own." He stopped short and looked at Misty, who raised her brows in return.

"On his own, huh?" She crossed her arms and glared.

Embarrassment dampened his anger. "Well, besides you. My apologies."

Procerus reentered the discussion. "No one else fought to raise Gray. If you felt you were being left out, you could have spoken up at any time. But that's beside the point. The council isn't raising this human child—Inco is. What he's doing is commendable. We'll send a message to him and ask if he wishes to remain on the council, and unless he says otherwise, we'll leave him be until he's ready to rejoin us."

Zebulan scoffed. "If he isn't here for the meetings, how can he remain on the council?

"By the grace and understanding of his fellow council members," Procerus replied.

"He should have to step down and rejoin later. We base seniority on time spent on the council. By the time he gets back, I—" he stopped short and cleared his throat to cover his error. "*Some of us* will have served more time." He looked to other members for support but received none.

"We have centuries. Humans have less than one. We'll survive without him for a while," Procerus trailed off in a dismissive tone.

Zebulan huffed but remained silent for the rest of the meeting, which involved little more than the renewal of a few short-term ordinances. After the meeting, the group gathered for smoked hors d'oeuvres and lemonade. Zebulan headed straight for the door.

"It's not fair, sir," Roe whispered as he passed.

He stopped and eyed Roe, unsure that he heard him correctly.

"I bet if I missed, I'd no longer be a member."

Zebulan glanced to see if anyone else was listening. The other members were in their seats with plates of finger foods, laughing and talking. He decided it could be easy and beneficial to put this dragon's eagerness to good use.

He told himself he'd be doing Roe a favor by giving him something to do.

"That's right," he agreed in a raspy whisper. "You'd be out instantly. Fledglings learn never to miss in the first year. Why make exceptions later?" He leaned in and lowered his voice even more. "I wonder if something else is going on, something bigger."

"Bigger?" Roe's eyes widened with curiosity. "Like what?"

"I don't know." He stepped back. "I'd investigate him myself, but I stand out among humans." He formed a V with two fingers and pointed at his eyes, which remained in dragon form even when in his Dú. "I guess we're just left to wonder." With a dramatic sigh, he turned towards the door and took a slow step, waiting for Roe to take the bait.

"I blend in with humans."

A smirk flashed in Zebulan's eyes. He turned back with a sober face. "I couldn't ask you to do that. We don't know what he's up to. It could be dangerous."

"But I want to do it. If Inco's doing something wrong, I want to help catch him."

"Shh. No one else can know. Imagine their reactions if they thought we were spying on a Good Samaritan. Report back to me. Tell no one else."

Roe nodded eagerly and left.

Zcbulan smiled and let out a long sigh of satisfaction.

CHAPTER 5

Gail was a sweet young lady with a soft voice and a warm smile. She stood lean and tall with blue eyes and dark-blonde hair that kissed her waist as she walked. There almost seemed to be a melody to her step. She moved with grace, and everyone who met her smiled without hesitation. No one in the village knew her full story, but they assumed it was a sad one.

They knew she was a widow devastated by the loss of her husband, but instead of letting it turn her heart cold, she redirected her love. She harnessed all the love she had for her husband and the family she would've built with him and poured it into the local children. She always had sweets and little handmade toys that she'd pass around to the young ones when she strolled through the village.

In the presence of children, she was chipper and playful. She'd sing and play or even join a sport in the courtyard. When she watched them from afar, however, there was sadness in her gaze.

Despite being a widow, Gail kept herself well. Because of how sweet she was to their little ones, the villagers loved and respected her and would buy all the goods she brought to town. She supported herself on fresh eggs from her chickens, pies she baked, and rent collected from whoever stayed in her guest cabin. The current guest was Inco.

Inco and Gray felt fortunate to have found her cabin vacant. Though it was next to hers, it was far from other people. Both dwellings sat on the plains up a steep hill just outside the Sheldon village. The town was relatively quiet, close enough for convenience, yet far enough for privacy.

They kept Jak indoors at all times. It had been four months since Inco's Qi had attached itself to the infant's chest. He watched for any changes that might be related to the Qi. So far, there had been no signs. During this time, Gray became convinced that Inco was overreacting.

"He needs the sun on his face, the breeze on his skin, fresh air in his lungs," he said.

"And if something happens? What then? No one will understand. *We* don't even understand. We don't know what to expect or how to handle anything that might happen. And as long as he has my Qi, I can't even take dragon form to protect him. I'm stuck in this miserable flesh sack."

"This is about Jak." He wagged a finger. "Don't make this about you."

Inco glared. "I think this is about you. Ever since the cave, you haven't been the same. Is this because you can't blow fire again?"

Shock and anger flared in Gray's eyes. "Are you serious? I haven't been the same because you've kept my brother a prisoner to your fears." He closed his eyes and calmed himself, then took a deep breath. "We won't know if something will happen until something happens. What if nothing happens? Do we force him to stay in these four walls his entire life? What kind of life is that for a child?" He paused. "What kind of life is that for anyone?"

Inco opened his mouth to speak, but no words came to him. He pressed his lips together and exhaled sharply.

Gray looked at Jak, who lay awake in an oval basket atop a table. He looked much different from the day he was born. His skin had become quite pale. His eyes were still wide-set, but his brow had taken on a more defined shape, making his eyes seem to pop more. His flat nose had poked out. The fine black hair that had covered his body had fallen out, but he still had a slim line down the center of his back. He had also filled out, changing from a thin, frail newborn to a chunky baby.

Jak cooed at him with a big smile. Gray rubbed his foot lovingly, then abruptly turned to the front door and yanked it open.

"He deserves better."

He slammed the door behind him, but it bounced from the door frame and remained ajar.

A few paces away, Gail approached, carrying a cloth-covered dish. Gray respectfully nodded as he passed her. She saw he was upset but didn't ask him why.

"Knock, knock," she said, poking her head through the partially open door. "How is my favorite neighbor?"

Inco was within arm's reach of the door. He opened it fully.

"Lady Gail, please come in."

He stepped aside the doorway and gestured toward a table in the middle of the room. On it sat the large oval basket shook. Jak kicked his feet and swung his hands from within.

"Oh, I do wish you'd just call me Gail. My late husband was no lord," she said with a smile as she sat the dish next to Jak. "Ooh, look, he's awake," she exclaimed with delight, then looked at Inco with pleading eyes. "May I hold him?"

Inco hesitated. "Oh, uh, yes, of course. Let me hel—"

"Oh, I can do it." She eagerly scooped him from the basket. "He's always sleeping when I come over. I've been looking forward to this so much." She cradled him in her arms.

Jak squealed and batted his hands toward her. She leaned her face in and let him touch and grab at her cheeks and chin. She smiled and shook her head gently at his hands, blowing kisses and making little popping sounds with her lips. Jak squealed again.

"He's quite taken with you," Inco said with a little surprise in his voice. "He hasn't had a woman's touch since—" He cut himself off and looked down at the floor for a moment before taking a deep breath. The aroma of the food gave him the perfect opportunity to change the subject.

"So what's this?" He lifted the cloth on the dish and peeked inside.

"Oh, I wouldn't know what to call it. It's just a mix of vegetables and meat with a few spices. Sort of a dry stew."

"You're too kind. You know you don't have to—"

"Oh, but I do," she sat in a chair at the table, her eyes still on Jak. "If I should ever have another husband, I need to keep my cooking skills sharp." She chuckled. Her voice then took on silly tones and pitches as she directed her attention to the baby.

"Besides, I love to cook, and today is Tuesday. I wouldn't miss a Tuesday." Her baby talk continued as she touched her finger to the tip of Jak's nose. "No, we don't. No, we don't." She then went back to popping noises and playful whispers.

Gail insisted on cooking a meal for Inco and Gray every Tuesday. They never understood the importance of it being Tuesday but assumed it was just a routine she preferred keeping. They told her time and time again that she needn't go through the trouble, but the truth was they looked forward to Tuesdays. Her cooking was delicious. It was a refreshing change considering Inco's cooking was… improving.

Inco returned the cloth over the food, then took a dish off a shelf and set it on the table next to Gail. She nodded in acknowledgment and continued to coo and play with Jak. Her playful gibberish trailed off when she noticed something below his ear.

"Looks like this little guy has a bit of dry skin," Gail said as she gently grazed her finger over it. "I can whip up some moisturizer for you tomorrow. I'll add lavender so it will smell beautiful and help him sleep."

He looked over her shoulder at the flake of skin. He didn't know if it was normal or not. Gray had had nothing like it, at least, not until his annual shedding after his DúKrue.

"That's very nice of you. Thank you. Well, it's about time for Jak to take a nap." He reached and patiently waited while Gail procrastinated with a few last coos and kisses. She let out a long breath of satisfaction, kissed the baby on the forehead, and handed him back.

"Thank you. I needed that." She rubbed her thumb in circles on the back of Jak's hand. Her sad eyes glistened.

Inco lost himself in her gaze, captivated by brown lines that shot out from the center to the dark grey ring surrounding the mostly blue iris. He had never seen eyes with three colors. His breathing grew shallow, as did hers. Her pupils grew larger, and their bodies seemed to float closer to one another without moving their feet. Jak broke the silence with a coo.

"I'd better get going."

"Of course. Thanks again for the… the, uh… dry stew."

She kissed Jak's hand and rubbed it as she turned toward the door, but something caught her attention, and she turned back around. She examined his hand closer. The skin was badly chapped. As she rubbed, the top layer loosened like a shedding snake. She stroked a little higher up his arm, and the thin top layer of skin peeled there as well. She looked at Inco, who failed to hide his nervousness. Something new was happening to Jak, and she was witnessing it. A piece of dead skin loosened. She brushed it away and watched it flutter to the ground.

"This shouldn't happen until he's much older," she whispered.

The comment shot through Inco like a tidal wave. His look of fear abruptly changed to one of shock and confusion.

She continued, "A migma doesn't shed until they've had their DúKrue. This shouldn't happen for another sixteen or seventeen years. What kind of migma is he? What kind of dragon was his mother?"

"His mother—" Inco couldn't respond. The shock of her words took his breath away.

"Hmm?" she pressed.

Inco hesitated. He didn't want to continue this conversation. Finally, he whispered, "Human."

"She's human? That means you're—" She pulled down Inco's collar, exposing the faint outlines of the scales. "You're a dragon? But how? This makes no sense. And where's your Qi?"

"What could you possibly know about migmas?" He flashed contempt with his eyes. Of course, he'd never

43

physically harm her, but he was feeling cornered and wanted to run from the encounter.

"I know that a migma is a half-breed between a dragon and a creature from their Dú. I know they're not common. Conception is difficult and unlikely but sometimes happens. A migma is born in their Dú from a dragon egg, just like a dragon. They have their DúKrue when they matured, just like a dragon. But…" She paused. "They can only be conceived by a female dragon and a male, hm, what do you call the creatures that aren't dragons?"

"Which ones? There are many."

"No, some dragons are born as humans, so that makes regular humans a… a…" She fanned her hand toward her face as if she could draw in the right word.

"Do you mean, kindred?"

"Yes. A migma can only be made by a female dragon and a male kindred. The egg grows to full size within hours and becomes hard within minutes." Her voice heightened as she continued. "It would outgrow her womb and kill her. It wouldn't even have a chance to harden. The unborn migma would die, too. How is this child alive?"

"How do you know all this?" He deflected her question.

Gail untied the laces that closed the deep-cut collar of her blouse. Inco respectfully looked away, but she put her palm on his cheek and pulled his gaze back to her. The one visible difference between a dragon and a migma was the chest scale. A migma in their Dú has only the bare Qi on their chest. A dragon in their Dú has a Qi surrounded by faded scales that blend into their skin. Gail had only a Qi.

He gazed at it long and hard. Everything that had just happened replayed in his head, as did the past few months of interactions with Gail. So many comments she made had suddenly gained a double meaning.

He desperately tried to think of a way out of telling her anything more than she already knew. He became lost in his thoughts and almost forgot to breathe. The sound of a snapping twig broke the silence and startling the pair.

Gail quickly pulled her blouse together, overlapping her hands over her chest.

Inco snapped out of his lost thoughts and looked past her in the direction of the sound. Nothing was there. He handed her the baby and rushed outside. At the side of the cabin, he stopped and listened.

A fawn frolicked in the distance, but he saw nothing else nearby. Then, from the corner of his eye, he spotted an odd shadow just behind the cabin. Cautiously, he approached the back-corner wall and peeked around.

"Roe? What're you doing here?"

Startled, Roe jumped to his feet and stammered, "I… I came to see you."

"Why are you hiding?"

Roe fumbled for words. "I wasn't sure if I had the right place, and you startled me when you came out. I—"

"What can I do for you?"

"I just wanted to let you know…" He desperately searched for an excuse. "The, uhm, the council has excused you from further meetings until the human child is grown."

"What do you know about the child?" Inco scowled.

"Oh, uhm, Misty and Boris told us what happened. D-don't kill the messenger," he pled.

"What's the matter with you? I won't hurt you!" Inco said. He was annoyed and struggling to stay calm. "Thank you for letting me know. I'll try to check in periodically."

"Yes, sir."

"Don't call me 'sir.'"

"Yes, s—Inco. I'd better go." He edged past Inco and hurried away.

Inco could see his nervousness. He knew Roe was a people pleaser and easily startled, so he tried to brush it off. He looked back at the fawn just as it disappeared into the trees, then looked again toward Roe, who was already far off in the distance, heading toward the cave.

When he went back into the cabin, Gail was sitting at the table with Jak. She stared at the infant's chest, where a single black scale shone. A black Qi. It was no longer green. Inco rushed closer. He rubbed the black scale, which had no edges, nothing that could aid in lifting or pulling.

"It turned black?"

She held out her fist and opened it. There in her palm was Inco's Qi.

"The prophecy? But it can't be real," Inco mumbled as he took his Qi. He rubbed his brow. The newborn drinking xenum tale was never a part of the prophecy, at least, not to his knowledge. Seeing the black Qi was the breaking point. There was no talking his way out of it now. He knew he had no choice but to explain everything and hope for understanding.

"Will you promise to keep this between us? I don't want anyone else to know. Only Gray and I know how this happened, but he doesn't know what I'm about to tell you. Even I didn't realize all of it until now."

"On my heart," she vowed.

"It's a long story. I'll make some tea."

CHAPTER 6

Roe landed in a shallow cave high in the Airland Mountains. He took his Dú, causing him to stumble rather than walk to his rendezvous with Zebulan.

Zebulan dusted a large chair carved from a log and sat. He rested one ankle on the opposite knee and slouched, massaging the hair on his chin.

Roe pulled a rag from his pocket to dust the other chair. As soon as the rag touched the seat, a large area in the middle moved. He jumped back as a spider-like creature the size of his head stood from the center, leaving a dip in the wood beneath it. It turned, hissed, and settled back in, vanishing as it blended perfectly with the grain of the wood.

He looked to Zebulan, who barely hid his contemptuous smirk behind his fingers, his chin resting on the palm of his hand.

"What have you to report?"

"The child's a migma, sir."

"A migma? I thought he was human. Are you sure?" Zebulan stared into space for a moment, then inhaled sharply and moved his hand to speak. "Who's the dragon mother?"

"The m-m-mother's human, sir."

"Ha! Not possible. No human woman has ever made it past the first few hours after conception. Even if they did, can you imagine a human woman trying to birth an egg that size?" He squirmed deeper into his chair, then jumped to his feet. "Blast these miserable chairs. What's the point of a resting cave if you can't get comfortable enough to rest?"

"Uhm, I don't know, sir."

"That was rhetorical." He pulled a pigskin pouch from his side and took a drink, raising his brow at Roe. "I almost forgot—I brought you some wine." He pulled a second pouch from the ground next to his seat and tossed it.

Roe caught it as it hit his chest with a slap. "Oh, uhm, I don't drink and fly," he said, but the truth was, he didn't drink at all.

Zebulan scoffed, "Men build trust over a drink. Are you not a man, or just not a trustworthy one?"

Roe flinched at the insult. To avoid another, he took a drink and swallowed hard, struggling not to gag on the strength of the wine. It left a slimy aftertaste in his mouth. He grimaced and ran his tongue over his teeth. Feeling pressured by Zebulan's awkward gaze, he forced a smile and a murmur of satisfaction, then fastened the pouch to his belt.

"Back to the mother—did she die in childbirth?"

"She's in xenum sleep. I saw her myself when I went through the portal. I spoke with Boris yesterday. He says Misty healed her. The story was that soldiers attacked her after giving birth, but Boris mentioned the birth itself is what caused her injuries."

"I don't think you heard me. A human woman has never carried a migma egg long enough to reach full size and harden. It always kills her."

"Yes, sir. But the child *is* a migma, and Inco is a dragon."

"How do you know the child is a migma? Did you see him hatch?" Zebulan drifted around him.

"N-no, he's shedding." Anxiety built in his gut as he watched Zebulan walk behind him.

"Shedding? The child is still an infant."

"It's early, but he's shedding, sure as I'm standing here. I saw it myself, and I heard the neighbor woman mention it. She thought it was dry skin, but I saw it. He's a migma, and he's shedding, I'm sure of it."

"All right, I believe you." Zebulan stopped in front of him but didn't face him. "This is highly irregular. Did the woman say anything else? Was she human or…"

"Human, s-s-sir. I belie—"

"What's with the st-st-stutter?"

"S-sorry, sir. Sometimes it happens when I get excited or nervous." He lowered his head. "Sir?"

Zebulan turned away and looked out at the bright sky. "What is it?"

"D-do you think he's the one?"

"The one what?"

"The one the prophecy foretells. The one who'll fight alongside Bakúnuh."

"Hm." Zebulan's face twisted perversely. "Keep an eye on the boy. Devote all your free time to him, but do it later. Right now, we have things to do." He walked to the edge of the cave floor and peered into the distance. "Have you ever been to Caligo?"

"No, sir. No one has ever been to Caligo. It's a wasteland."

"That's not entirely true."

Roe raised his brow. "Wha—which part?"

"You'll see."

CHAPTER 7

Inco set Gail's tea on the table while taking a longer than necessary sip of his own. He stared at her over the rim of his cup, pondering his words carefully.

"Do you know the story of the Rima?"

"A little. My parents separated shortly after my mother birthed my egg. My father's dragon friends kept him young with xenum until I hatched, then he raised me here on Earth. I was never exposed to the dragon culture as a child. I didn't even know I was a migma until I burst into dragon form for the first time a few days after my seventeenth birthday. What's it called again? A DúKrue?"

"Yes, you had your DúKrue, but I don't understand. How is it you know so little and yet so much?"

"My father explained as much as he could. He told me about the dragon cave, and I went to Origo, searching for my mother. I never found her, but I met my husband, Tibbel." Her voice cracked with sadness.

"Husband? I mean—" Ingo bit his tongue, realizing he'd spoken aloud and out of turn. He searched for words of comfort but noticed Gail had drifted off, her thoughts deep in the past as she stared blankly through him. He reached out to comfort her, thought better of it, and pulled his hand back.

"Uh, Origo is beautiful this time of year," he blurted, then berated himself for making such a stupid statement.

Gail was in her own world as she continued her story. "I knew it was where I belonged, and I tried to settle in. I even laid an egg, but it saddened me to know it would never hatch. I missed being here on Earth."

"Earth is beautiful—" He bit his lip hard and told himself to shut the hell up.

Gail hadn't heard him. "I missed being around children. Their pure, innocent nature fills me with joy, and that egg was a constant reminder of what I would never have. Tibbel brought me back to Earth, and we set up this home. We intended to use it as a part-time home, just for when I felt homesick, but then…" Her voice shook, "Tibbel died."

Tears welled in her eyes, but she took a deep breath and wiped them before they fell. "I come here for a few years, and then I return to Origo long enough for the villagers to forget me. I always come back, though, claiming to be a daughter or granddaughter if anyone recognizes me."

"Do you want to talk about Jak some other—"

"No." She sniffled, took a deep breath, and exhaled sharply. "No. I'm sorry, I've become quite a mess, and this isn't about me. This is about this little angel here." She touched the tip of her nose to the tip of Jak's nose. "Tell me the story. I'm listening."

Glad to see her back in the present. Inco told her the story.

"In the beginning, the Great Mistress of the Stars created Origo. The Magma Heart gave life to the planet, with four Qingdoms arranged by compass.

"The Mistress named the dragons and gave them each a Qingdom. Imoogi, the water dragon and her favorite, became High Qing over all of Origo. He ruled the West Qingdom and drew his strength from the sun. Tate, the wind dragon, ruled over the East Qingdom and drew strength from the moon. Bakúnuh, the soil dragon, ruled over the North Qingdom and drew strength from the planet's rotation. Knotlow, the fire dragon, ruled over the South Qingdom and drew power from the stars."

"But the south is Caligo."

"Yes, but it wasn't back then. After the creation, the entire planet was beautiful and harmonious for many thousands of years… until the great quake."

"Oh, yes, I know about the great quake."

"That's the scientific explanation, but there's another. It's an old legend that Bakúnuh turned on the other Qings out of hatred and jealousy of Imoogi. Tate and Knotlow were loyal to their High Qing, leaving Bakúnuh to dwell in anger and isolation until he went mad. He challenged Imoogi's position as High Qing in a duel. Imoogi refused the challenge, but Bakúnuh wouldn't take no for an answer. He attacked Imoogi, and they fought for days, destroying everything in their path, while Tate and Knotlow tried desperately to stop them.

"At the end of several days and nights of battle, the planet broke in two. One by one, Bakúnuh snatched each of the Qings' Qi from their chest to render them helpless. He trapped Imoogi in a stone prison and tucked him under Firestone Palace. Tate became trapped in the vortex of the Rima. Knotlow became one with the Magma Heart and pulled it to one side of the divide, away from

Bakúnuh.

"When the Magma Heart's life force was removed from the southern half, all the volcanoes erupted and filled the air with smoke and ash. They forever blocked the light of the moon, sun, and stars. Southern Origins were thrown into perpetual darkness and eventual death. The surviving Origins named the dead half Caligo, and the northern half became Salus.

"Sometime later, a prophecy emerged about a girl who will wake Imoogi and a boy that will help Bakúnuh wipe out civilization."

Gail pondered. "Why would he do that?"

"Because if he can't be High Qing, no one can, and if civilization is dead, there's nothing to rule. I think. Well, something like that."

"Is anything alive on Caligo? I thought that side was dead."

"Who knows?" He fanned away the thought. "It's just a legend. None of it is real. And without the girl, it's not even an intact prophecy."

"Then why are you telling me this? What does this have to do with Jak? And what girl are you talking about?"

"Just—we have to keep his Qi hidden. Someone could believe the prophecies and think he's a threat." He tried to deflect her questions. None of it was a secret, but he felt the less he talked about it, the less likely it became.

Her face twisted in confusion. "Why would anyone be afraid of a baby?"

"Because he matches th—" He raised his voice in frustration, paused, and then sighed as he turned to Gail. Her innocent eyes glimmered with curiosity as she stared back at him. His heart flooded his throat with anxiety as his eyes lowered to the black scale on Jak's chest. He ran his hand over his mouth, pulling at the coarse hair on his chin.

"Jak matches the prophecy. If it's true, he's destined to kill us all."

CHAPTER 8

For some time, nothing abnormal happened. Jak was a healthy growing baby who ate, slept, and played like any other. Inco easily took to fatherhood, while Gail became the boy's mother despite living in a separate home. Jak had a room in both cabins and spent time between them as if they were merely different rooms in the same house.

Inco appreciated Gail's help, but also much more. She made him feel in ways he'd never felt before, and being in the same room with her was like a breath of fresh air. Talking about life felt like a warm, satisfying fire in his heart, and watching her with Jak was indescribably fulfilling.

Gray was also happy to have Gail around. He noticed Inco's lightened mood in her presence, plus having her around made every day a Tuesday. That was all it took to win him over.

At twenty months old, Jak babbled, speaking only a few words. His chubby body thinned as he became more mobile, though he was short for his age. His black hair had lightened to a medium brown with natural highlights that sometimes shone red.

On a bright afternoon, Inco took him out to the garden to play while he pulled weeds and picked a few vegetables for supper. Jak waddle-walked around the edge of the garden, babbling nonsense in various pitches and tones while

Inco nibbled a few vegetables. Of course, Jak wanted to be just like his papa, so he attempted to mimic his actions. He picked up a small twig and shoved half of it in his mouth, grimaced a bit, and pulled it back out.

Inco bit a banana pepper from its stem and hummed with satisfaction while staring off in the distance. Jak looked at the stick. It looked like the stem, so he tried again. This time, he suckled the twig. Dirt spread over his tongue, and he pulled the twig out. It wasn't good at all. He attempted to spit and saw Inco toss the stem. Jak copied and happily threw the twig. He had no desire to try *that* vegetable again.

Inco plucked a chive onion and bit into the green end. Jak looked down at the grass. It looked similar, so he pulled a handful of grass, root, and dirt. He watched his papa bend the stalk of the chive and shove the rest into his mouth, biting it off close to the white bulb. Jak patted the handful of grass to bend it over and then shoved the whole thing into his mouth. Its flavor was like that of the twig, but with other unpleasant flavors mixed in. He spat—another awful vegetable.

Inco didn't see Jak eating grass and twigs. He heard him babbling and had him in his peripheral sight but was distracted with snacking on his little harvest, watching large buzzards fly over a crop field on the other side of the village. He threw the chive bulb and startled a young rabbit.

"Look, Jak, a bunny." He pointed. "Bunn-neeee. Can you say bunn-neeee?"

Jak looked at the rabbit and tried to mimic.

"Nee. Neee," he squealed, grinning ear to ear, and brought his hands together in clumsy applause to himself. Staring at the rabbit, his demeanor changed to a sharp focus.

Inco smiled at his attempt to say bunny and watched him admire it.

"Neeeee," Jak growled in a whisper this time. His senses spoke to him, taking control. He could feel the rabbit's heart race, smell its adrenaline, taste its fear. His arms tensed, and he sprang forward. In the blink of an eye, he leapt across the yard and grabbed the bunny.

Inco froze in shock. Jak secured the rabbit with both hands, salivating, with his mouth opened wide.

Inco sprinted toward him. "No, don't eat the bun—" But he was too late.

Jak bit down and tore off a mouthful. The bunny squealed as he dropped it and chewed, then tried to spit. Awful again. His mouth was full of fur, which was worse than all the nasty vegetables combined.

Inco reached him just as the bunny hit the ground. He looked down as it fled and could see it wasn't bleeding but was missing a patch of hair on its back. He turned to Jak as he spat and babbled and raked his tongue with both hands.

"Was that yucky?" he chuckled. Although Jak had just shown a new ability, his spitting and babbling were far too entertaining to take it seriously just yet.

"What's wrong?" Gail ran toward them. "I heard yelling." She slowed to a brisk walk as she approached the garden. Gray followed behind her. Inco was still laughing as he pinched pieces of rabbit hair from Jak's lips.

"We have a little hunter on our hands here. He caught a rabbit and a mouth full of fur."

"Caught a rabbit? That's not funny," She scolded while lifting Jak onto one hip. "You were supposed to be watching him."

Inco noted the seriousness in her voice and stopped laughing. He and Gray watched Jak continue to scrape fur from his tongue. They looked at each other, pressing their lips to stifle their laughter.

"Nee ucky," Jak scolded at the escaping bunny.

They lost their composure and burst into laughter.

"What fools." Angry, Gail turned and walked back toward the house.

After a few steps, she stopped to look at Jak. He was still scraping at the remaining pieces of hair on his tongue. She held him out in front of her. He met her gaze and smiled. A chunk of fur poked out from the corner of his mouth. She let out a snicker and smirked over her shoulder at Inco and Gray.

"Foolish boys."

CHAPTER 9

Lying under the stars, Gail and Gray chuckled aloud. He knew all the constellations and quizzed her on where they were. She was failing miserably, but Gray's supportive humor made it enjoyable.

"Jak's finally asleep," Inco said, approaching from the house. He moaned and groaned as he lowered himself onto the ground to join them.

"It's about time you joined us, old man," Gray teased.

"Can an old man do this?" Inco grabbed Gray's head and rubbed his knuckles against his scalp.

"Ah, stop it." He squirmed free. "Old man," he mumbled.

Inco threw his arm out and pulled back in a bluff, and Gray rolled his eyes playfully. Gail ignored their jesting and kept her gaze at the stars.

"Did he have trouble settling in?"

Inco sighed. "He says he's afraid of the dark."

"Isn't that about normal for a four-year-old?"

"That's probably the only normal thing about him," he mumbled.

Gail moved her hand to rest in the grass by her face as she turned her head toward him.

"What's wrong?"

"It's just—" He thought of how he wanted to phrase his concern. "How do we prevent, I mean, what if—"

"What if he's truly meant to fulfill the prophecy?" Gail guessed.

Inco closed his eyes and exhaled sharply as he sat up. He glanced at Gray before throwing a disapproving look at Gail.

"I was going to say, what if he wanders off in the night? We have no way of keeping him in his rooms or the cabins."

"He should know," Gail mumbled. She turned her toward him and propped on one elbow.

"What prophecy?" Gray asked.

"There's not much of a choice now, is there?" Inco complained.

"What prophecy?" Gray repeated.

"I thought that's what you were talking about."

"Well, I wasn't. I was thinking about his safety, not some garbage bedtime story."

"Bedtime story? Wha—?" Gray fumbled, trying to keep up. The more they argued, the more confused he became. He sat up and turned toward them as they continued.

Gail took a deep breath. "What if it's true? We should all—"

"It's not," Inco spat. "It's just a story."

"Then it's harmless to tell him. He should've known already."

"That's not for you to decide."

"He's my son just as much as he is yours."

"Hey," Gray tried to interrupt.

"Oh. I guess you get to choose who knows what and when, huh?" Inco raised his voice as he fumed.

"Hey," Gray tried again.

"You're treating him like a child. He should know." Gail raised her voice in turn.

"Hey! *He's* sitting right *here*!" Gray shouted. "What's going on?"

He glanced between them while they stared at each other. The tension was thick enough to cut. Inco let out a sigh. Though he would never admit that she was right, continuing the argument was pointless. He turned to Gray.

"Remember the story of the Rima?"

"Uhm," Gray pondered for a moment. "The great quake?"

"That's the official story, the one we taught you rather than filling your head with fables." He flashed a brief glare at Gail.

"Oh, you mean the 'Evil Qing of Dirt' version? I know that story, too. Why is it such a big deal? What does it have to do with Jak?"

"The story—no, the *myth* has been trimmed to be less daunting."

"All right. What am I missing?"

"Origo was split in half. Bakúnuh subdued Imoogi, Knotlow completed the Rima, and Tate remained stuck in the vortex he created. That's where the story ends, and the prophecy begins."

"A prophecy. I'm listening."

"The prophecy says that there will be a girl, the Daughter of Light. A migma born to a migma mother. She'll bear the mark of Imoogi on her shoulder, and upon reaching maturity, she'll bring the power of the sun to revive Imoogi. This will provoke the Battle of Origo. She'll have her DúKrue and fight alongside Imoogi."

Gray shrugged. "Still not seeing what this has to do with any of us, here."

"I'm not done. When Imoogi rises, he and Bakúnuh will once again fight to be High Qing, and if Bakúnuh wins, he will probably kill everything and feed on the decay. The prophecy speaks of another, the counterpart to the girl. He's called the Son of Darkness, a migma born to a human mother, who will bear a black Qi. It's foretold that he'll fight alongside Bakúnuh and bring about total victory."

"Wait, you don't think…" Gray faltered.

"He has the black Qi. He—"

"Not possible." Gray eased himself back down onto the grass. "He'll be lucky to be as tall as a dwarf by the time he grows up. He couldn't defeat an army of ants."

"I'm serious, Gray."

He looked at Inco, whose expression made everything sink like a jagged rock in his gut. Still, he tried to reason.

"He's not a migma."

"Yes, he is."

"No. We don't know that. He's just special. His Qi results from drinking xenum as an infant. Everyone knows a human Qi can become dark if xenum is their first drink. His Qi just looks like a dragon Qi instead of a human one. We don't even know if it has xenum in it or if he'll ever be able to pull it off to use it," his tone turned desperate.

"He is a migma, that much is obvious, and though he wasn't born a migma, he's still a migma born to a human. Origins have always assumed that the Son of Darkness would result from a male dragon and a giant human woman. But Jak became a migma by xenum being his first drink."

Gray's eyes filled with tears. "So, he's going to be evil?"

"No. Our destinies are our own, and we'll raise him right. The prophecy is just a tale. Besides, Caligo is forever dark and disconnected from the Magma Heart. Nothing could survive there, not even a Qing of dirt. If he's real, he's long gone. Plus, with no girl to wake Imoogi, the prophecy won't begin. Migmas can't have babies." Inco paused, realizing those words may be sharp to Gail. He looked to her for a response, but she continued to stare at the grass. "The only way there can be a daughter of a migma is if Jak has a child someday."

Gray rubbed his brow. "If it isn't real, how can it be an issue?"

"Because *others* may believe it, and if they find out about him, they could try to hurt or even kill him. That's why we've been here on Earth, to give him a normal life, but also to keep him safe. If his powers keep growing, he'll lose it all."

"He's just a kid." Gray sniffled and wiped the welling tear.

"Yes." Inco nodded.

"And without the girl—"

"The whole thing is null, but others may not see it that way. We must keep this to ourselves, and we must teach him to control his darkness."

"But if the prophecy isn't true, then he doesn't have a darkness," Gray said.

"We all have darkness in us. It's what we do with it that matters."

"I know the expression."

"It's not just an expression—it means something. Every intelligent being, whether from Earth or Origo, has a bit of darkness inside. It's the primal nature and instincts we once needed to survive. We're civilized now, but the urges still run in our blood. It's up to us to control them. Even if his darkness is small, coupled with his black Qi and true origin, we have to be extra careful with him to keep him safe."

Gray rubbed his eyes and dragged his hands over his face. "This is a lot. I'm going to bed." He headed toward the cabin. On his way, he stopped and turned back. "He's my brother. I love him, no matter what."

Inco blinked with a nod of reverence.

Gray's expression turned hard. "Never leave me out again."

Inco met his gaze and realized he was right. He was no longer a child, he was a young man, and he loved Jak just as much as they did. Inco took a breath, let it out slowly to release the tension in his eyes, and then gave another nod.

"Goodnight," Gail whispered.

Inco thought she was talking to Gray, but then he noticed her rising to her feet. Her expression was glum, her eyes watery. Gray's reaction to the prophecy had distracted him. He'd forgotten how he'd spoken to Gail. Never had he taken such a tone with her before, and it obviously upset her. He knew an apology wasn't enough, nor was it the right time. He watched her walk toward her cabin when a tiny voice broke the silence.

"Mama! Mamaaa," Jak called out as he squirmed past Gray and ran to Gail. "I want to sleep wiff you," he begged, wrapping his arms around her leg and looking up with his pitiful pleading blue eyes. "Pweese, Mama."

Jak hadn't grown much since he was sixteen months old. He remained thin and small. He gained a little color during the summer months but was still quite pale. His hair had grown more than his body and now reached his shoulders in thick brown loopy waves that fluttered in the light breeze.

"Very well, but straight to bed when we get inside," Gail conceded.

She picked him up and continued to her cabin. He laid his head on her shoulder and sucked on his index and middle fingers.

Inco watched until Gail reached her cabin. As she opened her front door, Jak looked into the house, then turned back and looked at Inco. His eyes shone with dark yellow light. His fear of darkness had evoked dragon night vision.

Though he startled at the sight, Inco respected Gail's personal space and ability to handle things for the night. He pretended he saw nothing and lowered his head back onto the grass, attempting to enjoy the stars, as they'd planned to do for the evening. It was pointless. He had lashed out at Gail and offended Gray, all in a single sitting. Faint echoes of the conversation hung in the air, and there was nothing more to do, so he sought the comfort of his bed.

CHAPTER 10

By the time Jak had reached nine years of age, he'd gained the speed, strength, and agility of a mature migma but was closer to the size of a six-year-old. His features had changed little, other than a slight thinning in his face.

Although his abilities were relatively benign and easy to control, Inco and Gray worked with him every day to keep them that way. Rigorous home studies with Gail had made him intelligent far beyond his years. But he had never been around other people enough to appreciate what was normal. He enjoyed adult conversation, creating short stories, and defeating Gray at chatarunga. His maturity, however, did not keep pace with his intellect. He was still quite clingy and emotionally dependent on his parents. He whined more than he should and even climbed in bed with them every chance he got.

Jak was very good at keeping everything within human boundaries—everything, except for his temper. Once his temper flared, he lost the focus he needed to control his abilities. And his anger was easy to provoke. He would lash out when things didn't go as he wanted, although he never grew angry at being corrected or refused something. His anger bore from frustration, pain, misfortune, or anything dishonorable or unjust. Dropping something, tripping over a rock, the inability to find an item, thinking Gray was cheating at a game, lies—any of these could set him off.

He and Gray spent their days coming up with ways to counterbalance his anger. They created a mantra to help calm his temper, the results of which were impressive. He would close his eyes, recite his mantra, and the anger would dissipate.

"One to grasp it. Two to stop it. Three to get past it. Four to drop it. Five to move forward. My fate is what I make it."

Together they'd ball a fist, counting out one finger at a time until their palms were fully open, then they would wiggle their fingers against each other's and laugh. After some practice, Jak went over the mantra in his head, still counting them out on his fingers.

Gray was a great inspiration to Jak. Inco and Gail were his parents, and he loved them, but Gray treated him like an equal, always including him. He'd advocated on his behalf many times and always made Jak feel accepted, regardless of the situation. It didn't matter that he was unique or short or angry, or even if he did something wrong—Gray never belittled or shamed him. Jak could always count on Gray for support.

***

"Jak wants to go to the village for his birthday tomorrow," Gray announced.

He stood with his hands on Jak's shoulders. Inco and Gail sat at a round wooden table drinking tea when they approached. Jak gave them a pleading smile over his interlaced knuckles as they looked up from their tea. While Gail took a slow sip, Inco set his on the table.

"You know we can't—"

"Please, Papa. I'll be good."

"Oh, I know you will, son. I know you will. But anything could happen. We just want to keep you safe."

"But it's my birthday. I'll be nine years old. I'm not a baby anymore."

"We know you're not. But you can still get hurt, and people won't understand the things you can do."

"I won't do anything special. I promise not to show how strong or fast or how high I can jump!"

"If you get mad, you might—"

"We have that under control," Gray cut in and stepped to Jak's side. "He hasn't had an incident in weeks."

Jak raised his index finger. "One to grasp it. Two to—"

"Honey, you can't predict what other people will do or say. That works at home, but it might not be as effective out there." Gail said.

"If I want a normal life, I need to be around other people," Jak said.

"I—" Inco furrowed his brow. "Who taught you that?"

Jak looked at Gray with a big smile.

"You raised his hopes?" Inco scowled.

"It's his birthday. He worked hard for this. He deserves a little fun. Even Gail agrees with me. Isn't that why we're here?"

Inco glared at Gail. She brought her teacup back up, attempting to hide behind it. He took a deep breath and exhaled while giving Jak a sideways stare.

"I suppose. But—"

"Yay." Jak bounced on his toes and threw his arms up in victory. He hugged Gray, then rushed to Inco.

"You will be on your best behavior," Inco said, returning his hug.

Jak then hugged Gail, nearly causing her to spill her tea. She set her cup down and returned the hug, then pulled back to make eye contact.

"You must listen to Papa. No tomfoolery."

"Yes, Mama." Jak turned to Inco. "But I get to have fun, right?"

Inco nodded.

"Promise?"

"Yes, yes, you'll have fun. Now, let's get you cleaned up. You don't want to be a messy birthday boy tomorrow, do you?"

Inco picked him up, wondering how long he'd be able to hold him like this, wondering how much longer Jak would be his baby boy. While he wanted him to grow into a solid, honorable man, he selfishly wanted him to stay this way forever.

CHAPTER 11

Jak's family lived in cabins atop a steep hill just outside the village. A nearby path took them north before heading west, arriving at the village's northern edge. As the sun warmed the late morning breeze, they set out toward the path.

"This is for you, Jak." Gail held out a small satchel. She set the strap over his shoulder and across his chest, the bag resting on his hip. "Happy Birthday, baby."

"It's just like Papa's." He opened it and looked inside, then adjusted the strap on his shoulder and fidgeted with the cover flap.

"It is. You can't go into town without a satchel."

He looked at her and smiled. "Thank you, Mama."

As they headed toward town, Jak tried to calm himself, but he skipped and jumped and moved every which way. He kicked rocks, threw twigs, and hopped onto some of the large boulders along the way. He ran a few yards ahead and used a stick to draw a large J in the dirt and then beamed at his mark as Inco and Gray caught up. As soon as they nodded in acknowledgment, he ran ahead to do it again.

Gail stayed behind. She watched from the hilltop while mending a few shirts. The village wasn't visible from the cabins, so she brought everything out and sat in the grass at the edge of the hill to watch from a distance. Jak periodically looked up from the trail and waved enthusiastically. She waved back every time.

Inco called for Jak just before reaching the edge of the village. Jak scampered over, the same big smile on his face.

"We've arrived. Remember what we talked about?"

"Stay close," Jak said. "If I can't see you, you can't see me. And—" He faltered.

"And no…"

"No strong or fast stuff."

"That's right. Here we go."

Inco held his hand as they strolled down the main road. Along the left were gardens and livestock in pens of various sizes. Along the right was a line of cloth tents with open fronts. People strolled inside the tents, inspecting the merchandise. The road was busy with people moving in every direction. He pressed against Inco a few times to avoid bumping into someone. A chicken frantically flapped in his face. He jumped back, still holding Inco's hand, and hid behind him. Inco noticed the trouble he was having and picked him up. A teen boy rushed past them in pursuit of the chicken. Jak watched over Inco's shoulder as the boy disappeared into the crowd behind them.

The view was much better from Inco's height. The street was busy and exciting. There were so many things he wanted to see.

"Can we go in there, Papa?" He pointed to a tent as they passed by.

"There?" Inco grinned. "You don't need women's clothing."

"What about that one?" He pointed at the next tent.

"Now, what do you need with a saddle bag?" Inco chuckled.

Jak frowned. Inco could see his disappointment. He looked toward the next tent, hoping it would be more suitable for Jak to browse.

"How about this one?"

He stepped off the road into the tent. Jak's frown disappeared, and he eagerly looked around.

Gray ruffled Jak's hair as he turned back toward the road. "I'm going to wander around." He disappeared into the crowd.

"I want down," Jak said. "I want to look."

"Stay with me."

"I will." Jak held Inco's hand and pulled him to a table of fruits. "What're those?"

"Hmm. I don't know. I've seen nothing like it."

A man approached on the other side of the table. "Those are called raisins. They're dried grapes."

"Dried fruit, huh?" Inco leaned in for a better look.

"I like fruit. Can I have one?" Jak reached.

Inco caught his hand and pulled it back. "How much?"

The man held up two fingers. Inco pulled two bronze coins from his satchel and set them on the table next to the raisins. Jak held his hands out together in the shape of a bowl, wiggling his fingers. The man picked up one cluster by the stalk and placed it in the boy's hands.

Jak eagerly plucked a raisin and ate it. It was sweet and tart at the same time. He pulled a small seed from his mouth and handed it to Inco. The remaining raisins went into his new satchel. He felt like a grown-up. Not only did he have his very own satchel, but now he had something to put in it. He couldn't wait to show Gray.

Inco picked him up and stepped back onto the road. Jak strained to see as far as he could. Something off in the distance caught his eye. Several children moved about, but he couldn't tell what they were doing. As they grew closer, they appeared to be kicking something around. Whatever it was, it looked fun.

"Papa, can I go play?" He pointed at the children.

"No, not today, son."

"But you said I could have fun today. I want to play. I've never played with other children before. Please, Papa, you promised."

"Look at them. They're all bigger than you,"

"But I'm stronger."

"Jak." Inco's brow furrowed.

"I'm joking. I can handle it. Let me prove it."

"Very well. Just for a few minutes." Inco made stern eye contact. "No fast stuff. No strong stuff."

"I know, I promise." He squirmed with excitement.

Inco put him down and watched him weave through the crowd to get to the children. He stepped to the side of the road to get out of everyone's way so he could watch Jak without being bumped.

"Hey, can I play?" Jak called out.

The children looked up from their game, slowing to a stop. One of them picked up the object they were kicking. It was a weathered cloth bag stuffed with straw and sewn shut.

"Sure. Now we can be even," one child spoke up. "Come. You're on my team." He gestured with a wave. "I'm Eadgar. This is Jorg, Oswine, and Dain. Over there's Saul and his team."

Everyone was bigger than Jak. Eadgar was the closest.

"How old are you?"

"I'm nine. Today's my birthday," Jak gloated.

"I'm also nine. So are Jorg and Dain. Oswine is ten."

"How do I play?" Jak changed the subject. Sensitive about his size, Jak felt better knowing that Eadgar was close to his age and not much taller.

"Just kick it to one of us, or try to get it over their stick. But don't let them kick it over our stick." He pointed out the sticks.

"Got it!" Jak quivered with excitement.

The boy held the straw ball with both hands and flung it high into the air. All the players froze as they watched. The moment it hit the ground, they all rushed towards it. One boy bumped into Jak, nearly knocking him over. He hesitated for a moment, then brushed it off, and ran with the group of boys.

Inco's attention peaked when the boy bumped into Jak. He sighed in relief when Jak brushed it off and continued into the game. His worries and fears continued to lessen as he watched his son laugh and shout with the other boys. It occurred to him that Jak had done nothing physically competitive, and perhaps it was time for him to learn to control his speed and strength rather than hide it.

Jak enjoyed the game. As he played, his confidence grew. He kept his focus on not using any extra strength or speed but still increased his game efforts. He wanted to make at least one point before he went home.

The ball rolled to him, and he kicked it in a zig-zagging pattern toward the other team's stick. His focus narrowed in on the ball. Everything around him faded from sight. Kick after kick, his confidence grew.

"Oof!" He collided hard with another boy and fell backward onto the ground, dazed by the sudden hit.

Saul stood over him. "Do you need a kiss from your mama?"

Inco started forward to intercede if necessary.

"No. I'm fine." Jak jumped to his feet and ran towards the ball as if nothing had happened.

Inco stopped, but he stood a few paces closer now. Pride and confidence swelled in him after seeing his boy take such a blow and not get angry.

The ball rolled near Jak again. This time he looked for someone on his team. Eadgar was open. He looked back down at the ball and pulled his leg back to kick it.

"Oof!" He hit the ground again.

"Watch where you're going, shorty," Saul sneered and then laughed obnoxiously. Two other boys approached at either side, laughing along. Jak glanced at each of them with a menacing grin.

"My horse shits taller than you," Saul declared and kicked the ground, flinging dirt at Jak's shoe, then ran toward the ball.

Inco didn't worry as much this time, but he remained alert and watchful.

"Don't mind him. He's an ass." Eadgar offered a hand and pulled Jak up.

"Ass?" His face twisted with confusion.

"That's what you call a guy you don't like. My Pa says it all the time."

"Ass," Jak repeated to himself. He looked to the side of the road and met Inco's eyes. Inco nodded with a pleasant smile, acknowledging that he was doing well among the other boys.

Jak rejoined the game but was more aware of Saul now. He kept him in his peripheral vision to avoid another collision. Occasionally, he noticed Saul watching him, and they briefly locked eyes.

"Watch this," Saul whispered to one of his teammates. He ran a few steps, kicked the ball towards Jak, and then ran full speed behind it.

Jak saw his sudden change of pace and braced himself.

"One to grasp it," he whispered, uncurling one finger from his fist. Being knocked down twice by the boy gave him an idea of his level of strength. He didn't have to be super strong to stop Saul.

"Two to stop it." The ball flew towards his chest.

"Three to get past it." He swatted the ball from mid-air, took a breath, and stepped into Saul's charge.

"Four to *drop* it." They collided, but this time Jak wasn't the one to hit the ground.

Saul fell back. He looked at Jak with shock and awe.

"Five to move forward. My fate is what I make it," Jak muttered with a glare, then walked away.

Saul's expression turned to anger. He grabbed a handful of dirt and threw it. His teammates approached him on either side, but they said nothing.

Inco lowered his gaze and furrowed his brows. Jak noticed and knew the expression meant he was pushing his luck.

Saul huddled with his team. Jak huddled with his. Eadgar talked about a strategy, but Jak wasn't paying attention. He wasn't used to feeling anger at others. He had never been exposed to anyone outside of his little family. Incidents among them were rare, and they usually handled them together. Controlling anger towards others was different and harder to control. He wasn't even sure it was anger he felt. It felt more like pride, defense, or ego. He looked at the other team's huddle to see Saul staring back.

"Got it, Jak?" Eadgar clapped, and their team spread out.

Jak snapped out of his gaze with a confused look.

"Just get the ball to Oswine, all right?"

Saul threw the ball into the air. Some teammates went after it. Saul and two others hung back a bit, running together, slower than the others. Saul ran along one side of the dirt patch; the boy with the ball ran along the other. The ball flew toward the goal, but Jorg blocked it and kicked it to Dain. Dain kicked it to Eadgar. Eadgar kicked it to Jak. Oswine stood ready by the other team's stick.

Someone pulled a cart in front of Inco. He tried to get around, but the crowd was unusually thick, and he found himself stuck in place.

Jak needed to zig-zag the ball a little to get close enough to kick it to Oswine. He started running while trying to monitor Saul's position, as his supporting teammates ran toward him. Jak's focus switched to them, and when he again looked back, he didn't see Saul. He slowed to a trot and looked around.

"Oooof!" Saul tackled him from behind, this time landing on top of him, scrambling to sit on his belly.

"Come on, Saul, stop being an ass!" Eadgar tried to assist, but one of Saul's teammates held him back. He struggled against the larger, stronger boy. "Move!"

Saul straddled Jak's belly. He pulled back his arm and swung, hitting Jak below the eye, dazing him.

"Nobody knocks me down, especially some rat-faced outsider." He pulled back and swung again, hitting again near the same spot.

Just as the first hit had put Jak in a daze, the second hit snapped him out of it. He squirmed to get free, but Saul's other teammates had rushed over and held down his shoulders.

"Get him," they yelled while laughing.

Inco finally made his way around the cart to see Jak on the ground with others holding him down.

Saul pulled back and swung a third time, aiming for Jak's chest, hitting the edge of his Qi. Jak's body trembled with a surge of adrenaline. His pupils elongated, and a transparent inner eyelid blinked. He strained against the pressure of Saul's weight to take in a deep breath. Seeing the transformation of Jak's eyes, the two teammates let go and backed away, but Saul didn't move. His mouth fell agape.

"You're a demon."

Jak let out a roar that echoed as far as the hilltop. Gail heard and scrambled to her feet for a better view.

Jak shoved Saul with both palms, one on each side of his chest. Saul flew off him and hit the ground hard, a short distance away. He rolled around, gasping, trying to catch the breath that had been knocked out of him.

The entire village came to a halt as people stopped to see what was going on. Jak scrambled to his feet. Saul's teammates who held Eadgar back now cowered behind him. Surprised but unafraid, Eadgar walked toward Jak. He stopped nose to nose with Jak and looked into his eyes.

"Are you all right?" He asked just above a whisper.

Before Jak could answer, Inco yanked him away and held him close. He looked up where Gail watched from the hilltop before turning his attention to the road, full of people and carts that eliminated any chance of getting through. The only thing between him and the hill was Oswine, still standing by the goal stick, frozen in fear. Gray burst through the crowd to join Inco and Jak on the field. The crowd surged forward, cries, curses, and threats increasing the closer they came.

"We have to go up the hill," Inco whispered.

"We'll never make it. Not without using extra abilities," Gray whispered back.

"It doesn't matter anymore."

Inco hurried toward the hill. Oswine, still frozen, watched as they approached, then passed him. Their quick pace turned to a jog, then a run.

"Think they'll follow?" Gray looked over his shoulder.

A few people approached the edge of the game field and stood next to Oswine. They talked among themselves and pointed towards Jak.

"They must go around, but they will come, I'm sure of it." Inco set Jak down at the base of the hill.

"I'm sorry, Papa. It wasn't my temper this time. Something happened when he hit my Qi."

"No matter." He urged him toward the hill. "Go! Climb!"

Jak looked up, daunted. It was nearly as steep as a wall. He put one foot on the hill and tried to put weight on it but slid down.

"Dig into it, like this," Inco said.

He opened his hand wide and curled his fingers as if he held an invisible ball. He slammed it into the hill. His fingertips sank past the grass into the thick clay soil. He then kicked his opposite foot in the hill and hoisted himself up. Jak copied and rose to his side.

"That's it. Keep going."

Gray pressed ahead to guide Jak from above while Inco held back to guide from below.

Jak kept going, grunting a little as he went. It wasn't the time to tell anyone, but it was sort of fun. His confidence grew a little, and he picked up speed.

"Careful, son," Inco cautioned.

"I am."

As if he'd jinxed himself, the soil under one foot crumbled and gave way. He tried to regain his balance but slipped. Both hands lost grip, and he fell.

"Paa—"

Inco caught him by the strap of his satchel. Jak swung his hand into the hill as Inco lifted him back up. He kicked into the soil and regained his balance, resuming his climb past his father again.

The villagers watched as the trio climbed the hill with inhuman agility. Commotion among them increased, and a few people shouted.

"Monsters."

"Demons."

Saul caught his breath and whined as he pointed toward the hill where three figures climbed with extraordinary speed. His father rushed to his side and yelled at the other villagers.

"After them!"

Gray reached the top and lay on his belly, his arms dangling toward Jak. He looked out at the crowd of villagers shouting curses and taunts.

"Stop the demons," Saul's father yelled as he rushed toward the hill with the villagers close behind him.

Jak neared the top, and Gray pulled him the rest of the way. They stood together, waiting for Inco, while the villagers gathered below. Several men grabbed handsful of grass, trying to pull themselves up. One tried using the foot holes left by Inco, climbing a third of the way.

Inco kicked into the hill and pushed down hard. A large chunk of soil loosened and fell, knocking several men back down.

"Hurry! Get to the road," Saul's father yelled. The crowd followed him along the bottom of the hill toward the road. Another smaller group had already run in the same direction.

"Get him ready to go. Grab only what we need," Inco said to Gray. He followed a step behind, looking over his shoulder at the crowd filling the road.

"Papa," Jak cried out from the cabin doorway. "Papa, I'm sorry."

"It's not your fault." Inco knelt to hug him. "Now, go fill your satchel with whatever you want to bring with you. Gray," he shouted, "grab Jak's clothes."

"On it," he called out from another room.

Gail ran toward them. "They're almost here."

"We have to go." Inco went inside to help pack up.

"Jak's blanket," Gail exclaimed. She turned to run back to her cabin.

"Leave it," Inco hollered.

"He'll never sleep again without it," She shouted over her shoulder as she ran.

"Where are we going?" Jak cried and pulled at Inco. "I'm scared."

"Gray, are you ready?" He picked up Jak and headed to the door. As he stepped outside, the crowd reached the turn of the path.

Saul's father pointed. "There they are."

"Where's Gail?" asked another man.

"They probably killed her," someone answered.

The crowd ran forward as Gray stepped out of the cabin.

"We have to go. Now!" Inco ran with Gray at his side.

"Mama," Jak called out, reaching towards the cabins. "Mama!"

The crowd had passed Gail's cabin and was running past the second cabin. An arrow pierced the ground in front of Gray. He jumped over it and looked at Inco, surprised, and fearful.

"Now?"

"Not yet."

"Mama. We can't leave Mama!" Jak wailed.

Inco pulled Jak from his hip and held him against his chest as another arrow landed in front of them.

"Now?" Gray repeated.

"Now!" He clutched Jak and leapt into the air. His body burst into dragon form, his large scaly arms still holding Jak against his chest.

The sudden change terrified jak. He'd never seen Inco in dragon form before. He looked at his large dragon head and screamed until finally, he passed out.

Gray still ran in his Dú. He jumped onto a boulder and sprang up, taking dragon form before he landed. The two of them hovered, looking down as the crowd came to an abrupt stop. Several people tripped over those in front of them.

"Snake," one man called out. As one, the crowd turned toward him, and someone smacked the back of his head.

"Dragons," Saul's father hollered. "Demon dragons. Kill—"

Gail's cabin exploded. Logs and debris flew in all directions as she shot up in dragon form. The crowd screamed and gasped, covering their heads. She flew over the startled crowd to join her family. Together, they ignored the crowd and turned away. Their bodies waved like ribbons in the wind. Their wingless flight aimed toward the dragon cave.

CHAPTER 12

Æmma was just as they had left her. She lay in a deep slumber, her breathing slow but otherwise motionless on the stone slab where Misty had healed her. She was very plain yet beautiful. Her hair had grown and covered the rock all around her head. Jak stood at her side, put his hand on hers, and stared at her face.

"This is my first Mama?"

"That's right." Inco crouched next to him. "You came from her belly."

"Is she sleeping?"

"Yes. She'd been injured. Remember how I fixed all your cuts and scrapes with my Qi? That's how she was treated, but now she has to sleep while her body heals."

"Why?"

"Because xenum is very strong, and when a sleeping human gets healed by it, their body sleeps until it wears off. It took a lot of xenum to heal her wounds." Inco rubbed a scar on Æmma's arm. "She'll sleep for a long time. But when she wakes up, she'll be well."

"She's not like you?" Jak's voice trembled.

He didn't know much about the Qi, just the bedtime stories Gray told him. He wondered how much of what he knew was true. He'd never understood why he was special or how it might relate to the dark scale. He only knew he had to be secretive about it and his abilities because others wouldn't understand.

Inco stroked his back. "No, son, she's a normal human."

Jak tried to make sense of all the new information. Nothing was as he thought. It was all so confusing and scary. He questioned everything else, starting with his father.

"Are you my first Papa?"

Inco winced at the question. He didn't consider Jak anything less than his own son.

"No, son, I'm not your first Papa, but I'm your Papa now, and I always will be." his voice cracked as emotions tightened his throat.

Although he'd asked, Jak hadn't expected the answer he got. He looked for another person lying on another stone slate.

"Where's my first Papa?"

"He died the day you were born. He was a hero. He saved both you and your mother."

Jak's gaze returned to Æmma. "What was his name?"

"Ælwulf."

Inco respected Ælwulf's memory and had no ill thoughts of him, but telling the boy about his birth father was painful.

Jak continued to stare at Æmma, memorizing her features while he tried to make sense of all the new information.

"Was he a dragon?"

"No, he was a courageous human, the bravest human I've ever seen." Inco tried to conceal his shock at Jak's casual mention of dragons. He wasn't sure how much Jak remembered from their escape from the village, but the boy had slept through the entire flight, and everyone was in their

Dú by the time he woke. Inco looked at Gail and Gray to communicate his concern, also showing his frustration at whoever told Jak about dragons. They both stirred uncomfortably; Gray looked away to hide the guilt.

"Am I a dragon?" Jak looked Inco in the eye.

"We—" Inco faltered, surprised at himself for not having prepared an answer for the inevitable question, but he hadn't expected this conversation to happen for several more years. Jak was only nine years old, and his questions were getting closer to information he wasn't old enough to understand. He and Gail exchanged expressions of caution and hesitation.

"We don't know." He looked back at Jak. "We won't know until you grow up."

Jak pressed his chin into his collarbone. Emotions stirred within him. Though his intelligence soared ahead of his age, his emotional maturity did not. He inhaled deeply, caressing the back of Æmma's hand. He squeezed his eyes shut and quivered as he exhaled.

"Am I a demon?" A tear fell. "Is that what's wrong with me?"

Gail brought her hand to her chest. "Heavens, no!"

She rushed to Jak's side. "You're a precious gift. There's nothing wrong with you. Just look at your blessings." She hesitated before adding, "Your first Mama will wake up, and you'll have two Mamas."

She encouraged this as a good thing, but in truth, it scared her to think of losing Jak when Æmma awakened. Saying it out loud caused her to choke up. She swallowed hard, bringing her other hand over the boy's chest, just above his Qi.

"You have the bloodlines of a very brave first Papa who loved you more than anything." She forced a smile. "And a very brave Mama who is full of love." Her tone quieted to a loud whisper as she touched Jak's nose with the tip of her finger. "All that bravery, all that love, for one little boy."

Jak felt comforted and irked at the same time. His thoughts spun. There were so many; it was hard to express only one. They all spilled out at once.

"Why do I have a Qi? Why's it black and not green like yours?" He glanced at Inco. "Why am I faster and stronger than I'm supposed to be?" His breathing quickened. Tears flowed from his eyes. Gail moved in and embraced him. He let go of Æmma's hand and turned to her, burying himself in her embrace, crying hard.

"Shhh," she intermittently rubbed and squeezed him. Tears filled her eyes and rolled down her cheeks. Her chin on Jak's head, she still looked at Inco. "Shhh," she continued, placing her cheek on his head, silently begging Inco to make it better.

All Inco could do was wrap his arms around Gail and rest his chin on her head. She leaned her cheek into his neck. His scent filled her lungs and fluttered in her belly. His arm gently rested across her back, and the warmth of his skin rushed into hers. He pulled her close, breathing her scent of sun and rosemary. He closed his eyes and held his breath for a moment.

Jak's cries faded, and he stirred between them. His face was still red and wet from crying, but he'd regained his composure. They loosened their embrace to give Jak room to move but didn't let go.

"Where are we going now?"

Inco kept his arm on Gail but leaned towards the boy. "We're going to Origo."

"Where's Oreo?"

"Oh-ree-goh," he enunciated. "It's a beautiful land, far away, but also fairly close. It's where dragons come from, and many other amazing beings and creatures."

Jak perked up. "Do I get to be strong and fast?"

"No, son. I'm sorry. You still have to follow the same rules."

Jak's expression shot from excitement to confused anger. "Why? If everyone there has a—"

"You're still different. Dragons don't have abilities or a Qi until they grow up. And you have a different Qi." He pondered how to explain. "Some fear what they don't understand. Origins might react the same as the Earthlings, or even worse, and it won't be easy to run from them. Most aren't human, and many of them aren't bound to the ground."

"Will I have to hide it forever?"

"Just until you're older, then it won't be as unusual." Inco reached out.

Jak pulled away and stepped back. Gray came to his side and held out one finger. Jak slapped his hand and stormed away, stomping his feet to the center of the cave. He let out a frustrated scream, then dropped to the floor and buried his face between his knees,

The adults exchanged concerned glances. No one knew what to do. Jak was the only one of his kind, whatever his kind was.

Inco stood and helped Gail to her feet. "It's time to go."

Jak stood abruptly and walked back to Æmma. He placed a hand on her belly and felt it rise and fall with her breathing. His anger mixed with all the feelings inside of Æmma. He felt her love, fear, concern, despair, and exhaustion. He leaned in and kissed her cheek, then backed away and turned to Inco.

"I'm ready," He whispered.

Inco put his arm around Jak and walked him to a smooth area of the cave wall. Stepping into the wall, he glanced at the boy, then bent down and stepped the rest of the way through.

Jak watched as Inco's foot was the last part of his body to disappear. He looked to Gail, who nodded and gently nudged him forward. He stepped into the wall and disappeared. She followed.

Gray approached Æmma's side. He remembered her soft voice when she sang the broken melody to Jak and the connection he felt through her touch just before he lost consciousness. She held a special place in his heart. She was the first Earthling to know him in dragon form, and he felt accepted by her. He kissed her forehead, breathing in her smell. He then went to the wall and put one foot through. He paused for one last look at Æmma before going the rest of the way.

Out of a dark corner of the cave, Roe stepped into the dusty beams of light and pulled back the hood of his cloak.

CHAPTER 13

Gray shielded his eyes as they adjusted from the darkness of the cave to the brightness of the sun. The others came into focus, standing on the cliff's edge, looking down at the landscape of Origo.

"Look, Jak. That's a male gazellion," Inco pointed out. "You can tell because the females don't have horns."

Jak leaned to see an animal eating orange grass. It reminded him of a deer, except it had two long black horns curving up between its ears. The gazellion took off running, splitting itself into a herd of smaller gazellions that ran in unison, then slowed and merged into one again. It looked back across the landscape and went back to grazing.

"A gazellion splits into thirty-seven smaller gazellion when it runs. The word 'gazellion' also means 'thirty-seven' because of this," Inco said.

Another movement pulled Jak's attention to a pond where a stick poked from the water. Attached to it was a string that led out into the grass.

"That's a mermaid fishing for a meal," Inco explained, seeing Jak's curious expression.

There was a sudden splash as the stick fell back into the water, pulling the string. At the other end, a small brown animal struggled as it was dragged from a hole. It jerked away, clawing at the dirt. The grass moved to either side, opening a pathway, as the string dragged the animal across the soil toward the water. It stopped at the edge, trying desperately to escape, and then was violently pulled in.

"Grass can move?" Jak awed.

"Usually, just green grass," Gray said. "Lots of other colored grass can't move: red, orange, yellow, purple, and blue. Never touch the blue; it's poisonous."

A gentle wind blew over a cluster of trees. Thousands of leaves rustled and whispered as they broke free of the branches, leaving the trees bare. Jak watched with amazement as they flew about in random circles before falling back into the trees, making them full and luscious again.

Jak looked out at the landscape of Origo. To the right, tall mountains with white peaks poked through thin clouds. The clouds were very peculiar. They flowed within themselves, pouring up and out of the center like a weak geyser, then folding back into itself from underneath.

To his left was a body of water with large white stones lining its edge and straight ahead, nothing but forest as far as he could see.

Inco looked down at Jak's expression and chuckled. "Welcome to Salus, the northern half of Origo. Son, this is our new home."

The strangeness and beauty of the place overwhelmed Jak. So much had happened over the last few hours. He closed his eyes and struggled to calm his racing mind.

Gray squeezed in between the two. He leaned forward to look over the cliff's edge and blew a large cloud of smoke. The smoke rolled into the air below them and took the shape of stairs.

"This is the mid-east Air region of Origo." He explained. "There are many things we can trust but cannot see."

Gail stepped out onto the smoke stairs and reached for Jak, but he recoiled behind Gray with a whimper.

She smiled. "It's safe." She tapped her foot on the stair, but Jak shook his head and withdrew farther, clutching onto his satchel as if it would save him.

"It's all right, son." Inco picked him up. "I'll carry you down."

Jak let out a trembling, high-pitched cry of fear.

"Cover your eyes. I have you. I won't let you fall."

Jak squeezed his eyes shut and pushed his face into his father's chest. Gail motioned for Gray to walk ahead of her so he could blow more smoke onto the stairs.

"Remind me why we're walking instead of flying," Gray groaned.

Inco adjusted his hold. "Jak is afraid of flying."

"He's afraid of this as well."

"Not nearly as much." Inco pulled his head back to look down at Jak, whose eyes remained tightly shut. "He's still conscious."

"Where are we going, anyway? We can't live in the woods like before. Not with a child."

Gail smiled. "We can if we have a house in the woods." She looked at Inco on the step behind her, then at Jak. "Follow me." She took dragon form and elegantly drifted away.

Inco looked down at Jak, who had passed out again. He pulled him to his chest and flew off into dragon form.

"Yes!" Gray leapt off the stairs, staying in his Dú as he fell. Just before impact, he took dragon form and flew along the ground. The grass moved to avoid being touched, exposing bare soil. "Woo-hoo! I missed this." He ascended in the sky and followed the others.

They landed in a meadow at the edge of a forest and returned to their Dú. Tall yellow wheat-like grass grew over the entire meadow with several patches of flowers and medicinal plants. It was large and oval, with one narrower end facing east. The field was large enough to raise a small city, but its natural foliage grew tall instead. They stood at the northern edge of the meadow, looking into the forest.

Inco recognized the area as the Gabril Forest. He'd spent some time in the area a few years back. The winters were milder, and the summers were never too hot. It was a perfect spot, known to be the home of many night creatures, making it difficult to sleep through all their commotion.

"How far from here?" Inco asked.

"Just a bit," Gail spoke over her shoulder as she followed a trail through the trees. "Not much longer."

True to her word, a few moments later, they arrived at a sunny clearing in the forest. A circular, waist-high wall wrapped the clearing. It was made of dull red adobe with light grey stones that poked out like scattered pearls, giving it the name 'pearled adobe.' Gaps in the wall split it into four sections, each with flat stone paths that led to the matching pearled adobe house and well.

Gray stared, marveling at its massive size for a single ground level home. The double-chimney roof slanted toward the back, lined along the lip with bamboo logs that protruded every three feet over at least a dozen tall, narrow windows that wrapped the house. The yard was dry, pale, and free of grass but decorated with a modest fire pit hemmed in by small pearled adobe benches. A log that appeared to be part of a fallen tree gave a break to bare soil monotony at the other side of the yard.

Inco admired the beauty of the home. He'd never come across it when he had visited the forest. He wondered why Gail had lived in the rough cabins on Earth when she had such a beautiful home in Origo.

Jak stirred in his arms, looking around, confused, and suddenly remembered the air-stairs. He whipped his head from side to side and twisted and looked down at the ground, then let out a sigh of relief. Inco chuckled and set him on his feet.

"Come," Gail called from the clearing. "There's someone I want you to meet."

"Huh?" Gray uttered. "I thought she was a widow."

Inco started toward the house. "Maybe she has a dog."

"A dog? Alone for this long?"

"Or a tethered fairy."

"I loathe fairies."

"Even the ladies?"

"Heh, fairladies are fun, but they can't cook." He rubbed his hungry belly as he followed. "And fairmen are traitorous assholes."

"Language," Inco scolded.

Jak walked ahead and picked up a lumpy oval rock. "I know what an ass is, Papa. Eadgar told me. That's what you call a guy you don't like."

"Actually, it's—just don't use that word. Can you do that for me?"

Jak inspected the lumpy rock, hardly listening, but nodded.

"Joss?" Gail called into the house. She walked in, looking back for everyone to follow. "Joss, I'm home."

Inco messed Jak's hair as he walked by. The boy stood still, rolling the rock in his hands as he examined it.

"This rock is *lonely*." He clutched it into his fist. Inco and Gray had walked past him without noticing, so he sauntered behind them.

"Joss? Where are—" she paused, looking into a room. "There you are. Didn't you hear me calling?"

Curious, Inco and Gray followed Gail.

"Gail?" a woman's voice shrieked. "Gail. Gail. Gail."

Inco and Gray approached the doorway to see Gail and another woman embrace. They both cried and pulled back to look at each other. Gail kissed her forehead and embraced her again. They buried their faces into each other's shoulders, crying and murmuring words unintelligible to the men.

Inco stepped into the room. "Is this your cousin or sister?"

Gail turned from the embrace. Her face soaked with tears, she smiled.

"This is my sister-wife, Joscolyn; Joss for short."

It was not the answer Inco expected. Plural marriage was common, but Gail had never mentioned her. He bowed his head toward Joss but gave Gail a look of bewilderment.

"We've been raising a child together for nine years," he said in a low tone. "And you never mentioned having a sister-wife."

"I was afraid you wouldn't understand," She timidly spoke while rubbing a chill from her arm.

Joss looked back and forth between the two in shock.

"Raising a child? Are you—"

"Oh, no, no, no. Never without you, love. He rented my spare cabin and was raising an orphan child. I sort of became attached. I became his mother." She tried to look past Inco's expression of hurt and surprise.

Jak approached Gray in the hall just outside the door. He stared down at his rock, feeling it. It wasn't a physical feeling, but a deep internal sense. He stared at it as he entered the room, stopping beside Inco.

Gail overlooked Jak as she dwelled on how Inco must've felt. She glanced at him every other second, trying to read him while dodging eye contact. Inevitably, contact was made, and Gail saw the glimmer of pain in his eyes. All she could do was apologize with hers.

"Mama?" Jak held out the rock with a bewildered expression that grew as he spoke. "This rock is *lonely.*"

She closed his fingers around the rock and pushed it down to his side. "Jak, this is Joss. Joss, meet Jak."

Joss leaned down to his level. "I thought you said nine years. He doesn't look—"

"He's small for his age," Gail cut her off in a whisper.

Jak looked at her, tilting his head slightly. He opened his satchel and dropped the rock inside, then stepped forward and reached for Joss.

She pulled him in and stood, smiling as he studied her face. Her eyes were narrowed, and the outer edges angled up. They were a glowing golden color. Her skin was a beautiful, deep tawny beige, but her lips were ashen. Her hair was thick, black, and puffed up all around her head. He touched her kinky hair. It sprung back into place when he let go. He put his palm on her cheek and held it there. Her smile grew large.

"You're lonely, too," he said just above a whisper.

Her smile twitched a bit as it faded, but it didn't disappear. He brushed his hand along the side of her face to her ear, moving the hair out of the way. Her ear was long and pointed at the top. Jak inspected her ear. He was curious, but he kept it to himself.

He felt her emotions—loneliness, a little fear, fluttering joy, an intense yearning, and deep, complicated sadness—but didn't know what to make of it. He ran his fingertips across her forehead and down her jawline to her neck, then pulled his hand away and whispered, "All you need is love."

Joss let out a crying laugh. She pulled him in for a long, tight embrace, smiling at Gail as if she'd just received the best gift in the world. Jak turned to Gail while still in Joss's arms. His expression was perplexed.

"I can feel her, Mama." His voice shook with sadness.

Inco stepped forward. "What do you mean?"

"She's sad and lonely. I can feel it."

She set him down and stroked his hair, looking to Gail and Inco with an awkward expression.

"Hey," Gray called from the hallway. "Do you have some fat I could chew? I'm starved."

"Fat?" Joss sneered. "I can do better than fat." She raised her eyebrows matter-of-factly as she passed him in the hall. "Who wants crendala?"

"Cren… Cren… She's an elf?" Gray beamed, bouncing on his toes.

"She's a DúElf." Gail smiled, amused by his enthusiasm.

"Yes! Best day ever," he cheered.

Inco and Gail both looked at him playfully.

"I mean, meal. Bad day. Best meal… the—" He pointed down the hall and eased away in the direction Joss had gone.

That fall, a new chapter began in their lives. Everything calmed. They had enough privacy for Jak to enjoy more freedom. Inco enjoyed building a unique friendship with Joss while deepening his friendship with Gail. Joss' elven cooking thrilled Gray to no end.

Life was good… for a while.

CHAPTER 14

Gail and Joss had been melancholy for days. They didn't smile or laugh. They hardly spoke, and they were especially sad when going in or coming out of one particular room. They had locked it since Gail and her entourage had arrived. Jak wasn't allowed in. The adults told him it wasn't a place for children. He was curious, but the sadness of the room deterred him.

He felt sadness in the house. It had been there since they had arrived a year earlier, but now it was almost overwhelming. Inco tried to be supportive and empathetic while keeping a distance. He'd cooked the last few nights, and Jak had grown tired of potatoes and eggs. Gray spent most of his time away from home.

Jak tried to distract himself by playing outside. He had kept the rock he'd found the day they arrived. He didn't go anywhere without it. The rock had feelings inside it. It wasn't alive, but Jak felt it, and it somehow connected with him. He'd sit and stare at it for hours, rubbing the lines, ripples, and lumps.

The rock had also caused him a bit of trouble. No one understood his attachment to it, but mostly let it be. When it broke Joss's blue flower vase, Inco sent him to his room for the rest of the afternoon. A few days later, he was playing with it, tossing it in the air. It came down and hit Inco on the head while he sat whittling. He'd been warned never to throw it in the house again.

One night, while they were eating, Jak had the rock on the table, tapping one end of it, causing it to spin. He tapped too hard, and it flew into the serving bowl, splashing soup onto Gail and Joss. Gail took the rock away and put it on a shelf until morning. That was a horrible night. Jak couldn't sleep without it. Since then, he'd been careful only to toss it around outside.

One evening, Jak felt overwhelmed by the sadness in the house. It weighed heavily on him, to the point of overshadowing any feelings of his own. He was going outside when he glimpsed his satchel from the corner of his eye. Excitement rushed through him as he put it on, put his rock in it, and ran outside.

The sky was pink with dusk, and nocturnal animals in the forest emerged from their nests for a night of hunting. The air cooled with a light breeze, carrying fragrances of flowers from the Gabril meadow.

Jak sat on a log and opened the satchel. The cluster of raisins was still there. He examined them carefully, remembering the day in the village. He put one in his mouth, savoring the tart and sweet flavor. It was as good as he remembered. He pulled another raisin off and rolled it between his fingers, still savoring the taste of the first one. He noticed there was something familiar about the one in his hand.

It occurred to him that the raisin looked like his rock. He pulled the rock out and held it next to the raisin. The rock was much larger, but they looked just alike.

"I'll call you Raisin," he whispered. "I'm tired of calling you Rock."

"Jak," Joss called from the front door. "Time for your bath. Come inside." She disappeared back into the house.

Jak slumped with dread. He put the raisins and the rock back into the satchel and reluctantly got to his feet. Listlessly, he walked toward the house, talking to his rock.

"Come on, Raisin. We have to go back in."

The forbidden room distracted him as he made his way to the bathroom. The door was ajar. He peeked inside but didn't see anyone. The sadness in the room was overwhelming, but his curiosity grew. He pushed the door open a little farther and poked his head in, making sure no one was sitting where he couldn't see. The room was empty.

It was a large den. Solid double-doors on the far wall caught Jak's attention, and he wondered where they led, having realized he had never wandered near the back of the house, or he would have seen them from outside.

He stepped into the room, nearly tripping over the curled corner of a rug that covered most of the floor. Sconces lined the longer walls, and on the far wall was a mantelshelf over a fireplace, but something blocked it. Several pillows were on the floor with something on them, covered by a blanket. Jak wondered what it was. He pulled out the rock and clutched it for security as he crept closer. An odd feeling came from the object under the blanket. He wasn't sure what it was, but it was strangely familiar.

His hand became sweaty. The rock slid against the moisture of his palm. He stood on the tips of his toes and set it on the edge of the mantelshelf. He rubbed his palms on his clothing until they felt dry, then slowly reached for the blanket. The tips of his fingers timidly touched it. The strange feeling intensified. He pulled the blanket back slowly, revealing an enormous egg.

It was a deep red. A grey spot appeared on top and spread out, opening into a gray ring on the red surface that rippled to the bottom, then repeated. His fingertips grazed the egg; it felt peaceful, feminine, tired. With each ripple, it grew weaker. The egg was dying.

Jak laid his palms on the egg. As soon as they made contact, the room shook, and he stumbled back. The rock vibrated off the edge of the mantelshelf. He tried to catch it but missed. It fell onto the egg, creating a small crack at the top.

The shell around the crack turned grey, but this time it didn't turn into a ring as it rippled down. It spread, flowing down until the entire egg was solid grey. The color deepened, taking on a gritty, porous texture. Jak stood paralyzed by panic. The door swung open.

"Jak?" Joss's eyes immediately went to the egg, then widened with shock. "NOOO!"

CHAPTER 15

Gail and Inco were in the sitting room when they heard Joss cry out. They rushed toward her cry. As they turned into the hall, they found her collapsed in a doorway of the forbidden room, sobbing. Gail knew instantly—the egg must've died.

Migmas and dragons can only lay eggs in dragon form. If they're white, they're unseeded and abandoned in a forest for the trees to consume. If they're seeded, they'll be red and will stay red for sixty-seven years, then pulsate for the last three years, hatching in the seventieth year. However, an egg laid by a migma will never hatch. Instead of pulsating for the final three years, rings of grey ripple from top to bottom. At the end of the seventy years, it will turn to stone and be thrown into the night sky to be cared for by the Great Mistress of the Stars.

Gail had laid the egg close to sixty-seven years ago, and it had begun its three-year ripple as it died. This was the cause of the tremendous sadness in the home. Tears welled in Gail's eyes as she neared Joss in the doorway.

"It wasn't time… it wasn't time. It's all we had left of Tibbel," Joss wept.

Gail held back tears as she tried to console her. "We still have each other."

"We still had time." Joss wrapped her arms around Gail. "It wasn't supposed to happen this way."

Gail was confused. They always knew the egg would die, but Gail wasn't as knowledgeable about the process. She'd assumed it could die at any time. She looked in the den with sudden curiosity. Her gaze fell on the crack, then the rock. Her sorrow and grief turned to anger.

"I'm sorry, Mama," Jak whimpered. "I'm sorry. I didn't mean—"

Her cheeks flushed, eyes narrowed, and lips pursed. She didn't even look at Jak. Her eyes fixed on the rock that lay near the egg. Without a word, she stormed toward the rock, picked it up, then stormed away. Jak watched nervously at first. When she left the room with his rock, concern took over.

"What're you doing with Raisin? Mama!" He bolted after her. "Mama, I'm sorry. Don't take Raisin," he wailed as he chased her, catching up just outside the house. "Mama! Mama, don't!" He pulled at her dress. He didn't know what she was going to do, but he could tell it wouldn't be good.

Gail marched to the edge of the clearing and stared into the woods. Her already heavy breathing became heavier as her anger rose to a peak. She pulled her arm back, and she screeched as she threw the rock as hard as she could into the darkness of the woods. She stumbled forward from the momentum before shakily regaining her balance.

Jak, who was still pulling tightly on her dress, lost his balance and landed on his knees. He cried, but not because of falling. He cried for his rock, reaching out in the direction she had thrown it.

Gail looked down at Jak, coldly at first. Anger had overridden all her senses, but when her racing heart slowed, she felt sorry for him. That rock was his favorite thing in the world, and she had taken it away from him, not for the night, not for a few days, but permanently. Her thoughts went to the egg, her anger returning. She took a sharp breath and stormed into the house. She wasn't only angry at the rock or Jak. She was angry at Joss, and Joss needed to know.

Gail entered the den. Joss knelt over the egg, hugging its cold stone surface. Inco stroked her shoulder, unsure how to comfort her.

"This could've been avoided," Gail scowled, stopping in the middle of the room.

Joss looked at her, grief and tears covering her face. She cried a little harder in response.

"It shouldn't have been here," Gail added.

"It was all we had left of him," Joss sobbed.

"This wouldn't have happened in the nesting house. They would've kept it comfortable until it died."

"But it deserved to be with those who loved it."

"It deserved to die peacefully. Not like this."

"I couldn't—"

"You? *You?* It was my egg. *Mine,*" Gail shouted.

Joss gasped. Her crying wavered to shock. "It was ours. We were all—"

"We? No, you." Gail pointed. "You were only thinking of yourself." She turned her glare to Inco. "And *you.* You should've taken that rock from him weeks ago."

He opened his mouth to respond but sighed instead. It was an emotional time for Gail. If she needed to take it out on him, he would let her.

Gail looked at the egg for a moment, still simmering in anger, then left the room again. She could hear Joss's crying intensify as she stormed down the hall. Her anger was over-whelming. She didn't know what to do with it. Striding into the sitting room, she balled her hands into tight fists of hair, pulling at her scalp. The pain added to her outrage, tip-ping her over the edge, and she screamed out her rage, then screamed again, and again. Finally, her anger gave way to grief and exhaustion. Her thoughts returned to Jak, whom she'd left outside... alone... at night.

"Jak?" She called from the doorway, peering out at the dark shadowy clearing, but heard no response. "Jak?" she called louder. Still no response. A trickle of fear made its way up her spine as she stepped out into the clearing.

"Jak?" She called out again while her eyes searched the surroundings of the house. She ran to the edge of the clear-ing where she'd thrown the rock.

"Jak," she called out loudly. Her panic peaked, and all anger fell away. She realized she'd never been so harsh with him before. Regret sunk in the pit of her stomach while panic filled her head.

Inside, Inco tried to console Joss. He pulled her to her feet and into an embrace. She no longer cried but still trem-bled with emotion.

"I know it was her egg," she whispered into his chest. "But it was all we had left of Tibbel."

"I know. It's all right. Gail's upset. She didn't mean any of it." He rubbed her back, gently swaying with her in his arms. It was the first time he'd been this close to her, and though the circumstances were unfortunate, holding her felt nice.

"She was so upset when she found out the egg would never hatch. She didn't want to watch it die. We were going to take it to the nesting house to live out its years until it died. We all agreed, but then Tibbel died. It was all that was left of him. I couldn't let it go. She couldn't watch it die, so she went back to Earth. And I was all alone. It was all I had. And now it's gone."

Inco lifted her chin to meet his gaze. "You have us."

She looked into his eyes. They were kind and soft. He locked eyes with her, lost in the golden loops that seemed to pull him in. He moved his hand from her chin to her jawline, lightly poking his fingers into the soft hair behind her ear. He could feel her heartbeat increase as her breathing slowed. He leaned in. Her breath moistened his lips. Gail burst into the room.

"Jak's gone, I can't—" The closeness of Inco and Joss startled her.

They both let go and turned away, embarrassed. Gail's head couldn't handle much more. First, the egg, then Jak. She had no mental space for anything else, good or bad.

"I can't find him. I think he ran into the forest to find the rock."

CHAPTER 16

Jak stood at the edge of the clearing, staring out in the direction Gail had thrown his rock. He thought about going after it, but hesitated. He'd never wandered off alone. Being alone in the dark forest was scary, but the thought of never seeing his rock again was equally frightening. He quivered with the inner conflict and took a deep breath to calm himself, but it didn't work. He couldn't hold back any longer. He burst into a full sprint, running into the forest.

Small animals were everywhere. As Jak ran past, they scurried back into their holes, up the trees, or into the scattered thickets of bushes. He paid them no attention as he intently watched the ground he was running over for his rock. The forest was dark, and there were rocks and sticks everywhere. How was he ever going to find *his* rock?

Jak turned, looking back at the clearing where Gail had stood when she'd thrown the rock. He shuffled side to side, trying to align himself with the direction it had flown. Once he thought he had the right line of sight, he searched the ground again.

Suddenly everything came into clear focus. Though it was still dark, Jak could see everything clearly. He looked at his hand, and yellow light reflected off his palm. His eyes had changed to night vision. It wasn't something he'd ever learned to control, but usually worked when he needed it.

Now, with night vision, Jak noticed far more rocks than before, but none were his. He continued in the direction he thought it would have flown. Finally, he spotted it—next to a little mound in the dirt that had an opening on its side.

He squatted and grasped it in his hand. A sense of relief washed over him, but instantly turned to shock as a large black and grey animal shot from the hole and attacked his arm. He jumped back, but the animal held on tight. It scratched and dug its claws into his skin, then sank its teeth into his arm.

"Ahhh!"

He shook his arm and swatted at it, desperately trying to break free. The animal released its hold to let out a terrifying scream before sinking its teeth in Jak's arm again, shaking its head and tearing at his flesh.

Jak screamed too. He tried using his free hand to push the animal off, but the animal readjusted and mounted the other arm.

It bit down, snarled, then let go to reposition itself on his arm. As the creature came back to bite yet again, Jak dropped the rock to free his other hand. He grabbed its loose skin and pulled. It didn't let go. He tried again and still couldn't pull it off.

In the fray, Jak forgot he had extra strength he could use, but when the animal bit his arm for the fifth time, his fear and panic turned to anger. He felt fury deep in his belly that shot heat to his head. He grabbed the animal by its throat, squeezed, then sharply twisted. The animal's neck made a single pop, then went limp, but Jak wasn't done yet. He was still full of anger and truly hated the beast. He flung it into a tree as hard as he could and watched as it fell to the ground, motionless.

"Ass," he vehemently shouted at the animal.

He cried in pain as he looked at all the wounds on his arms. Blood ran down his forearms and drizzled off his elbows. Falling to his knees, his cries grew louder. The pain gave way to a final burst of anger. He grabbed a boulder and threw it at the animal but missed it entirely.

As the fear and adrenaline faded, his chest began to burn. It felt like a sunburn itching as it heals, but much more intense. He rubbed at the burning sensation, and his Qi fell into his hand. He looked down at it, remembering all the times Inco used his emerald Qi to heal scrapes and cuts over the years.

It slipped between his bloody fingers and fell onto his lap. He wiped his hands on his clothes and picked it up again. His cries faded as he felt a tumble of emotions—anger, curiosity, and pain all swirled inside of him. Rotating it between his fingers, he looked for the opening. Once he found it, he held it over the first arm and squeezed. Black xenum shot out in a stream. Most landed on his arm, but some shot past it, falling into the dirt. He held the Qi more carefully over another wound and squeezed a little more gently. Small drops of black liquid fell onto the wound. He watched as the tears and holes in his skin pulled themselves closed. He switched hands and healed the other arm.

Jak let out a sigh of relief. Blood and black xenum still covered his arms, but the painful wounds had disappeared. He pushed the Qi back against his chest and let go hesitantly, unsure if it would stay. It did. He grabbed his rock and climbed to his feet. Blood and black xenum from his forearms ran down to his hands, coating the rock and dripping onto the ground. He opened his satchel and put the blood and xenum covered rock inside, closing the flap.

Jak was about to head back to the house when he heard a soft chuckling purr sound. He thought the noise came out of the hole from which the animal had jumped. Two little noses and four tiny eyes poked from the darkness. They were babies of the animal that had attacked him. When Jak knelt to look closely, a third nose appeared behind the others. Three orphans were inside the hole.

"Maybe Mama will let me keep you," he muttered into the hole.

He looked at the animal at the base of the tree. Anger swelled in his gut again. Even though he wasn't in pain anymore, that animal had attacked him without reason. He wondered if someone could stuff it. He lifted her by the skin of her neck, holding the animal just below eye level. He inspected the animal's face, mostly black, with grey fur on top that ran down her back. He touched her sharp teeth and looked at the indent it made on the tip of his finger.

"You lose," Jak snarled.

Xenum and blood ran down his forearm, soaking into the animal's fur. It suddenly wiggled and screamed, startling Jak. He fell back, dropping the creature. Crawling backward, he glared while she stood still, looking at him. Blood and xenum rubbed off his hands and onto the ground. Cautiously rising to his feet, he continued to back away. The animal licked its lips and stood perfectly still.

"Jak!" A voice called from behind him.

Joss, Inco, and Gail all ran toward him. He looked back at the animal, still standing in place.

"Oh, Jak," Gail cried in relief. She embraced him and held him tight, then crouched to his eye level. "Are you all right?"

Before Jak could answer, she looked at his arms and gasped.

"He's hurt!"

Inco reached for his Qi but paused. He saw blood, but no wounds.

"I'm all right, Mama. I used my Qi."

He pulled his Qi from his chest and held it out for them to see. Gail looked at it with surprise and then looked at Inco with the same expression. Jak put it back on his chest.

"Oh," Joss cried out. "A honey badger."

She pointed at the animal Jak had fought, which had shuffled back to her hole. It looked at Jak one last time. He wasn't sure if it was a twitch or a gesture, but the honey badger winked, then went into the hole with the babies.

"Curse whoever brought those dangerous animals here from Earth," Gail sneered.

Joss nodded. "I try to keep them away. I've set traps and chased them off and even taken dragon form to scare them away. Nothing works. Honey badgers just don't care."

"Is that what made you bleed?" Gail held Jak's arm, turning it over, checking for any wounds he might've missed. "What's all this black stuff?"

"That's my xenum, Mama. It's black because my Qi is black."

"Yes, I know, but I didn't think—" she stopped herself from saying more. She didn't want to alarm Jak, but she'd never heard of black xenum. "Never mind, let's get you home."

"I'm sorry I broke the egg, Mama. It was an accident. The ground shook, and Raisin fell off the shelf. I wasn't throwing him. I promise."

"Raisin?" Her brow rose.

"That's my rock's name. Raisin."

He nervously watched as she closed her eyes and took a deep breath, then hugged him again.

"The egg is at peace now."

"Let's get you that bath." Joss reached for his other hand. "You're twice as dirty now."

Joss and Gail both walked him back to the house. Inco followed but stopped when something caught his eye. On the ground near where they had found Jak was a long narrow patch of fresh green grass. The rest of the ground was bare except for sticks, dirt, and a few spots of dried-up grass, but this patch was bright and healthy. Nearby, a few more tiny patches of bright green grass riddled the dirt. He walked away, his mind spinning, unsure what to think of it.

The honey badger poked out of her hole again. She sniffed the air, then looked back into the woods away from the house. She sniffed again, then postured, and let out a death rattle growl.

Inco looked back to make sure she wasn't following before continuing to the house. He didn't see what she was growling at. He didn't see Roe watching from a distance, partially hidden by a tree.

CHAPTER 17

Joss added a pot of boiling water to the bath. She smiled down on Jak as he felt the water.

"This should warm it just enough."

"That feels good," Jak said.

He hung his satchel on the chair next to the tub and climbed in. His arms swayed over the surface of the water. Blood and xenum mixed into the water. He looked at Joss, smiled, and nodded.

"I'll leave you to it. Call me if you need anything." She walked out, leaving the door ajar.

Jak had a narrow view of the hallway through the gap. The door to the den was open, and light from the sconces shone into the hall. He felt terrible for a moment, then thought of Raisin. He leaned over the edge of the tub, reaching into his satchel. His reach found something strange—small firm balls where his raisins should have been. He pulled it out. It was a cluster of grapes. He didn't understand why they were in his satchel. He opened it wide, searching the inside for his raisins. All that remained was a loose grape and his rock. He curled his fingers around it, still upset from losing his raisins.

"Ah-ha-ha-ha-haaa," a high-pitched voice squealed.

Jak fell back into the water, making a big splash. Footsteps rapidly approached in the hallway, and then the door popped open slightly more than it had been. Joss poked her head in.

"Are you all right?"

"Mm-hmm," he nodded, innocently waving his arms in the water.

"Don't make a mess." She pulled the door to a finger-width from the frame.

"I won't."

Jak waited for her shadow to fade, then looked into his satchel. There at the bottom was his rock. It was the same rock he'd always had, but something was different about it. He shook the satchel a bit to get a clearer view.

"Whoa," the same high-pitched voice yelled from the bottom.

Jak leaned in for a closer look. Two small eyes opened on the surface of the rock and looked back at him. He gasped and pulled back but was careful not to fall again.

"Why don't you draw a picture? It'll last longer," the rock said.

"What are you?"

The rock brought the remaining grape to his mouth and took a bite.

"I'm Raisin. Don't you remember?"

"Raisin?"

"That's my name. You should know. You picked it." He muffled with his mouth full, then swallowed, then took another bite of the grape and moaned with satisfaction.

"But—" Jak had no words.

Raisin stuffed the last bit of grape in his mouth, moaning and making smacking noises as he chewed, then gulped it down. "I know I'm handsome to look at, but do you think you could get me out of here?"

Jak lifted him out of the satchel and held him at eye level. Raisin's body was made of the rock Jak had been playing with for the past year. Rock dust formed his arms and legs, and tiny pebbles made up his elbows, knees, fingers, and toes. Blotches of blood and xenum covered his body. Jak touched one of the stains. It was sticky.

Raisin looked down at himself. "Ew! What's this stuff all over me?"

"It's blood and xenum."

"Blood?" Raisin cried out before fainting in Jak's palm. One eye peeked, then quickly closed again.

Jak giggled.

"Are you laughin' at me?" Raisin rose back to his feet. "Are you… laughin' at… me? You should find a reflection." He tried brushing the blood and xenum off. "You're the one who looks like someone pulled all the hair off a monkey and stuck it on his head." He rubbed harder. "Why won't this come off?"

"Why do you talk like that?"

"Like what?"

"I don't know. Strangely."

"I don't talk *strangely*. Lots of creatures talk like me."

"Like who?"

Raisin raised a brow while lowering the other. "Who wants to know? *Who wants to know?*"

Jak giggled again.

"Keep laughin'." He looked at the tub. "Ooh, that'll work." He jumped out of Jak's hand into the water, landing on his back at the bottom of the tub, still rubbing. All the blood and xenum floated off him, and a few bubbles emerged from between his legs. He smiled with relief, and then his eyes widened as more bubbles escaped his mouth. His arms flailed around in a panic. He couldn't breathe.

Jak pulled him out.

"Man," he panted. "I sank like a *rock*."

"Um," Jak smirked. "You are a rock."

"Oh, right," he snickered while staring at Jak thoughtfully. "You know wha—"

The door opened again. Jak clasped his hands around Raisin and pulled him underwater, tucking his hands between his legs and trying to act casual.

"How are you doing?" Joss peeked from the doorway.

"I'm fine."

"Are you ready to get out?"

"No, the water's still warm. A little longer?"

"I'll come back in a few minutes." She pulled the door back to where it was.

Something pinched Jak's finger hard. He flung his arms out of the water, still holding Raisin.

"Didn't we just go over this? I'm a rock, not a fish." He coughed a few times. "And another thing—never put me that close to your rocks." He spat. "I had my mouth open and everything."

Jak giggled again. Looking closer at Raisin, he could see that his body's creases still had a tiny bit of xenum in them. It occurred to him that the xenum had brought Raisin to life. And it had done the same to the raisins and the honey badger. His face lit up.

"If it can bring a stone to life, maybe it could save the egg," he exclaimed, jumping to his feet.

Raisin waved his arms while standing in Jak's hand, trying to keep his balance.

"Whoa, I'm startin' to think I don't want to be near this water anymore."

Jak gripped him tightly as he jumped out of the tub. Still wet, he ran into the den. The air was chilly to his wet naked body, but he didn't care. He pulled the Qi off his chest as he ran across the room.

Inco sat on the floor near the egg. Gail lay across a few pillows, resting her head in his lap. He ran his fingers softly through her hair. They both turned when they heard wet feet patter across the room.

"Jak? What are you doing?"

Jak didn't answer. He ran straight for the egg, leaping over pillows and blankets on his way. He shuffled to a stop and leaned into the egg, then pushed himself back a little.

Gail scolded, "What are you doing? Get away from there."

Jak held his Qi over the top of the egg. "I can fix it, Mama."

Inco jumped to his feet, but he was too slow. A short stream of black xenum shot out of the Qi and splashed against the egg. It ran through the crack and drizzled down the front to the pillows beneath it.

"Honey," Gail sighed sympathetically. "It doesn't work that way. Xenum can't—"

Before she could finish, the egg changed. The top turned light pink, and the crack pulled itself together. An angelic hum filled the air, then manifested into wavy pale hues similar to the waves of heat in summer, except they took on varying shades of green. As the waves condensed, the color deepened, and the sound shifted to come from their flow. Finally, the hues created a dragon shape without legs or defining features. The figure stretched almost the den's full length, floating along the ceiling and down to the egg.

Joss approached the doorway to see everyone motionless, watching in amazement. When she saw the hues, she froze as well. Before the last bit of the crack closed, the colors entered the egg, slowly at first, then with more speed. The humming intensity increased until the last bit of color shot inside, and the room fell silent. The crack closed completely, and the pink color deepened as it flowed down the egg.

The egg returned to its original deep red color, wobbling in place until it stopped. Bright green shadows flowed like a smoke cloud across the red, then faded. Everyone exchanged speechless glances. Gail crept on her knees and edged toward the egg.

Bright light burst from the egg, knocking Jak on his back. Gail fell to her side. Joss held the door jamb for support. The brightness briefly blinded everyone. They rubbed watery eyes, attempting to ease the mild burning sensation. As their vision regained focus, they once again gazed upon the egg. The explosion came from it without harming it. It pulsated with waves of green pulling in and out of the red. A shadow in the shape of a tiny human foot pressed against the inside of the scaly shell.

CHAPTER 18

A dragon egg only pulsates in the last three years before hatching. They wouldn't have an outcome for years. However, if Jak's family had learned anything from raising him, it was to expect the unexpected. From his black Qi to his humanity with dragon powers, a dead egg brought to life, and now, a migma egg pulsing, everything about and around Jak was different.

Gail spent a lot of time in the den. Although it would be a long time before the egg would hatch, *if* it hatched, she felt she needed to make up for lost time. She'd been away for much of its existence.

Joss spent a lot of time with the egg as well. As a full-blooded DúElf, she could've had a viable egg with Tibbel, but he died before she was ready. In her mind, this might be her only chance at having a baby. She loved Jak, but she had missed out on his baby years and hadn't quite built a motherly bond with him.

Inco tried to accommodate the ladies by taking on cooking and cleaning duties. He felt as if he were becoming a father again, looking forward to baby laughter and first words. His relationship with Gail had been stagnant for a long time. He felt an overwhelming desire for her, but she still grieved the loss of her husband. He also wasn't sure how to handle things with Joss. His feelings for her were growing at an increased rate. Though he knew the two women were a package deal and showed much love for each other, he remained confused at the complicated nature of their relationship. He had never considered loving more than one woman. But with Gail and Joss, it felt natural and unnatural at the same time. For the time being, he resolved to be there for them both—platonically—and help as much as he could.

***

Jak spent most of his time outdoors or in his room with his new old friend, Raisin. Gray hadn't been home for almost two weeks and had missed out on all the excitement. He hoped Gray would come back soon. Although anxious, he wanted to introduce him to Raisin. Jak hadn't shown the "true" Raisin to Joss or his parents for fear they would take him away.

One evening, he played outside with Raisin later than usual. Stars appeared one by one in the evening sky. The sunset wasn't visible from their little clearing in the forest, but Jak could tell it was near that time. As he admired the colors of dusk, a familiar figure caught his eye.

The honey badger stood at the edge of the clearing. In her mouth, she carried one of her babies. It hung by the skin of its neck, barely moving, but it made small whimpering noises. The mother badger set the baby down, then stared at Jak with an intensity that made him uncomfortable.

Jak stepped back, unsure of what to expect. The baby lay on its side, moving its arms and legs, but made no attempt to stand. The mother badger continued to stare, and Jak stared right back. She didn't show any signs of aggression or fear. Instead, she used her nose to push the baby forward a bit, then stepped back, sat on her haunches, and stared at Jak.

Overcoming his anxiety, he stepped forward with caution. He hesitated when the mother licked her lips. Was she trying to tell him something? As he drew closer, he felt her emotions. She was pleading for something. He gained a little confidence and shifted closer, still cautious. The last thing he wanted was another bite from her powerful jaws and sharp teeth.

"Please," a voice whispered. "Help her."

He jumped back a step. "You," he gulped. "You can talk?"

She tilted her head. "You can hear me?"

"Why wouldn't I?"

She looked at her cub. "Please help her."

"But… how?" Jak stepped closer.

"Whatever you did to me, it changed me. I am now somehow connected to you. I have been watching over you since that night. But all of that is not important. Please help her."

"What's wrong with her?"

"She fell ill. I do not know what is wrong with her. Just help her."

Jak knelt and touched the cub. It didn't respond. He pulled his Qi off his chest, rolled the cub onto its back, and placed a drop of xenum on its belly. It squirmed a bit but didn't seem to be better. Jak gently opened the cub's jaw and put another drop in its mouth. The cub made suckling noises but still didn't seem healed. Jak returned his Qi to his chest and sighed.

"I'm sorry. I don't know…"

Before the mother badger could respond, the cub rolled onto its feet and nuzzled under her.

"Thank you," she whispered.

"I still don't understand how you can talk," Jak whispered back.

The cub walked to Jak. He let it sniff his hand, then looked to the mother for reassurance. She gave a nod of approval. Jak nodded and cuddled the badger cub against his chest.

"It's probably something in that black stuff," Raisin chimed in from behind him.

The mother badger jumped back and growled.

"Whoa, whoa, whoa. I'm with him," Raisin said.

The mother badger looked to Jak for confirmation.

"It's all right. This is my friend, Raisin," Jak said. "But how did my xenum connect us?"

"You covered me with muck. Did she get that on her, too?" Raisin suggested.

"Maybe that's it." Jak wanted to dismiss the subject he couldn't discuss with anyone outside the home. He changed the subject. "What's your name?"

"I have no name in your language."

"Well, you look a bit like a skunk. How about Skunky?" he chuckled.

The badger growled with disapproval.

"All right, all right. How about Matilda?"

"Matilda." She repeated. "What does it mean?"

"Something about battles. She's a girl soldier in one of my brother's stories."

"I like it," she said. "You may call me by this name, Matilda."

"Can I name this baby, too?"

"You saved her life, so you may name her, as long as it is not 'skunk.'"

Jak nuzzled the cub close to his face. "How about Honey? She's sweet, and she's a honey badger."

Matilda let out a sigh. "I suppose that is not terrible."

He put the cub down. It pranced to Matilda and stood beside her.

"It's time for me to go inside."

Matilda made a rattle noise to stall Jak. "Someone watches you from the forest."

"Huh? Who? Why?"

"His intentions are not good. I can smell his pitiful disgrace. He has no honor."

Jak looked into the forest but saw nothing. "I'll tell my papa." He turned toward the house. "Goodnight, Matilda. Goodnight, Honey."

Matilda picked up Honey in her mouth and disappeared into the darkness of the forest.

CHAPTER 19

Inco made a loin for supper. It relieved Jak to see something other than eggs and potatoes. They ate on the den floor because Gail couldn't bear the thought of coming out of the room, even to eat. Everyone ate quietly, watching the egg. Occasionally, a foot or hand appeared on the inside surface of the egg.

Jak settled next to Joss. Since his arrival, he'd grown quite fond of her. She was motherly but also more fun and enthusiastic than Inco or Gail.

"Do you think it'll be a boy?"

"I don't know," she said with her mouth full. "Is that what you want? A little brother?"

"Brother?" Jak queried.

"Of course," Gail spoke up. "You're my son, and this will also be my child. It will be your little brother or sister."

"Little sister?" He cringed at the thought. He had a strong feeling the baby was going to be a girl but hoped otherwise. "What will I do with a little sister?"

"Intimidate the boys who try to kiss her," Inco jested.

Jak groused at the thought. Everyone laughed together, and he smiled at the attention. It had been a little boring over the last few days, with everyone focusing so much on the egg. The sound of the front door opening and closing interrupted the laughter.

"Hello? Where is everyone?" Gray called out.

"Gray!" Jak jumped to his feet and ran out of the room. He ran as fast as he could down the hall and barreled into Gray, hugging him enthusiastically.

"Whoa," Gray laughed, stumbling a bit from the impact. He sat a large cloth bag down and tossed his satchel on the bag. "Hey, I missed you too."

"So much has happened. Raisin fell and broke the egg. Then Mama threw him in the woods, but I found him. Then a honey badger attacked me, but I killed it. Then Raisin—" He cut himself off. He hadn't told anyone that Raisin was alive yet. "Then I healed the egg. Now we're going to have a little brother or sister. I hope it's not a sister, though. Boys are more fun. Girls are gross. Except for Mama and Joss, because they're grown-ups," he rambled on.

"Egg? Sister? Slow down. What are you talking about?"

"Come, I'll show you. Everyone's back here."

Jak grabbed his arm and pulled him to the den. Everyone smiled and offered welcoming words as he entered. Gray acknowledged, but his attention was drawn to the egg.

"I thought it was dying."

"It did. I healed it with my xenum, just like the honey badger."

"The honey badger?" Inco cut in.

Jak nodded. "I had xenum on my hands when I picked her up. It healed her. Her name's Matilda. She's nice now. My xenum took away her meanness."

"*Her* name? Wait, you healed a female with your xenum?" Joss tried to make sense of it.

"Yes, and then she brought me her baby to heal. I named her Honey," he paused and looked at Gray. "Were you the one watching me?"

"I just arrived, little brother," he answered, alarmed by the question. "What—"

"What do you mean watching you?" Inco cut in again.

"Matilda said someone in the forest was watching me. She said he smells like disgrace, but I thought maybe she just smelled Gray's onion breath."

"How? Stop, just—just stop," Inco stammered. "Start from the beginning. Tell us *exactly* what happened."

"When I found Raisin—"

"Who's Raisin?" Gray asked.

"Raisin's my rock. The one that—"

"We all know which one," Gail grumbled.

"Anyway, when I found Raisin, the honey badger attacked me. I couldn't get her off me, so I broke her neck."

Inco's eyes bulged. "You what?"

"It snapped like a twig, and I threw her against a tree." Jak gloated a little, but frowned at the disapproving looks. Joss put her hand over her chest. Gail covered her mouth in surprise.

"Then, my chest started itching. I scratched it, and my Qi came off. I remembered Papa healing my scrapes with his Qi, so I used mine to heal my arms. But too much came out, and it was all over my arms and dripped everywhere. I picked her up. Blood and xenum dripped on her fur, and it healed her.

"When I took my bath, I reached for my raisins, but they were gone. There was a bunch of grapes instead. Then Raisin—" He caught himself again but had already cut himself off more than once, and Joss noticed.

"What about Raisin?"

"I was playing with him in the tub when I thought maybe I could heal the egg, so I did." He omitted how Raisin had come to life. "Then, today, when I was outside, the honey badger brought me one of her babies. It was sick, and she asked me to heal it."

Joss gasped. "The honey badger came here?"

"And it can talk," Inco reiterated.

"Mm-hmm. She talks a little weird, but she asked me to heal her baby, so I did."

"Jak," Gail said. "You shouldn't—"

Inco held out a finger. "Just let him finish."

Jak hesitated at the feelings he sensed from everyone. He felt a lot of fear and confusion in the room. He looked at his feet in shame, rocking back and forth on his heels.

"It's all right, Jak," Gray knelt behind him with a hand on his shoulder. "You can tell us. Everyone's just a little concerned."

"And scared," Jak said.

Gray looked at Inco, Joss, and Gail. That Jak could recognize and expose their feelings so easily made them uneasy.

"We're just a little scared because we love you," Gray reassured him.

"You are, but not Mama and Papa. They're not scared *for* me. They're scared *of* me and think I'm bad."

"Oh, we don't think you're bad, sweetheart," Gail soothed. "We just want to protect you and help you grow to be a good man. Anyone can be bad if they don't get the right direction from their parents."

Jak looked up from his feet. Inco nodded his agreement with Gail, as did Joss.

"I healed the baby, and Matilda let me name it. I named her Honey. Matilda said she's connected to me now because I healed her."

"We're surprised, Jak, because as we were taught, we can't use our xenum on the opposite sex unless it's our own blood child. That's why Mama never healed your scrapes. And the reason you're connected to…" Inco hesitated, not remembering the badger's name.

"Matilda."

"Yes. The reason you're connected to Matilda is that you somehow did a blood bond healing."

Jak's brow furrowed. "What does that mean?"

"When your blood mixes with xenum and then heals someone, it can bond you for life. Mostly that just means you're fond of each other from that point on, like family. However, in your case, it seems to have done… more."

"No, I've heard of this," Joss spoke up. "There are tales of animals becoming sort of a 'familiar' to the dragon when they're brought to life with blood and xenum. It's called Blood Beget, but it requires a ritual. I've never heard of it actually being done, especially by a migma."

"A familiar?" Jak asked.

"Aren't familiars—?" Gray stopped himself. He covered Jak's ears and silently mouthed, "Demons?"

"Demons?" Jak exclaimed.

"No. That's an Earth familiar. I don't think they're real. A dragon familiar is a creature that bonds to you for life. They share some, or even all, of your powers and abilities. I thought it was just a tale, but there could be more to it."

Jak fretted, unsure what to think. "So…"

"It's all right, honey. She won't be evil unless you are," Joss said.

Inco flashed a frustrated glance for her wording. "Neither of you will be evil. Or bad. Or demons. Or any of that."

Joss bit her lip and crossed her arms, unsure how to respond.

"Is there anything else, son?"

"I was about to come inside, and Matilda said someone was watching from the forest. She said he smelled like disgrace."

Inco and Gray exchanged glances and nods.

"Gray and I will look into it. Is that everything you needed to tell us?"

Jak thought about Raisin. He wanted to reveal him. Hiding him was becoming more and more difficult. But he was worried that one of the adults would toss him into the forest again. On the other hand, if he didn't say something now, they'd be angry later, especially after Inco asked to know everything. His eyes shifted while he tried to find the words. He inhaled deeply.

"Well—"

"Achoo!" A high-pitched noise sounded from Jak's pocket.

Jak jerked in surprise. He scanned everyone's face, seeing their bewildered expressions.

"What was that?" Joss asked.

He exhaled sharply, his shoulders dropped, and he stared at the floor. "That was Raisin. He also came to life."

"The rock?"

He sighed, reached in his pocket, and pulled Raisin out.

"I had blood and xenum on my hands when I touched him too. And he rubbed it on the raisins in my satchel, turning them back to grapes."

"That's not possible," Gail said.

He held out his hand. Raisin stood in his palm and looked around, then locked eyes with Gail.

"Ah," he screeched in fear and ran up Jak's arm.

Jak scrambled to keep Raisin from falling and squirmed as the rock moved around under his shirt before coming to a stop on his shoulder. Raisin peeked out from under the collar, looking fearfully at Gail.

Gail's look of surprise turned to comical contempt. She put her hands on her hips, pursed her lips, and shook her head.

Gray still knelt behind Jak. He looked curiously at Raisin and poked him with a finger.

"Hey! Watch who you poke with that grubby finger," Raisin complained.

Gray let out a soft chuckle.

"You think that's funny? Just back off, pal, and we won't have any problems."

"Shh," Jak said. "That's my brother, Gray. He's fun."

"And we're not?" Joss teased, trying to hold back a grin.

Jak rocked back and forth on his heels. He was still nervous. "Can I keep him?"

Gail's eyes slivered. "Absolutely n—"

"Of course you can," Joss said. Flashing a stern look at Gail, she muttered, "It's his only friend."

"Keep him away from the egg," Gail said, giving Joss a look of defeat. She looked back toward Jak, but he'd left the room.

"Thanks, Joss," he called from the hallway as he ran to play outside.

"We need to keep that thing close anyway," Inco said. "Stone Golems haven't existed for many centuries. It would surely cause issues if we cast it away, and someone else found it."

CHAPTER 20

Gail and Joss had retired for the night. Jak had fallen asleep on the pillows strewn about the sitting room floor. Inco decided just to leave him there, not wanting to wake him. He looked comfortable.

"Are you ready?" Gray whispered from the front doorway.

"Yes, I'm coming," Inco whispered back, spreading a blanket over Jak. He stepped lightly and joined Gray outside, closing the door, careful not to make a loud noise.

"All right, what's the plan?" Gray still whispered.

"I'll go out there and hide. You go to the edge of the clearing. Create a disturbance. Make noise, and walk through the forest. I'll be watching."

"Got it."

"Got it." Raisin startled them by not whispering. He poked his head out of Gray's pocket.

Inco rubbed his brow. "What's he doing here?"

"He wants to help. And if he's out here with us, he isn't in there waking Jak."

He rolled his eyes, then took a few steps away from the door and took dragon form. As he shifted, he also became transparent, using his incognito blending abilities. By the time he was in full dragon form, he was entirely invisible. Appearing as no more than a haze, he moved toward the edge of the forest, then leapt out and flew over the trees.

"What do you know about anything? You're just a dumb rock." Gray slurred his speech to mimic drunkenness, clumsily wobbling in dragon form.

"Smarter than you, you drunk overgrown lizard," Raisin said, then shielded one side of his mouth with his little gravel hand and whispered, "How'm I doing?"

"Terrible, you sound like a three-year-old," he whispered back.

"You're about to taste the back-o-me-hand, you slithery sloth," Raisin shot back, raising his hand in position to swing a backward slap.

"I have *five good reasons* to shut your mouth-hole." Gray curled his scaly fingers into a fist.

"All right, that's it. You called down the thunder? Well, now you've got it," Raisin growled.

Without warning, he jumped onto Gray's large dragon head, ran to the end of his nose and jumped off. As he fell, he caught himself on the edge of Gray's nostril and swung into it, feet first.

"Wha—" Gray called out, pulling his head back and shaking it side to side, pawing at his nose.

"I call this move *The Gas Chamber,*" Raisin dragged out his words in a gravelly voice, then grunted as he farted into Gray's sinuses.

"Ah," Gray groused. Rearing onto his hind legs, he took in a deep breath and blew out sharply from his nose, sending Raisin flying out past the forest tree line.

"Woooo," Raisin howled as he flew through the air and then grunted when he landed.

"That was disgusting," Gray complained.

"I know," Raisin chuckled. "Especially the part where I pushed too hard, and a little mud-nugget came out."

"Yaach," Gray rasped and blew more air through his nose.

"What are you going to do about it, Shit-nose?"

He flexed, making the rocky surface of his chest turn muscular. Gray charged at him, so he ran deeper into the forest. Gray chased him, loudly knocking his tail into the trees as he ran. Raisin recognized a pair of eyes peeking from a hole in the ground.

"Incoming," he shouted, diving into the hole, then turned around to see Gray closing in. "There are babies in here," he warned.

Gray kicked dirt and skidded to a stop, then peered into the hole with one eye.

"We're not supposed to be fighting for real," he whispered.

"It's more fun this way," Raisin whispered back. "I've been waiting forever to use that move."

***

Roe watched from under a heavy cloak, standing behind a nearby tree, straining to hear. He leaned towards them, exposing himself a little more when a twig above him snapped, jolting his attention upward. He couldn't see anything, but he could feel a presence.

As he looked around, a pair of eyes appeared. A set of teeth appeared beneath the eyes. He stepped back, keeping his face in the cloak's shadow. A face and neck manifested before him.

"Who are you?" Inco hissed.

Adrenaline surged through Roe. He bolted, running deeper into the forest. Inco retracted his visibility and slithered along the trees over him. Roe could hear the cracking of limbs above and knew he was much too slow to escape in his Dú. He started taking dragon form and looked back, causing him to lose balance. Rolling down a shallow hill, he landed on his back in full dragon form. A hazy force pounced on him, and Inco snapped into unrestricted view.

"Who are you?"

Roe quivered in fear, shielding his face with scaly arms, then cautiously lowered them.

"Roe?"

***

Gray heard Inco yell. He looked up from Raisin's hiding hole and ran toward the sound of his voice.

"Wait for me." Raisin jumped from the hole and grabbed his tail as he sprinted, knocking his tail into a tree.

"*Ooof!*" Raisin grunted from the impact.

His tail hit another tree.

"*Ooof!* Watch where you're goin', Shit-nose," Raison called out, barely hanging on by one arm. He pulled himself up and mounted near the end, just before the flailed tip. Gray's tail raised and slammed down as he came to a stop.

"Ohh, my rocks," Raisin painfully groaned, holding his groin as he fell sideways.

Gray came to Inco's side and looked down at the frightened trespasser.

"Who is he?"

When Inco turned to answer, Roe seized the opportunity. He kicked Inco back and leapt up through the trees and into the sky above. Gray took chase, yanking Roe's tail and hoisting himself onto Roe's back.

Roe snarled and roared as he opened his mouth wide, but Gray was quicker and bit down on his neck. Roaring in pain, Roe twisted and kicked, digging his long sharp claws into Gray, slashing four gaping wounds down his side. Gray howled in pain, released his bite, and fell back to the ground with a thud.

"Gray," Raisin yelled, running to his aid.

He jumped onto a boulder and fell into it as if it were liquid. The boulder rattled as it changed shape. A pair of eyes appeared on the surface, and then arms and legs emerged from it. A mouth formed and then opened and gasped for air. The boulder rippled and rolled onto gravelly legs and ran to Gray.

"Are you all right?"

"Raisin?" Gray's eyes bulged with surprise before rolling back in his head. He lost consciousness.

Roe soared over the trees when an invisible force collided with him. Inco remained invisible as he held Roe's head down, smashing his face into hundreds of branches. Holding him by the throat, Inco swung him like an ax into the trees and then dove in after him, spearing him into the ground and pinning him.

"Who sent you?" Inco snarled.

"No one. I noticed Jak was special. It made me curious, so I've peeked in from time to time," Roe whimpered.

Inco forced a look of surprise. "What's so special about Jak?"

"He'll fight at the side of—"

THUD... THUD... THUD... The ground shook. Something approached. Something huge. Inco and Roe both looked in the direction of the sound to see a giant rock golem walking toward them. In his arms, he held Gray's limp body.

"You killed Gray, you coward," Raisin said.

Inco adjusted and tightened his grip on Roe as Raisin lowered Gray to the ground next to him. He looked back at Roe, pure hatred beaming from his eyes.

"You won't kill me, will you?"

"There's nothing abnormal about my children," Inco snarled.

Brief confusion flashed in Roe's eyes.

"You leave my family alone. If I catch you in this forest or anywhere near us again, I'll kill you. Understood?"

"Yes, sir. I understand p-perfectly."

Inco let go, and Roe scurried to his feet and tried to run but bumped his face into something hard. He looked up, and Raisin glared back at him. Roe slithered around and hurried away, disappearing into the trees toward the sky.

"He isn't dead," Inco said. He put Gray's xenum into the gaping wounds. "But he might've been if you hadn't brought him to me."

"I'm glad I could help," he spoke in a deeper voice than usual because of his size.

"Can you carry him to the house?" Inco rotated an arm. "I'm a little sore."

"Sure thing."

By the time they reached the house, Gray was waking up. He moaned as he came to, somewhat off-balance, in Raisin's arms. He looked at the ground moving below him and saw Inco walking ahead.

"Welcome back, Gray," Raisin said.

"Whoa." He jumped down. Although he recognized Raisin instantly, he was shocked at his size. "What happened to you?"

"I jumped on a boulder and fell in. I came out looking like this… but I think I can fix it."

"How?" Gray asked.

Raisin stood at the edge of the clearing and took in a deep breath, then shook like a wet dog, humming through his fluttering lips as he went. Pebbles and rocks flew from his body and landed all around, causing him to shrink until he was back to his original size. He stopped and fell over, dizzy.

"That was fun," he exclaimed in his normal high-pitched voice. "I carried you all the way home. How about you return the favor?" He reached up.

Gray scooped him up to face level and smiled warmly.

"Thanks, little friend."

Raisin grinned. "Anytime, Shit-nose."

CHAPTER 21

Roe limped to the door and knocked. He could hear grumbling and cursing from inside. Footsteps approached, and the door flew open.

"What do you want at this time of night?" Zebulan scowled.

"They caught me, sir," he wheezed.

"What? Who?"

Gaping wounds oozed blood down Roe's neck, his face bloody and battered. Both eyes were puffy and bruised, and a twig poked out from his hair. His clothes were filthy and torn.

"Inco. Gray. A giant, uhm, r-rock monster," he stammered.

"Rock monster?"

"He said children."

"What?"

"Children, as in more than one—" He fell to his knees in exhaustion.

Zebulan pulled him inside and shut the door. He dragged him across the floor to his sitting room. Roe lay half-conscious and barely responsive. Zebulan removed Roe's Qi, then dripped xenum into the wounds on his neck and forehead. The wounds closed up, and Roe groaned as he opened his eyes and looked around.

"You can do the rest," Zebulan tossed his Qi to Roe.

It bounced from palm to palm as Roe fumbled to catch it. Zebulan walked to his counter and stood facing away as he topped off his tea and poured a second cup.

Roe pulled himself to his feet and sat on a couch beautifully carved from a wooden log. It was remarkably comfortable. He looked around the room. Though he'd reported to Zebulan many times, never had he been in his home. A large white furry mass lay scrunched up near the lit fireplace. He used his foot to drag it away from the fire, causing it to spread back out across the floor. It was the fur of a rare Emmoth, a horse-sized version of an Earth elephant, covered in white hair everywhere except the ears, trunk, and antler-like tusks.

His eyes continued to wander. A collection of mummified, miniature animals stood along the mantelshelf. Next to them stood an abatwa, also mummified, holding a tiny shepherd's staff.

A unicorn hung from the wall next to the mantelshelf. Unicorns aren't as Earthlings imagine. A unicorn is a sharp horn with tiny eyes at the base. It has a centipede-like body covered in long hair that resembles a horse's mane. The horn can fly but usually hovers low and meanders aimlessly through forests and wooded areas. When a horse or similar animal nears, the unicorn mounts. It digs its tiny sharp legs into the animal's neck, then the horn's base latches onto the animal's head. Although it's a parasite, it does no harm. In exchange for being nourished by the animal, the unicorn gives it the ability to fly.

"All these creatures are protected," Roe sputtered.

"Yes, well, they are *very* well protected here. Nothing will happen to them," Zebulan responded with bitter sarcasm.

He handed Roe the hot cup of tea. "Now, tell me what happened."

Roe struggled to wrap his head around the wickedness behind the sitting room décor. He tried to tell himself that it was a misunderstanding. Maybe the artifacts were already dead when they were preserved. At least, that's what he hoped.

"I was watching Gray argue with something small in the woods when Inco attacked me from the trees. I fought with them both, but Inco pinned me. A giant rock creature was on their side. I didn't have a chance."

Zebulan eyed him suspiciously. "What did you tell them?"

"N-nothing, sir. It's what *Inco* said that grabbed my attention."

"Yes. Something about children?"

"Yes, sir. Children. He said there was nothing abnormal about his *children*. That must mean there's more than one child."

"Hmm. Find out what you can about the others. I'll be in Caligo for a few days. It's time to make plans."

"Yes. To stop the prophecy?"

"Stop it?" Zebulan mused. "Why would I want to stop it?"

Roe's eyes glazed over, straining to hold back his shock.

"This world is full of filth. Migma elves. Migma wolves. Migma people. Even migma trees. We've soiled our heritage as dragons with the filth of all these meaningless kindreds. The only way to restore and preserve our true glory is to wipe them all out and block all portals to Earth. Origo will become a glorious world of the purest of dragons. And I'm in a perfect position to secure a powerful seat in the new world."

He took a sip of his tea and glared at Roe, who noticed and also took a sip. Zebulan grinned maliciously. "Your hard work won't be forgotten. Many rewards await you in the new world, but we must get there. Now finish your tea and get back to work. You've wasted enough time."

"Yes, sir." Roe hid his shock.

It wasn't what he'd thought. For the first time, Roe questioned his loyalty. Zebulan opened the door and stood by it, waiting. He set down his unfinished tea and walked to the door.

"Inco knows I've been watching. It will be harder to hide in the shadows."

"I'm sure you'll think of something," Zebulan assured in an uncaring tone. He put his hand on the back of Roe's shoulder and guided him out, shutting the door behind him.

Roe stood on the front porch for a moment, rolling his tongue over his teeth, trying to dispel the awful aftertaste of the tea. He thought about everything that had just happened, everything he'd seen, and scratched an itch on his forehead. Excruciating pain shot all around the top of his head. He yanked his hand away, groaning in pain. Reaching again, more gently this time, he felt for the cause. Just behind the hairline, a twig protruded from his skin.

He grabbed the exposed part of the twig and pulled, immediately letting go and cringing in pain. He tried again, using his free hand to hold the wrist of the first. He took in three deep breaths, then pulled hard and fast. The rest of the twig came out, covered in blood.

"Inco," he growled.

He no longer questioned his loyalty. All of Origo could perish for all he cared, so long as Inco went down with it.

CHAPTER 22

Procerus sat in his chair in the council chambers and listened to the other members' chatter. Finally, he raised a hand for silence. "The migration of the bears into wolf territory is not permitted."

He turned to Boris. "Your ties with the DúBear tribe would be helpful. Go and speak to them. Ask them to put a stop to it."

Boris nodded. "First thing tomorrow."

"Grace, please speak to the DúWolves and let them know we're handling it. There is no need to fight over territory."

"I'll meet with them this afternoon," Grace agreed.

"Next on the agenda, we—"

Inco burst through the chamber doors, fury in his eyes. "Who sent him?"

Procerus ignored his outburst and smiled. "Inco, how nice of you to join us. We could use your help with a few items on the agenda now that you're back."

"I'm not back yet." He approached the council circle, glancing at Roe, who kept his eyes to the floor. "I'm here because your spy put my sons in danger."

"Spy? Sons?" Procerus raised his brow.

"Yes, my sons—Gray and Jak—the human child I'm raising. We caught Roe spying on us from the forest. He's been doing so for some time."

"Roe? What have you to say to these accusations?"

"You mean migma." Roe jumped to his feet. "That child is the Son of Darkness. Inco hides him for a reason."

"You spied on a fellow council member?" Procerus scowled. "On whose authority?"

Roe deflected the question. "The well-being of Origo is my only concern, sir!"

"What danger could come from a child?" Procerus crossed his arms.

"He's the one who'll fight alongside Bakúnuh in th—"

"*Rubbish*," Procerus yelled. "I gave you no authority to spy on Inco *or* his human son."

Inco saw that Procerus wasn't buying into Roe's claims. "Sir, we just want to live in peace. I'm not hiding anything."

But Roe wasn't finished. "The child has a Qi, sir. It's as black as night. He has dragon night vision, speed, strength—ask him why he fled from Earth, sir. *Ask him!*"

"Silence!" Procerus held up a hand at Roe and turned with an intrigued look. "Inco, is this true?"

"Sir, the child is being raised by dragons. Naturally, he'll be stronger and faster than other human children."

"And what of this black Qi?" Procerus asked.

"He has no such thing, sir."

"Liar," Roe screamed and rushed at him.

Inco punched him in the face. He fell back, holding his broken nose with one hand and grasping for his Qi with the other. Inco spread his feet and readied to deliver another punch.

"Enough," Procerus commanded. "Inco, you have my apologies. You won't be bothered again. Roe, you're suspended from the council and banned from being any-where near Inco or the human child."

"Thuthpended?" Roe lisped through his now broken nose. "But thir!"

"My decision is final."

"Thank you, sir." Inco nodded in reverence and left, glaring at Roe as he passed.

The council members all watched as Inco left. Roe looked to Zebulan for support, but Zebulan looked away. Holding his bloody nose, Roe bumped into his own empty chair as he headed toward the door.

Procerus called out to Roe, "You'll wait five minutes before leaving. Give Inco some time to clear the area." He waved his hand at Roe's face. "Tend to your nose while you wait."

Finally allowed to leave, Roe waited on a bench near the council chambers. He watched as the council left, one by one, until Zebulan walked out, followed by Procerus, who locked the door behind him. Roe watched as Zebulan talked to Procerus, but he was too far away to hear them. The two shook hands and parted in opposite directions. Roe caught up to Zebulan.

"Why didn't you back me up?"

"Because I don't want the council to know about the boy," he said while looking ahead. "And you made a fool of yourself in there."

"I thought we wanted Inco off the council."

"At first, yes, but things have changed. The possibilities are much greater now."

"What do you mean?"

"Leave him be while he raises the child. Once the boy's ready, we'll deliver him to Caligo."

"What? I thought—"

"Your job isn't to think," Zebulan spat. "Leave the thinking to me. I'll let you know when I need your services again." He walked away.

Insulted and angered by the humiliation, Roe jogged to catch up with Zebulan again.

"Maybe I won't be available. Maybe I'll put my services to better use elsewhere."

Zebulan turned, his expression cold and forbidden. He looked Roe in the eyes, clenching his jaw. His icy gaze pierced through Roe as if he were looking straight into his soul. Roe's demeanor shifted from anger to fear as his impulses forced him to be submissive again.

"Sorry, sir," he whispered, lowering his gaze in shame.

Zebulan turned again without a word, took dragon form, and flew away.

CHAPTER 23

It had been almost three years to the day since Jak healed the egg. Though he'd just turned thirteen, he more closely resembled a ten-year-old in both his stature and the way he still thrived on the affection of his family—particularly Gray. While the parents encouraged him to be less clingy, Gray maintained that affection toward family was a strength, not a weakness. Jak liked this perspective, and as it came time for the egg to hatch, he looked forward to passing it along.

Joss scrambled and scurried about the house, cleaning and preparing for the baby. She made many trips to markets and sales, coming home with blankets, infant gowns, toys, and two cradles.

Gail scarcely left the den. She read stories to the egg, sang to it, and slept near it every night. Several times a day, she scraped the surface with a blade and placed the shell dust on her tongue. She could only do this with a pulsing egg as the shell weakens to hatch. It would stimulate her Dú breasts to produce milk. Dragons with more primitive Dús simply licked their egg to produce milk in their Dú. This is necessary since newborn dragons are stuck in their Dú and unable to take dragon form until adulthood.

A dragon's egg pulses faster in the days before hatching. Every day that passed brought them closer and closer to something, but they weren't sure what. The next step would be for the egg to hatch, and everyone in the home hoped it would, but there remained a sense of uncertainty. Past events made this hatching unpredictable.

Inco found himself torn between the two women. While Gail wanted him to keep her company, Joss frequently asked for help with preparations. As often as possible, he'd retreat to the sitting room to relax. With his feet up, he'd lay his head back against some pillows and take in deep breaths of contentment. He was in the sitting room when Gail's voice reverberated throughout the house.

"It's time," she cried out.

Inco rushed to the den where everyone else had already arrived. All their combined attention was on the egg. It rocked in place, and the pulse of colors quickened, and then it stopped. A crack appeared. It extended halfway down the egg, and as pieces of the shell fell into the egg, a gap formed.

Jak squeezed his way behind the egg, where no one else was small enough to stand. From there, he could see everything. He peeked into the gap and saw movement, but nothing more.

"Come on, baby," Gail encouraged in a soft, melodic voice. "Come on."

Another crack split the top of the egg, intersecting with the first. The shell crumbled along the new crack line and fell in. Everyone bumped heads and crowded shoulders as they struggled to see.

Gail pulled back some top pieces of the eggshell and broke off other sections until she'd removed the entire top half of the egg.

There at the bottom, an infant looked back at them. Its skin thin and wrinkly, the hair black as coal, and eyes of a grey so light, they appeared almost colorless. A dark blue ring surrounded the gray. Everyone gasped at the beauty of the baby. A few red chips of eggshell had fallen in, one covering the infant's genital area.

"It's a boy, right? A brother?" Jak tensed in hopeful anticipation.

Gail reached in and moved the egg chip.

"It's a girl." She cried with joy. "I have a daughter." She looked at Joss, whose face quivered and eyes welled with tears. "*We* have a daughter."

The women embraced. Joss kissed her once on the forehead, and they turned back to the newborn, with smiles that lit up the room.

"We have a daughter," Joss echoed. She crept closer to get a better look. "She's beautiful. Perfect in every way."

"A sister," Jak groaned.

Gail gently lifted the baby from the egg. The remaining chips fell away. As the baby fussed, Gail nestled her under her chin, then leaned forward and looked into the empty egg.

"What's her name?" she asked.

Joss reached into the egg and brushed the shell chips away from the center. At the bottom of the egg was an etched and colored picture of a white jasmine flower with wavy blue lines flowing from its center.

"I'm not sure. I don't know what it means," Joss said.

Jak looked confused. "Don't you get to name her?"

"No, dear. Dragons and migmas are born with a name to describe them. When we're older, we can choose our own names to go by, but we are always born with a name that's significant to us. Sometimes it's a special ability, sometimes a strength, and sometimes just a part of our personality."

"My name means blending in," Inco said.

"Mine means a father's pride." Gail smiled.

"Mine means light-hearted," Joss added.

"And mine is all over me," Gray chuckled.

Jak pondered. "Who named me? What does my name mean?"

"I did. Your name means 'Just a kid.'" Gray said, playfully rubbing his knuckles into his scalp.

"Hey." He pushed Gray's hand away.

"This is the fun part. We get to guess," Gail said.

She settled on a large pillow and untied the laces that ran up the front of her dress, pulling them out of the top four holes. She pulled out one breast and rubbed the nipple over the baby's lips. The infant latched on and suckled.

Jak tried to understand. "How will you know when you guess it right?"

"When her name's spoken aloud, the egg will turn white," Joss answered. "Then we'll grind it to a powder and spread it in the garden. It's excellent for the soil. The vegetables will be bigger and plumper than ever."

"Maybe her name is Flower," he guessed, watching the egg for changes. Nothing happened.

Inco looked into the egg at the etched picture.

"That's a white jasmine. I'm not sure what the blue lines are."

"Fragrance?" Joss guessed.

"Beauty?" Gray guessed.

"Purity?" Gail guessed.

On and on, everyone sat around guessing names, but nothing turned the eggshell white. Inco brought several books into the den. They flipped through old yellow pages and made guesses all night long until morning.

"What happens if we don't guess her name?" Jak stretched, then yawned.

"It could stall her destiny," Gail explained. "She may not develop whatever special ability or characteristic she's supposed to have that makes her unique. She may grow to feel lost, insecure, or may never feel like she belongs."

Inco stared into the egg for what seemed like hours. He pondered and researched and obsessed over her name. He wasn't her biological father, but you wouldn't know it by how he acted.

"Sound." He turned away and grabbed a book he'd left open. "The sound of jasmine. The sound of white jasmine. Here it is, Lee-Link. Lilink." Everyone watched as the eggshell seemed to swallow its own color and turn white.

He showed Joss the page.

"That's a G," Joss pointed out.

"Yes, but it's old Chinese. See here; they pronounce the G at the end with a K sound."

"I would've never guessed."

"We'll spell it how it sounds, with a k," Gail said in a soft cooing voice, directed at the baby. "Welcome to the family, Lilink."

"Welcome to the family, Lilink," Joss said.

"Welcome to the family, Lilink," Gray said.

"Welcome to the family, Lilink," Jak said.

Inco smiled, relieved to have finally figured out her name. He went to Gail and reached for the baby.

"Let's go see Pa—" she stopped in mid-sentence, unsure of how Joss felt about Inco being her father since Tibbel was the actual father. She looked to Joss for reassurance. Joss smiled and nodded her approval.

"Let's go see Papa." She whispered to Lilink, handing her to Inco.

He held her close and kissed her nose. Tears welled in his eyes.

"They can call you whatever they want, but you'll always be Baby Girl to me," he whispered. "Welcome to the family, Baby Girl."

CHAPTER 24

The first five days with Lilink were calm and hectic at the same time. She was the center of her parents' attention. Gray, however, had all the time in the world to spend with Jak. Within two days, they had hand-carved all the pieces needed for Chaturanga. He taught Jak all the rules and moves, then played until Jak finally won a game on the evening of the fifth day.

"I almost won." Gray teased.

Jak smiled with smug pride. "No way. I still have my Raja, my Mantri, one Ratha, one Gaja, and three Bhatas. You lost big time."

"Yes, but I took both your Ashvas so fast."

"Mm-hm. I let you… to give you false hope."

"It's not fair when it's two against one," Gray grinned.

"Raisin doesn't count. He's the same size as the pieces."

"Hey," Raisin shouted, sounding genuinely offended. "I resemble that remark."

Gray and Jak paused for a moment and then rolled back in laughter when they caught Raisin's joke. Raisin joined in the laughter and accidentally kicked a Raja into a Mantri, knocking them both onto the ground.

"Well, brother, I have to go," Gray breathed, inwardly cringing at the oncoming protest.

He expected Jak to argue and whine and beg him to stay, but he didn't. He just slumped in sadness.

"All right," he mumbled, looking at the ground.

Gray felt terrible. He knew Jak was going to be lonely without him.

"I'll make a deal with you," he offered.

"Hmm?" Jak kept his eyes down.

"I'll come back in three days since there's so much going on here. If you behave and help the family until I get back, I'll bring you whatever treat you want."

"Any treat?" Jak's face lit up.

"Any treat."

"I want raisins. Can you get me raisins?"

"Boy, you drive a hard bargain, don't you?" Gray teased until he noticed Jak's smile fading. "Raisins it is."

"Yes!" Jak jumped up and hugged Gray. "Three days?"

"Three days." Gray hugged him back. "I love you, Jak."

"Love you, too."

***

The adults didn't spend much time in the den anymore. Jak missed everyone being close and cozy in the evenings, but it was a lot more comfortable in the sitting room. Lilink had a cradle there, and she spent most of her days in it. She had another cradle in the moms' room, where she slept at night. When Gray made his rounds to say goodbye, everyone was in the sitting room. He kissed Joss's hand, followed by Gail's cheek, then walked toward Inco, making a kissing face.

"I'll tell you where you can plant those lips," he playfully wagged a fist, then stood and hugged Gray.

"I'll be back as soon as the tournament ends—should be two days, but I told Jak three just in case it runs over."

"Just enjoy yourself. Jak will be fine."

"Every time I leave, something hap—"

"You won't have your youth forever. Enjoy it while you have it, but easy on the ale."

"Nag, nag."

"And not too much sticky-puff," Inco whispered. "That stuff loosens too many belts."

Gray grinned and rolled his eyes as he stepped away, knowing that's exactly what he intended to do.

"Three days," he whispered as he passed Jak.

Jak smiled and stood by the open door, then closed it behind Gray when he left.

"Jak," Gail called. "You still haven't held your sister. Don't you want to hold her?"

He grimaced.

"You saved her life. You're her hero. She wants to meet you."

"She does?"

"Of course, she does. Come over here and sit next to Mama," she cooed, patting the seat next to her. "Take off your shirt. Babies love skin-to-skin contact."

He removed his shirt and sat in the spot she patted, wiggling into place to get comfortable. Gail placed a pillow on his lap and posed his arms over it to best hold Lilink, then took her from her cradle and gently laid her in his arms.

He looked at her, and she looked right back at him. The bond was instant. Jak no longer cared that she wasn't a boy. All his disappointment melted away, and warmth filled his heart. At that moment, he understood Gray's feelings as an older brother. Lilink was his sister, and he knew he would die for her if necessary.

He leaned in and kissed her forehead when suddenly, the ground shook as it had done the day Raisin fell on the egg. The very same shake that turned out to be a blessing in disguise, for had the egg not cracked, Jak would've never gone through the events that led to healing the egg and having a sister. However, past blessing or not, the shaky ground frightened everyone.

Gail grabbed Lilink from her brother's arms, huddled to the floor, and secured her tightly against her chest. Lilink cried from the sudden movement and sense of panic in the room. The trembling intensified and became far worse than what had happened before.

Inco jumped from his seat and rushed to Jak. Gail and Joss crouched in front of them, shielding the baby between them as if the ceiling could cave in. Inco and Jak leaned over the women to protect them, all huddled together. Gray burst through the front door and ran to them, adding to the shield over the women and baby. Seconds later, the trembling stopped.

Lilink still cried. Inco pulled away from Jak, noting the mark on his forehead from being pressed into his shirt buttons. The mothers looked over Lilink, who screamed as if she were in pain. Gail fretted as she tried to find the source. She removed the infant's gown and was shocked by what she saw. Joss gasped, and Inco leaned to see.

On Lilink's shoulder, just above her collarbone, was a red blistery mark that hadn't been there before. It was shaped like a dragon's head rising from water. The adults recognized it instantly. It was a well-known symbol of the legendary High Qing of Origo. It was the symbol of Imoogi.

CHAPTER 25

Inco picked up an old dusty book from the den floor. "Here it is. The prophecy of Imoogi."

Joss held Lilink against her chest, gently bouncing her. "What does it say?"

"It's Latin. It says, 'Let all who look upon these words be warned. The High Qing Imoogi has fallen at the hands of his brother. He will rise from his death when she who carries his mark brings him the power of the sun. She will then share in his Dú and fight in the Great Battle of Origo.'"

"That can't be right," Gail said.

"Let me see here. 'Nox' can mean sleep and night as well as death, and 'pugna' can mean struggle, fight, conflict, or strife. But yes, I'm translating correctly."

"I mean, it can't be real," Gail clarified. "What're the chances of us having both of the children of the prophecy? It can't be possible. It can't be real," she rambled. "The prophecy's coming true."

"No, it's not."

Inco tossed the book like trash. He tried desperately to deny everything, unable to fathom the possibility of his baby girl and beloved son being so ill-fated. The very thought enraged him.

"Listen, I know you two want to stay positive, but we *must* take this seriously," Joss said.

Inco fumed. "You don't think we take this seriously? Those children are real. We must care for them. This?" He pointed at the book he'd tossed. "This is whatever we let it become. It cannot decide for us. We decide our own fate, not some story written by who *knows* who. None of that will happen unless we make it happen."

"You're a damned fool, Inco." She approached him slowly, tilting her head near his face. "How will he aim away from what he doesn't know?"

Inco stepped back uncomfortably. Joss remained in place, her glare unwavering. He didn't want to admit it, but she had a point. To avoid their children starting a war, they had to admit that it was possible.

"Jak won't grow to be good unless he learns what's bad. We must fight his evil destiny with our eyes wide open— all of us. Jak needs to know what he's avoiding in order to avoid it, or the next time he gets angry, it won't be a honey badger's neck he snaps. You saw the look in his eyes when he told us."

She was right. Jak looked like he enjoyed telling how he killed the animal. Inco's eyes glazed over, and he pursed his lips, too defensive to admit anything.

"And Lilink. If she doesn't know what to avoid, she could stumble upon it without even trying."

Inco deadpanned. "Stumble? Across the Rima?"

"Maybe not, but that prophecy doesn't say she has to cross the Rima, now does it? It doesn't say she has to go to Caligo at all."

She was right again. He struggled to think of a rebuttal, but anger clouded his thoughts, and he could see that she was just as enraged. It wasn't like an Elf, or DúElf in her case, to anger in such a way. They were the most levelheaded and diplomatic creatures in all of Origo. Inco decided it was time to diffuse the conversation, and the only way to do that was to walk away. However, his conscious desire to end the argument didn't overpower his subconscious desire to have the last word as he started toward the door.

"Well, then I guess we'd better aim them away from killing each other."

Joss's expression shifted. She knew about the prophecies, but it didn't occur to her that the children might hurt each other.

"What do you mean?"

"If he fights alongside Bakúnuh, and she fights alongside Imoogi, they'll be fighting each other."

He stormed out of the den and collided with Jak, who had been standing outside the door listening. Jak fell back onto the floor. Inco's anger vanished instantly.

"Are you all right?" He helped him back to his feet.

Jak jerked away as if insulted by the help.

"Were you listening? How long have you been standing here?"

Jak glared. "Long enough."

The coldness in Jak's eyes took Inco aback, and he embraced him to break eye contact. He ran his hand through Jak's hair, wondering if something had hit Jak's head during the tremors. There were no lumps or cuts on his scalp. Inco pulled back and looked, but the boy stared right through him.

"I *will* defend her. Nothing bad will ever happen to my sister." Jak declared. He turned around and walked away.

Inco watched until Jak turned out of sight at the end of the hallway. Joss and Gail stood behind him. They'd heard everything. Inco felt Joss's fingers slip between his and responded with a gentle squeeze.

"We need to tell him everything. Now, while he's young enough to change the course," she spoke, just above a whisper.

Inco sighed and squeezed her hand again. "I suppose."

INCOGNITO

GRAY

KERI BROWN

ÆMMA

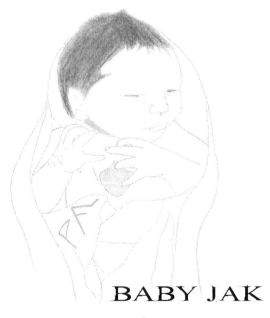

BABY JAK

GAIL

JOSCOLYN

JAK

LILINK

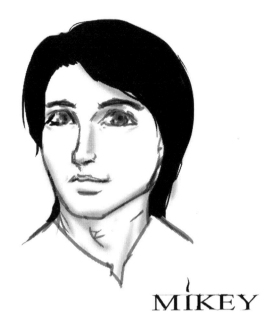

MIKEY

RAISIN

KERI BROWN

MATILDA

LEX

ANANÍAS

TELLEM

DWARF

EMMOTH

UNICORN

ZEBULAN

ROE

CHAPTER 26

Gray cancelled his plans after the tremors and Jak hearing about the prophecy. Jak said nothing, and Gray was fine with that. He just held him… all night. Gray was the only one that could still coddle Jak like a child without him getting offended. Jak seemed better the next morning, so Gray told Inco it might be a good time for the conversation.

Everyone sat in the sitting room. Jak was still shirtless and wore the same pants from the day before. He was somber after learning of the prophecy and attempting to digest everything. The worst part was how much it contradicted how he felt about Lilink. His shoulders slumped, and he gazed at the ground, lightly rubbing his Qi.

"So what you're saying is… I'm the Son of Darkness, and I'm destined to be evil."

"Not a chance," Gray exclaimed. He moved closer to Jak and put a blanket over his shoulders. He wrapped one arm around him and pointed at his Qi. "This doesn't decide your fate. You do."

"We all have darkness in us," Inco said.

"It's what we do with it that matters." Gray finished the expression with a nod.

"I could never hurt my sister," Jak said in a trembling voice.

His eyes twinkled with tears as he looked up. He blinked, causing the tears to stream down either side of his face and fall into his pants pocket.

Raisin squirmed inside the pocket, wiggling his way to the opening to peek at Jak. He'd never mentioned it, but he could feel Jak's emotions. He wanted Jak to feel better but didn't know how. He ducked back into the pocket when Gail approached to sit beside Jak.

"We know that. We know you love her," she said.

"We just want you to know these things so you can set your path away from it all," Joss added.

Jak sniffled. "But… how?"

"With the goodness in your heart and mind," Inco answered. "We're raising you to be good, and I have faith that you'll become a great man."

"But if my Qi is black, then so is my heart."

"Your Qi has nothing to do with it. It's only black because you drank xenum before anything else. That's just what happens. A dark Qi isn't a bad Qi, nor the other way around. There are lots of evil dragons who have a normal green Qi."

POP!

A loud sound erupted from outside. Everyone abruptly looked at the front door.

POP! POP! POP!

More loud noises followed in quick succession, each louder than the last.

POP! POP!

Gail sprang from her seat and took Lilink from her cradle. She and Joss huddled over the baby. Inco and Gray opened the door enough to see a group of men running together in the forest.

POP! Sparks came from the end of a stick held by one of the men.

"Stay down," Inco said.

He opened the door wider. Gray slipped out first, and Inco followed, closing the door behind him.

Joss motioned for Jak to join them in their huddle. He looked at her, then Gail, then Lilink, feeling an overwhelming desire to protect her. He loved Gail and Joss, but Lilink was his priority. Jak stared at the door, his nostrils flared, the pupils of his eyes narrowed.

"I will protect her."

He jumped from his seat and ran to the door, swung it open, and spun out to look back one more time.

"Jak, no!" his mothers called out as one. They reached out but couldn't pull themselves away from Lilink.

"Wooo!" Raisin cheered from Jak's pocket.

Jak slammed the door and ran to join his father and brother. They both stood at the clearing's edge but ran into the forest before he could reach them. He ran behind, following them toward the sounds.

"Get them," one of the men called out in the distance. Another *POP!* Then another.

"Stop," Inco called out.

"Hey," Gray yelled.

The men had stopped running and gathered around something on the forest ground. As Inco and Gray approached, two of them held strange long sticks pointed at them. They appeared to be hollow. One man poured fine black powder into his, then jammed another thinner stick inside. He pulled it out, tucked it along the outside of the main stick, and joined in taking aim at Inco and Gray.

"Halt where you are," he called out.

Inco and Gray didn't stop. They slowed to a brisk walk but continued toward the group of men. Jak slowed about thirty paces behind. He wasn't extra careful or quiet, but no one noticed him following.

"Who are you? What is your business here?" Inco called out.

"I am Assistant Roger Bailie of the Roanoke Colony, with permission of Her Majesty Queen Elizabeth. I command you to halt, or we'll shoot." He held the strange stick closer to his face, still pointed at Inco and Gray. "Halt, I say."

Inco saw no threat in their measly sticks. He furrowed his brows and continued toward them. Gray kept up, walking at his side.

"Why does he claim two names?" Inco mumbled.

Gray humphed, "And what kind of name is Roger?"

POP!

The strange stick made a loud noise like those they'd heard before. Sparks flew from the tip, and the man holding it thrust back. Inco stopped abruptly, paused for a moment, then fell backward to the ground. His lifeless body hit with a thud. Blood oozed from a hole in his forehead down into his open eyes.

"There's the little one," one of the other men in the group yelled. They all turned and ran after something.

Gray did not understand what had just happened. What had appeared to be a stick had made a noisy spark, and now Inco lay on the forest floor, bleeding. He knelt at his side.

"Inco, what happened?" He pulled Inco's Qi from his chest and poured several drops into his forehead wound.

Nothing happened. Inco remained motionless, his lifeless eyes fixed and open.

"Inco!" Gray continued to shake him.

Inco didn't respond.

"Papa," Jak's voice trembled as he approached. "Papa? Are you all right?"

"Jak? Wha—I- I- I don't—a man, Roger! Then the stick—it sparked, and—" He crouched over Inco's body, his arms reaching out as if he expected to catch raindrops in his palms. "I don't know what happened."

"Papa," Jak cried out. "Papa! Get up, Papa!"

He rushed to Inco and pulled at his arm. Raisin jumped from his pocket, landed on Inco's belly, and made his way to Inco's chest.

"Oh, no." He shook his head.

Jak stopped shaking Inco's arm and let it slide from his grip. He realized he felt nothing from Inco. No feelings. Beings always have at least one active emotion, unless they're dead. A calm rage suffocated his grief, and he stood tall with conviction and calm determination.

"He's gone."

Gray cried. He grabbed Jak and pulled him into his chest as he wailed in agony greater than anything Jak had ever heard from him. Even when he once broke his leg, he didn't cry in such a way.

He pulled away from Gray and turned to look at his father. Raisin stood just above Inco's collarbone, touching his cheek gently as tears beaded down his rocky body. Jak couldn't cry. He was too angry to cry. His blood boiled, and heat pulsed through his face and hands. He looked in the men's direction, seeing them in the far distance, and his eyes went cold.

POP! POP! Distant sounds could be heard, along with incoherent yelling.

Jak removed his Qi and handed it to Gray, making fierce eye contact.

"Try this," he said without expression, then ran after the men.

"Jak!" Gray called.

"Hey," Raisin jumped off Inco and ran toward Jak. "You forgot me!" He slowed to a jog and stopped. "Aw, man!"

Gray tried to go after Jak, but his legs were weak with shock and buckled under him. He looked down at the black Qi and crawled back to Inco. Even though it could never work, he did what Jak asked. His hands trembled as he tried to hold the Qi between his thumb and first two fingers. He rested one arm across Inco's chest and steadied the Qi over the wound.

Raisin ran back to Inco and jumped up next to Gray's arm. He watched with curiosity and a glimmer of hope as Gray leaned on Inco, struggling to see through the tears. He squeezed the Qi over the wound, releasing several drops of black xenum into it, and then collapsed his head onto Inco's shoulder.

Raisin saw no change. His hopes faded, and he moaned in disappointment.

The danger of Jak running after the men finally broke through the grief and shock. Gray turned to see where Jak had gone, but he was nowhere in sight. He rose to his feet, but his legs felt heavy and numb.

"Jak! Come back!"

Leaves and twigs rustled behind him.

CHAPTER 27

After handing Gray his Qi, Jak ran after the men in the forest. His feet pummeled the ground, causing dirt to fly in all directions. Yelling and more *POP* noises echoed through the trees, giving Jak a vague direction to run until he jumped over three troll bodies on his way. Assuming they were the target of the men's chase, he felt certain of his direction and gained speed. Everything in the forest became a blur. A clear, sideways eyelid protected his eyes from the pressure of the wind. His pupils became elongated and pointed at the tops and bottoms. His hair flew straight behind him.

The man at the rear of the group turned around just as Jak leapt into the air. He groaned in fear and aimed his spark-stick just before Jak landed on his chest. The man collapsed under him, losing his grip on his spark-stick. Jak grabbed the stick and threw it, pure hatred pouring from his eyes.

"Are you Roger?" he growled through clenched teeth.

"I'm Christo—oof!"

He jumped off his chest, leaving him struggling for air, and leapt onto another man from behind. He put a knee between the man's shoulder blades and pulled his head back by his hair. The man wailed in pain, grasping blindly for the spark-stick he dropped.

"Are you Roger?"

"I'm T—"

Jak heard enough. He smashed the man's head back to the ground, knocking him out. The other men had heard the painful cry and came running—their spark-sticks pointed at Jak.

"Which one of you is Roger?" he asked in a calm rage.

Three men turned to a fourth who had his eyes fixed on Jak.

"That would be me," he said, maintaining eye contact. "Assistant Roger Bailie of Roanoke." He pointed his spark-stick at Jak.

"You killed my papa," he huffed as his adrenaline rose.

Roger chuckled, lowering his spark-stick. "It's just a boy. Grab him. Maybe he has some answers."

The men started toward him, lowering their spark-sticks and hunching their shoulders, ready to pounce. He glared at them and took a deep breath.

"RRRAAHHH!" All the frustration, anger, and hatred boiling in his gut came out in a roar so loud the leaves flew off their branches.

The men jumped back and lifted their spark-sticks again. *POP!*

Smoke flowed from the end of one of the spark-sticks. Jak jerked back as something pierced through his shoulder. It went through the skin and out again, landing somewhere behind him. He looked at the blood trickling out of the small round wound.

Flashes of Inco's lifeless face filled his head. The blood trickling down his arm became the blood that ran into his father's dead, open eyes. Although it didn't seem possible, more anger filled his veins, making his face red. He clenched his fists and flexed all the muscles in his still boyish arms.

Black scales emerged from the skin around his wrists, then more scales above them, and yet more above those. Jak's height increased rapidly. His arms filled out with mass. Muscles protruded across his chest and abdomen. Within seconds, scales covered every bit of his torso, and he stood sleek, muscular, and taller. Scales emerged up his neck and face as he turned his gaze to the men.

"Sorcery," one man called out.

"Demon," Roger declared, raising his spark-stick again.

Jak shuddered as the word struck a nerve. His response was quiet but filled with rage. "Never call me a demon!"

POP! Another spark-stick smoked at the tip. This time what flew from the spark-stick ricocheted off Jak's scales and drilled into a nearby tree. Bark and splinters spit out from the hole. The men stepped back in shock.

***

Gray heard the rustling of leaves and twigs behind him but dismissed it, assuming it was just Raisin. He scrambled to regain his footing, to chase after Jak.

"What happened?" Inco groaned as he sat up and rubbed his forehead.

Raisin looked at him, speechless. Gray spun around.

"Inco," he shrilled.

"Did that man hit me with a rock? My head's killing me." He looked at his hand, covered in blood laced with black streaks. "Ow! It must've hit me hard," he grumbled, reaching for his head again. A tiny, perfectly round lump had formed where the hole once was. He looked at Gray with a puzzled expression. "Why're you screaming for Jak?"

"Inco! You were dead. I don't know what happened, but you died when that, that... stick *sparked.* Then—" He glanced in the direction Jak had run.

Inco squeezed his eyes shut and rubbed his aching brow. "Dead?"

"Dead as a rock," Raisin nodded.

"I'm fine. It's just a lump. What about Jak?"

"He went after them, and he doesn't have his Qi." Gray held the black Qi in his palm.

"What?" Inco tried to stand but fell back to the ground.

"His xenum works after death. It probably has to be immediately after death, I think. I'm not sure, but I do know you were dead. Your heart stopped. Your breathing stopped. Something's changed in Jak since Lilink hatched. Everything about his life has been strange. What more could possibly happen?"

"Don't ask questions we don't want an answer for," Inco groaned with the effort it took to maintain balance. Gray pulled Inco's arm over his shoulders to steady him as Matilda ran past them in a hurry.

"Wait for me," Raisin called.

"No," Gray yelled.

Matilda looked back but kept running.

"Aw, come on!" Raisin threw his arms out in frustration, looking back at Gray.

"Go absorb your rock pile," Gray groaned from the pressure of Inco's weight.

Raisin looked back to the clearing where a large pile of rocks sat at the edge.

"It'll be faster if you throw me."

Gray leaned Inco against him, picked up Raisin, and

threw him as hard as he could.

"Wooooooooo," Raisin wailed through the air. He landed on the rock pile and rolled around, becoming larger and larger as the rocks sank into him. He ran back to Inco and Gray, shaking the ground with loud thuds.

"Take Inco back to the house and protect the women. I'll go find Jak," Gray said. He removed Inco's arm from his shoulder again and guided him toward Raisin.

"No," Inco said. "I have to get my son."

"You're in no shape to keep going. Raisin, take him and go."

Raisin nodded and picked up Inco, lifting behind his knees with one rocky arm and across his upper back with the other. He looked at him with a chivalrous grin.

"Not... a word," Inco sneered.

"I can respect that," Raisin said, still smiling.

***

Jak stood his ground as the men edged in to surround him. As if from nowhere, Matilda jumped onto one of them. She made a death rattle growl as she bit into his arm. The man tried to pull her off, but she latched onto his other arm. She scurried over his shoulder, down his back, and around to his crotch. With a sharp growl, she sank her teeth into his genitals.

He screamed while swatting and grabbing at her with both arms. Her death rattle intensified and quivered as she shook her head and yanked off a mouthful of flesh and fabric. The screams of pain continued. Matilda jumped down and spat out the chunk of flesh. The man fell to the ground in a fetal position, howling.

"He will bleed out fast," she stated in a matter-of-fact tone.

"Matilda?" Jak marveled.

"Last I checked," she nodded with a wink.

"You *can* wink. I knew it!"

POP!

The dirt next to Matilda flew in all directions. She jumped from the impact site and attacked the man who fired the shot.

Jak refocused his attention on Roger, who was shoving a smaller metal stick into a spark-stick, then hurriedly pouring something into it. Walking toward him, Jak grabbed a spark-stick one of the other men had dropped. He tossed it up and caught it by the center. Gripping it tightly, holding it like a spear, he sidestepped and lunged, throwing it as hard as he could. It hit Roger like an arrow in the lower right side of his chest, throwing him back. The spark-stick drove through him and embedded itself in a tree behind him.

Jak moved closer to Roger. He could hear Gray calling his name in the distance but ignored it. Things weren't over yet. He was far from finished with Roger. He listened to the dying man struggle to breathe, swaying side to side, fascinated with the gurgling and gasping noises. There was a sadistic satisfaction in Roger's pain that Jak had never experienced. Hot chills of inner pleasure hit him in waves with every sound of anguish. He placed a foot on Roger's chest and used both hands to yank the spark-stick out. Roger slid down the tree to settle in a sprawled heap on the ground.

Jak took a moment to admire the weapon. It was made of

both metal and wood. A curved fishtail of wood at one end narrowed as it met and ran along the bottom of a hollow metal pole. Little metal pieces poked out in various places. They were all shiny and well crafted. Along the wood were pearly white dots, lines, and artwork of animals. The beauty and art put into this horrible weapon surprised Jak.

He looked back at Roger, who was losing consciousness. He used the end of the spark-stick to lift his chin and make eye contact. Roger's eyes rolled back as he struggled to hold his head up. Jak let the spark-stick slide through his fingers until the curved wooden end slipped into his palm. While maintaining eye contact, Jak stepped back, lifted the spark-stick, and swung it like an axe chopping wood.

The impact caved in the top of Roger's skull. Jak felt a powerful release in the sound of crushing bone. He swung the spark-stick again, splitting Roger's head open. Blood and grey chunks fell from his skull. The sense of release flowed through him. It was intoxicating. He swung again, splashing blood everywhere. He swung again, and again, and again until Gray grabbed the spark-stick from his hand. By then, Roger's body was split down to his navel, and blood dripped from Jak's face and arms. Gray marveled at the scales and growth.

"Jak, what happened?"

Jak's euphoria stopped instantly, and rage took over. He wanted that feeling of release again. He snarled and lunged at Roger's dead body, but Gray caught him and pulled him back.

"He's dead, Jak. He's dead," Gray grunted, struggling to hold Jak. While desperately trying to control Jak, a part of Gray continued to wonder at Jak's size and strength. "Come on, Jak! One to grasp it…"

Jak continued to struggle.

"Jak, stop!" Gray shouted.

The gruesome sight of what his little brother had done was almost too much for him. That, compounded with the scales and shocking growth, overwhelmed him. He felt anger and sadness simultaneously.

Finally, Jak stopped struggling. He groaned at the emotions coming from Gray, calming his rage and hatred. His breathing slowed and quieted. The scales all over his body receded back into his skin. His eyes returned to their normal shape. Everything returned to normal except for his size. He buried his face into Gray, crying.

"He killed Papa."

"Inco's alive, Jak," Gray whispered. "Raisin took him home. Your xenum saved him, and it saved three trolls I found dead while we searched for you." He lowered his voice to a whisper. "Your xenum's very special."

"Will it work on him?" Jak looked at Roger's body.

"No. He's dead-dead."

"I can finish off the unconscious ones and track the others if you like." Matilda offered.

"It talks," Gray exclaimed.

"Yes," she seethed, squinting her eyes. "And *it* has a name."

"Oh, sorry,… Matilda, right?" He nodded in reverence. "I think these guys get the point. We just need to take these sticks, and I'm sure they'll leave when they wake up. Thanks for looking out for Jak."

"Any time, but I was not asking you." She looked at Jak. "I am asking this big guy."

"Thank you, Matilda, but I think Gray's right."

"As you wish." Matilda nodded in reverence before running off toward her burrow.

Jak pondered her 'big guy' remark. He looked at his arms, flexed his biceps curiously, and then patted his abdominal muscles. But his shock and delight gave way as exhaustion overwhelmed him.

"Gray," he muttered.

"Yes?"

"What's wrong with me?"

"Well, it looks like all the action triggered a growth spurt."

"I mean, why did I do this?"

"You were just protecting your family. That's normal."

"But I enjoyed it."

"You enjoyed what?"

He locked eyes with Gray, his voice barely above a whisper.

"Killing him."

Gray paused, trying to hold back his fear, but Jak felt it and lowered his head in shame again.

"That's just the rush of everything going on. It's a strange feeling," Gray tried to console him.

Jak sniffled, keeping his head down. "The prophecy's true. I'm evil."

"No, you're not. Don't say that. Don't even think it!"

"Yes, I am. Can you fix me?"

In that moment, he felt Jak's pain as if it were his own. It hit with such force that his knees shook beneath him and his heart wrenched with pain. Jak was his little brother, and even in this moment of savagery, he wanted nothing more than to protect him. He looked at Jak's blood-covered chest and shoulders, then noticed the blood on his own hands and shirt.

"We'll sort this out later. Let's get home and get cleaned up."

Jak nodded, dreading his father's response to everything that had just happened. He and Gray gathered the spark-sticks and made for home in silence.

CHAPTER 28

A deep concern for Inco quickly set aside surprise at Jak's growth. He'd fallen terribly ill by the time Jak and Gray had returned home from the forest. For days, he ran a high fever with chills and sweats. The knot in his forehead was cherry red, with several red streaks running out from it. No one knew what to think of it.

They kept him isolated in his room as a precaution. Being a DúElf, Joss's immune system was the strongest, so she handled most of his care. She spent countless hours at his bedside, wiping the sweat from his forehead and spoonfeeding him sips of water.

Gray cared for Lilink, and Raisin guarded the house in his giant form while Gail and Jak went out to the Gabril meadow to gather medicinal plant clippings. Jak wanted to use his xenum on Inco, but they worried that it might've been what caused his illness. He'd protested that Inco was alive because of his xenum, and it made little sense for it to resurrect him and make him sick at the same time. Still, they opted not to use it.

Upon entering the meadow, several women and children scattered. They were a surprise for Gail and Jak as the Gabril meadow had never been occupied before.

"Wait," Gail called out. "Don't be frightened."

Jak grabbed her arm by the crook of her elbow. "Ma, let's go back to the house."

"No." Gail pulled away. "We can't live in constant fear. They may need help. Perhaps they're from southeast Origo. Maybe they're just passing through."

"What if they're the ones from the forest, Ma?"

"All the more reason to make peace, Jak. Now, come."

She walked toward the flocking people. As they approached, they saw more and more people. Jak and Gail came to a small camp where more than a hundred people gathered. They stopped near the point where the campground seemed to begin.

"Ma," he whispered in protest one last time. She ignored him.

"Hello. My name's Gail," she called out. "This is my son, Jak. We live nearby."

The group whispered amongst themselves. Gail strained to hear, but they huddled tight and covered their mouths when they spoke.

"Where are you from? Are you passing through?" Gail persisted. "Do you need aid? Food? Water?"

"Water," a woman called out.

"Bandages," another woman answered.

The huddle of people seemed to loosen. A woman put down her child but held his hand to keep him close. The crowd stared with blank faces and fearful eyes.

"We can help. We have a well." Gail pointed toward the forest without turning. "It's in front of my home. Take what you need. I have no bandages, but I'd be happy to heal any wounds you may have, uh, ladies only, though."

"Are you a doctor?" one woman asked, and the group's murmur increased.

"No, just my Qi," she answered, holding a hand over her chest.

"Algonquian medicine woman," someone said aloud.

"She's too pale," another objected.

A woman pushed through the group of people. She held out her arm, which had a badly discolored open wound. Her face was pale, thin, and sickly; her eyes sunken and dark.

She stopped a few feet from Gail. "Can you heal this?"

Several people protested her walking out of their huddle, but they didn't chase after her.

Gail gasped at the sight of the wound. She pulled her Qi off her chest and held it out. The woman held out her arm while swaying in place. Gail reached forward with the Qi and squeezed a few drops of xenum onto the wound.

The woman winced and looked at her arm. At first, nothing happened. She raised her eyebrows at Gail, then back at her arm. The wound lightened in color and the bruising and redness faded. Within a minute, the blackened skin turned pink again. The woman smiled with a chuckle of amazement. Her arm looked as if she'd never injured it. She laughed nervously and ran back to her people, raising her arm for all to see as she pushed through the crowd.

The people gasped and shrilled like a chorus. Another woman ran out with her adolescent daughter. She showed an ugly cut on the side of the girl's finger. Gail dripped xenum onto it, and it healed almost instantly. The girl ran back, showing her finger to the crowd.

A man limped forward, steadying himself with a long walking stick. Jak recognized him and moved behind Gail, hiding his face while keeping a watchful eye.

"A vermin attacked me in the woods," he said, pulling up his pants leg.

"I can't." Gail tried to look away but noticed the red staining of the man's pants.

He continued to pull the pant leg past his knee, then jerked at the cloth and ripped it open, showing his upper inner thigh—or at least, what was left of it. A large chunk of flesh was missing. The wound was dangerously near his genitals.

"I can't heal a man."

Gail clutched the Qi and stepped back. The man snatched her arm by the wrist. She shrilled and struggled to pull away. Jak stepped out from behind her.

"Let her go."

"Demon," the man growled, releasing Gail's arm, causing her to fall back. He hobbled backward, angered and startled.

Jak tried to lead his mother back toward the forest, but she pulled back toward the people.

"My Qi! He made me drop it."

She fell to her knees, hidden by the height of the tall grass, and searched. Men from both sides of the huddle came running toward them, holding spark-sticks. Jak jumped in front of her to protect her. She found her Qi, quickly placed it back on her chest, and stood behind him. She looked over his shoulder at the men running toward them.

"Jak, let's go." She pulled at him.

"No. We can't outrun their spark-sticks."

"Spark-sticks?"

"Back away," Jak said to the men. "We only came to help. We don't want any trouble."

"He killed Roger," the injured man called out.

"You killed someone?" Gail exclaimed in a whisper.

"This man you call Roger. He injured my father and me with his spark-stick," Jak announced.

"Spark-stick?" a man chuckled and took aim at Jak. "You mean this?"

"Get down, Ma."

He flexed his arms. Black scales flipped out of his skin and covered his arms and torso.

"Jak?" Gail fretted. "What's happening?"

"Demon," the man yelled louder, adjusting his aim.

Jak fumed at the mention of the word demon. He took in a deep breath to roar but held it when someone shouted.

"Stop," the voice called out from the crowd. "Stand down, gentlemen." A man approached him from the group. "At ease, Roger."

"Roger?" Jak blurted.

"We have… I mean, had two Rogers in our company," the stranger explained, trying to use a friendly tone. "I'm Ananias Dare, lead assistant to the Governor of Roanoke." He offered a handshake.

Jak looked at his hand but didn't move from his defensive position in front of Gail. Ananias closed his hand and dropped it to his side.

"A moment ago, you healed my wife, Eleanor, and we are sincerely grateful." He stared at Jak's scales as he spoke but looked away when Jak's gaze met his.

"You're welcome," Gail said over Jak's shoulder. She wondered why he gave two names, but with the tense atmosphere, she decided not to ask.

"My daughter—" Ananias paused, putting his hand over his mouth briefly. Desperation shone from his eyes. "She's but two months old and has fallen ill. The injury on my wife's arm poisoned her blood. I'm grateful that you healed Eleanor, but could you please look at my daughter?"

"We can only heal injuries," Gail said. "We can't cure illness."

Jak studied Ananias, feeling his desperation. It was a heart-wrenching feeling that Jak could barely stand. His expression turned soft and empathetic. The scales on his arms and torso folded back into his skin and disappeared. He lowered his arms and sighed.

"Take me to her."

"Jak, we can't heal illness," Gail said

"I can," he whispered over his shoulder.

"You can't let them see your Qi," she whispered close to his ear.

"It'll be all right," Jak whispered back, then turned to Ananias. "No weapons. Put them all away if you want my help."

Ananias eagerly agreed. He turned to his people and announced in a loud, assertive tone, "At ease, gentlemen. Put your weapons away."

Jak and Gail followed Ananias toward the group. Jak glanced at a man who put a spark-stick on the ground. He looked away, only to see another man walking away with a spark-stick. The danger was everywhere, but he trusted Ananias. He could feel his intentions.

Ananias led them to a small shelter built from sticks, mud, and the tall meadow grass. Eleanor sat inside, holding a baby in her arms.

Jak knelt next to Eleanor and looked at the baby. She reminded him of Lilink, except her soft, innocent face was pale, and her lips were tinted blue. Jak sensed her racing pulse and could hear her labored breathing. He pulled his Qi from his chest, keeping it concealed in his hand, and squeezed it over the baby's mouth. He couldn't tell how much xenum he squeezed out because he was trying so hard to keep his Qi and the xenum from being seen.

The baby coughed and squirmed in Eleanor's arms. Her cheeks turned a soft pink color, and her lips changed to match. The paleness in her face brightened to a healthy peach tone. She opened her eyes and made tiny newborn mewling sounds.

"Oh, thank heavens," Eleanor exclaimed, embracing the baby.

"What happened to everyone here?" Gail looked around at their tired, dirty faces.

"We were chased from our settlement by a Croatoan tribe. As we ran, my wife fell and injured her arm. A few others were injured as well. They chased us into a forest that led us to this meadow, but when we tried to return, we couldn't find our way back. We aren't quite certain where we are."

Gail clung to Jak's side. "What part of Origo are you from?"

"We're from England, My Lady. We were granted royal permission to establish a settlement in the New World."

"Where's England? I've never heard of it."

"Never heard of it?" He laughed but noticed she was serious. His tone sobered. "Where are we?"

"This meadow and the surrounding forest are all part of Gabril. We're in the East Qingdom, halfway between the North Qingdom and the Rima."

His brow furrowed. "Rima?"

"Are you from Earth?" Jak cut in.

Ananias looked at him blankly. "Where else would I be from?"

"This isn't Earth. This is the planet Origo. There's no England here."

"There's no England on Earth, either," Gail muttered.

"Not Earth?" he repeated with a confused chuckle. "There's nothing outside of Earth, except the heavens, and England has been a great kingdom since the year 927."

"Nine twenty-seven?" Gail gasped. "You're from 927?"

He looked at her curiously. "No, My Lady. The year is 1587."

"That's—" She found herself unable to speak further.

"I owe you a debt for saving my family. Is there anything we can do for you in return?" Ananias offered.

"You're welcome," Gail mumbled, still pondering the claim that the year was 1587.

"My father. One of your men injured him with one of your spark-sticks. We healed him, but he's ill now."

"Yes," Gail proclaimed. "If you're truly from the future, you may know how to help him better than we can."

"Especially since it was your people that hurt him in the first place," Jak added, trying to suppress his anger at the thought.

"Spark-stick?" Ananias pulled one from behind his wife. "You mean one of these? It's called a caliver. It's a gun."

Jak stepped back cautiously, pushing Gail behind him again.

"Relax." He put the weapon back and showed his palms. "We won't hurt you. What happened in the woods was a misunderstanding."

"Misunderstanding?" Jak snarled. "Your men attacked my father and three trolls."

"Trolls? You mean those orange hairy creatures?"

"Yes. What did they do to you? Trolls are the most intelligent and peaceful beings of us all."

"I…" Ananias was speechless, confused, and lost for words.

Eleanor turned to Gail. "Did you remove the pellet?"

"What pellet?"

"These guns shoot a lead pellet. If you didn't remove it, it could be what's causing his illness."

"Yes," Ananias agreed. "You must remove the pellet."

Gail said no more. She turned and ran through the crowd of people toward the forest, calling for Jak as she moved through the tall grass.

"If there's anything else we can do—" Ananias offered Jak, holding out his hand again. Jak still felt a bit of hostility but accepted the handshake.

"Tell no one. Credit my mother for your daughter's health," he said as he turned to run behind Gail.

He caught up with her halfway through the meadow, and the two of them ran the rest of the way home together.

***

"I know what to do!" Gail burst into Inco's room with a small blade.

Joss jumped from her seat. "Don't touch him. You might get his sickness and pass it to Lilink."

Ignoring Joss's warning, she wrung a rag over a bowl of water at Inco's bedside and wiped the lump on his forehead. She then put the blade to the lump.

"Gail," Joss grabbed her hand. "We don't know what's in there."

"I do."

She pulled away and cut the skin over the lump. Pus and blood shot out. She cut a little more, opening the skin wide over a black object. Joss leaned in to look.

"Is that from Jak's xenum?"

"No. It's from their guns," Jak answered from the bedroom doorway, feeling disgusted toward the weapon that did this to Inco.

"Guns?" Joss whispered to herself.

Gail pressed the sides of the wound, and a solid black ball popped out. She glanced at it, then tossed it into a bucket on the floor. She pulled Inco's Qi from his chest and dripped xenum into the cut. It healed quickly as the red lines around it disappeared. Inco's eyes fluttered as he regained consciousness.

CHAPTER 29

A knock at the door came early the next morning. Gray answered and jested cheerily with the visitor.

"Where's Inco?" Chance asked, looking around. He glanced at the cradle in the corner of the sitting room but didn't ask about it.

"He's in his room. Why? Not here to see me?" Gray playfully punched his shoulder.

"Nah, I'm here on business. The council wants Inco to attend today's meeting. There are special—uhm—circumstances."

"I'll lead the way." Gray headed down the hall. "He's just getting over an illness, but I think it's mostly gone."

"Where's this little brother of yours?"

"He's not so little anymore. He's still sleeping. Teens, you know?" He smirked at Chance as they reached the end of the hall.

Inco was sitting at the foot of his bed, lacing his shoes, when Gray opened the door.

"How long was I sick?" he asked without looking up. "I feel like I've seen no one in a decade. We should—" He noticed Chance in the doorway, and his look turned serious, thinking of all the worst probable reasons for such a visit.

"The council continues to excuse you to raise the human child, but they have requested your presence for today's meeting."

"For what reason?"

"We have many reports of... newcomers. We are addressing the situation today. Procerus wants you there, given your position near one of the clusters."

"Very well. When's the meeting?"

"We should get there just in time if we leave now." Chance stepped back, smiling as Inco approached.

"Let's go then," he flashed back the same courteous smile as he passed into the hall. "I guess I'll see everyone when I get back. We should do something. Maybe we'll have a fire."

Inco headed down the hall, adjusting his shirt sleeves on his way. You wouldn't know by how healthy he looked that he'd been dead a mere four days earlier and remained on death's door until less than a day ago. In fact, it was almost as if he were healthier than he'd been before the incident in the forest. He stood taller, walked more confidently, held his head higher, and moved about more purposefully. His eyes were brighter, and the tired lines under them had vanished.

He and Chance went out the front door and jumped off, taking dragon form. They rose into the sky and flew over the forest trees toward the council chambers.

People in the Gabril meadow saw them. Women cried out and ran back to the camp. Men watched in awe. Children cried out gleefully, unaware of their parents' perception of danger.

They arrived at the council chambers just as the meeting began. The pair went in and quietly took their seats. Roe, whose suspension was long over, shot a glare of disgust at Inco, who returned the glare.

"Thank you all for coming to today's unscheduled meeting," Procerus said. "We have but one item on the agenda today—to decide how to handle the newcomers from Earth."

"Are they all human?" Grace asked.

"It appears so unless you count the horses, dogs, and a few other small animals and pets," Misty said.

"How did they get here?" Boris asked.

"They all seem to have accidentally gone through temporary portals that opened just long enough for them to slip through."

"So why don't we just put them back through the Airland portal?" Percy suggested. "I'm sure they would all rather be home."

"Well—" Misty searched for the right words.

"They're not from our time," Procerus said. "One woman is prehistoric, but the rest are from Earth's years 1295 to 1997 A.D."

"Is this *ab urbe condita* or *anno domini*?" Boris asked.

"*Anno domini.*"

Procerus paused as all the council members gasped and whispered to each other.

"That's rather confusing, especially with the difference in our years as well," Percy said.

"Yes, it's a lot to sort out. Sending them back to Earth so many years from their own time would be devastating to them all."

"How are they any better here?" Zebulan spat.

"Here on Origo, we're all aware of portals and that they're from a different time. Explaining that on Earth would be impossible. Here, we can understand and possibly accommo—"

"Absolutely not!" Zebulan interrupted. He stood abruptly, pushing his chair back. "You say we're here to decide, but it sounds like you've already decided." His tone then changed from angry to mocking, "Let's just keep them all here, like little pets that we have to feed and care for while our own subjects suffer."

"Our subjects are fine," Procerus said calmly.

"You're right, they are, but for how long? This is precisely why we have rules about who can come through the portals." His face twisted in disgust. "With all these humans—"

"We will adjust!" Procerus stood as he yelled. "These people didn't choose to be here. They're not enemies. They're now people of Origo. We are not a barbaric civilization. We'll teach them our laws and help them settle and live peacefully among us." He glanced around the faces of the council. "Besides," he grumbled, "the portals are all closed at the moment."

Everyone in the room gasped, including Inco.

"Jak's mother is over there," Inco said. He glanced at Zebulan, wary of what his opinion might be, but he didn't react. "The laws prohibited us from bringing her here because she wasn't related to a subject of Origo."

"Yes, I know," Procerus said.

"If the portal opens again—" Inco started, still glancing at Zebulan.

"Yes, you may bring her here. She's now the mother of a subject of Origo since you've had her son here for many years now."

Zebulan grumbled and took his seat while giving Inco a disapproving look, to which he didn't respond. He knew Zebulan was a powerful advocate for keeping Earth and

Origo separate, and he appreciated that his position helped maintain balance in Origo.

Misty read off details of the newcomers.

"One hundred and fifteen souls, led by one Ananias Dare, appeared just outside the Gabril Forest. They're from a place called Roanoke in Earth's year 1587. They've set camp in the northeast Gabril meadow."

Boris looked confused. "These people are using second names?"

"A foolish fad," Procerus grumbled, "it won't last."

Misty smirked in Procerus's direction before speaking to Boris. "Earthlings will begin using first and last names around the end of their tenth century to maintain generational lines. It has also started here in the western regions. Many Origo traditions spread to Earth over time. Perhaps that's what happened here, only in reverse."

She then continued to read from her list.

"Two boys, ages four and six, have been found on opposite sides of the Connar Canal. They've been taken to the nesting house and orphanage in Yekka. Charlie Ross, the four-year-old, held a coin printed with the words 'United States of America,' and the year 1874, and Homer Lemay, the older boy, says he's from a place called Wisconsin in the year 1920.

"Three men, Thomas Marshall, James Ducat, and Donald MacArthur, have appeared together in Balee. They're from a land called Scott in Earth's year 1900.

"Two hundred and eighty-three men in two galleys, led by Vandino and Ugolino Vivaldi, appeared in the Misbaden Ocean. They're from a land called Genoa in Earth's year 1295.

"Two boys, ages nine and twelve, appeared in the Valley of Clayton. They claim to be princes, Edward the Fifth and Richard. They've claimed many titles and are from a land called England in the year 1483. These boys are staying with the family of elves that found them.

"A single man appeared in Airland. His name is George Bass, also from this England place, but he says he was in a land called Tahiti in the year 1805 when he fell through a portal to our world.

"A woman appeared in Curratia. She's perhaps unique of all the newcomers, accompanied by two carnivorous reptilian beasts that obey her. We cannot establish communication or a timeline from her. She and her reptiles are in the Currlin caves.

"Last, a teen boy by the name of Mikey Noneya appeared in Vinnlenn. He's from a land called Yomama. He says he's from the year 1997 and is under Chance's care."

"Four hundred and eight humans," Zebulan scoffed under his breath.

"Actually," Inco raised a hand for attention. "There are now fewer people in the first group."

Misty's expression turned curious. "What do you mean?"

"They mistook trolls for dangerous creatures and chased them into the forest. Gray and I heard their weapons and ran out to investigate. Upon introduction, they injured me. When Gray caught up to them, two were dead and several wounded," he explained, giving his honest understanding of what was explained to him when he woke from his sickness. "We took some of their weapons, but they have more."

"Yes," Misty said. "Many of these newcomers are heavily armed with weapons we've never seen before. We've convinced them to allow us to store their weapons in the council's vault. Let's hope the Roanoke people do as well."

"All these people need to learn the laws of Origo as soon as possible," Procerus said. "They must know the laws if they're expected to follow them. All infractions before their teachings will be excused, but the teachings begin now."

Everyone mumbled in agreement.

"Inco, I'd like you to instruct the Roanoke people since they're near your home," Procerus said.

"Yes, sir."

"Boris and Percy, I'd like you to instruct the Galley men."

"Yes, sir."

"Chance, you continue to take care of the boy you've generously taken in. Perhaps you can assist Inco with the Roanoke people."

"Yes, sir."

"Mention the royal boys to the Roanoke people. See if they belong together. If not, they'll remain with the elven family. I trust they'll do well instructing them."

Chance nodded in agreement.

"Grace, would you consider instructing the younger boys at—"

"I'd be happy to!" She grinned.

Children were Grace's favorite beings in existence. She already spent much of her time volunteering at the Nesting House and Orphanage. "May I take them home with me?"

"Once they've grown comfortable with you, you may present the option to them," Procerus then turned his attention. "Roe, I'd like you to instruct the three Scotsmen."

"Yes, sir."

"Zebulan," Procerus sharpened his tone.

Zebulan crossed his arms, pressed his lips, and looked ahead without speaking.

"I'd like you to instruct George. He's an educated man, so it should be quick and easy."

Zebulan closed his eyes and gave a reluctant nod.

"Misty and I will take care of instructing the wild woman. Everyone is to report back here in three days to give a status update. Inco, you may attend or let Chance speak on behalf of you both." Procerus stood. "That concludes today's meeting. Thank you all."

CHAPTER 30

The Nesting House and Orphanage was a rectangular adobe building with two floors. The top level was for the eggs, and the downstairs housed children who either didn't have parents or had parents who worked there.

Inco and Chance stopped to pick up Mikey. He had stayed there during the meeting. He ran outside as soon as they landed. The grass in front moved toward the building to get away from Inco and Chance, then shot to the sides of the building as Mikey ran from the door. He'd already seen Chance in dragon form and wasn't afraid at all.

His shaggy and thick brown hair bounced over his forehead and ears, flipping out in half-curls in all directions. His bluish-green eyes gave bright contrast to the dark grey ring surrounding them, reminding Inco of Gail's eyes.

Mikey's clothing was like nothing Inco had ever seen before. The shirt had neat seams and a white silhouette of a woman's body with large white wings and NIRVANA written above it. His pants were blue and made of a material that Inco had never seen. On his feet were black shoes with the words CONVERSE ALL STAR written around the star.

Mikey noticed Inco looking at his feet.

"Like my kicks?" He held one foot out in front of him and rotated his ankle.

Inco didn't answer. He wanted to agree, but he wasn't sure what the boy meant by 'kicks.'

"Don't some dragons have wings?" he asked Chance while glancing at Inco.

"Nah, those dragons are a myth," he chuckled. "Wings are overrated anyway. They'd get in the way."

He lowered himself to his belly to allow Mikey to climb on, which he did with ease as if he'd done it several times before.

"Do all dragons have that?" He pointed to Inco's chest.

"It's called a Qi, and yes, all dragons have one." Inco grinned.

Mikey smiled, then shifted his focus back to Chance. "You're like a living *rollercoaster*." He leaned toward Chance's ear and said in a loud whisper, "That's a ride that takes you high and fast."

"This boy talks a little funny, but I love it," Chance said to Inco with a grin, then turned back to Mikey. "You ready?"

"I'm *hella* ready, dude. Let's fly," Mikey answered eagerly, then paused and took a more serious tone. "None of that crazy loopy stuff, though. I'll barf on you."

He adjusted the straps of his backpack, then leaned his belly against Chance's neck and firmly gripped the middle of the three bone horns under Chance's ears.

They lifted from the ground, and the three of them headed toward Gabril.

"We should probably talk about a few things before we get there," Inco said, flashing a cautious look at Mikey and lowered his voice. "About Jak."

"I know he's special," Chance replied. "And don't worry, Mikey can't hear anything over the wind in his ears."

Inco tried to hide his alarm. "You what?"

"After the incident with you and Roe, I asked Gray about it. He told me about the first drink and dark Qi."

"He told you?"

"I told him I heard about Jak's Qi, and he thought I already knew. It's not his fault. Don't worry, your secret's safe with me."

"What else did he tell you?"

"He told me Jak found a golem. What's his name again? Raisin? He sounds fun. I can't wait to meet him."

"Oh, he's fun, all right." Inco rolled his eyes. "I suppose if you were going to tell someone, you would've done it already. We just don't want anyone to misunderstand as Roe did. It'd be so easy for someone to want to hurt or even kill him."

"Oh, I know. Gray had the same concern. It sounds like Jak's a good young man, though, so I doubt you've anything to worry about."

"Yes," Inco sighed, wishing he truly believed Jak had more good than bad.

The rest of the trip to Gabril was silent, except for the occasional hoot or holler from Mikey whenever Chance would rise or dip in the air. They arrived in the Gabril meadow just in time. Men from the colony had gathered tools and headed into the forest to cut down trees to make their new homes. Seeing the two dragons approach, they grabbed their guns and took aim. Inco and Chance quickly took their Dú and tucked Mikey behind them for safety.

"Origo is a world full of dragons," Inco shouted.

Everyone stopped and listened in a state of shock.

"You're welcome to stay, but you must live among us and accept that you're *not* the dominant ones here," he exclaimed with an informative tone. "Dragons rule this world, and we *will not* hurt you. The myths and legends of Earth paint us in a strange light. We won't burn your village or eat your children."

The people calmed and lowered their weapons as Ananias approached. He'd seen the dragons land and shape-shift from the campsite and saw that there was no danger.

"I'm Ananias Dare, lead assistant to the governor of Roanoke." He reached out to Inco, who shook his hand warmly.

"My name is Inco, and I'm here to teach your people the ways of Origo so that we may co-exist peacefully."

"Of course, right this way."

At the campsite, Inco and Chance explained that the trees in Origo were conscious living beings, and only soil, rock, and trees that had fallen naturally could be used to build. They went on to explain the ways of life on Origo.

"We're a peaceful world. Our laws are minimal, but they're firm. We don't give warnings. Those who break our laws are subject to punishment or even exile. We can send you back to Earth over a thousand years before your time," Inco bluffed.

"It seems we have a lot of newcomers, so the council has prepared a speech that explains how things work here in Origo." He pulled a scroll from his satchel, unrolled the top, and read aloud.

"Origins fall into seven categories. The first is dragons. Dragons hold a high, authoritative role over all others. The second category is the kindreds. These are not dragons but have dragons among their kind. Humans are kindreds because there are DúHuman dragons. However, not all creatures have dragons of their kind."

Inco rolled back the paper as he read the paragraphs of information about the laws and ways of Origo. He reached the end with a flat tone and let out a sigh of relief as he rolled it again.

"Questions?

"How do we know if someone is a dragon or a kindred?

"All dragon children are indistinguishable from kindred children of their kind. An adult dragon is obvious if their Qi is visible."

"This is a Qi," Chance pulled at his shirt collar.

"Yes, well, here is the scroll of everything I just went over. There are also lists of the creatures in each category." Inco handed everything to Ananias. "There are illustrations of everything there. If you need a clearer picture, we can take you for a tour in small groups over the next few days.

"Henceforth, you are officially Origins. We have a council you can petition with requests and grievances. Chance and I are both on the council. While you are primarily my responsibility, you may come to either of us if you need anything." He looked over the crowd of blank stares. "Any more questions?"

"Yes," Ananias said. "What about fish?"

"Fishing is *not* allowed in any small body of water surrounded by stones. You may fish in waters that lack stone borders," Inco answered. "Fishing in the restricted waters will cost you your life."

"A death penalty for fishing?"

"No. We don't have a death penalty here, but we do have mermaids. They can and will kill and eat anyone who fishes in their waters. They're exempt from punishment for killing those who fish in their waters and are the only ones allowed to kill groundhogs for meat. It's their delicacy. If you see a line coming from their waters, leave it alone. They're fishing for food with these lines. If you or a child grabs it, they *will* pull you into the water. They won't purposely kill you for this, but their reflexes are sharp, and their hooks are sharper. Many creatures have died of injuries or drowning."

"One last thing," Chance looked around to make sure he had everyone's full attention. "Never, under any circumstances, go near the Rima. Don't try to look in it and don't attempt to cross it."

"What's the Rima?" Ananias asked.

"It's the gap between Salus, where we are, and Caligo, the dark dead side of this world. It has a powerful vortex that will suck you in and kill you. There's a stone wall barrier a hundred feet from the Rima. It extends around Salus. Do *not* cross it."

"Can you heal my husband?" a woman shouted from the group of people.

"Yes." Inco smiled. "Chance and I can heal any men who need it. No wound is too small or too large."

He and Chance exchanged glances and nods as they removed their Qis to heal the approaching men.

***

Things were going much better than he thought they would, especially given their encounter in the woods. He felt better with each person he healed. Most of the wounds were minor, but it felt good to help the people of Roanoke. He looked forward to working with them to build their colony. A man with a chunk of skin missing from his upper inner thigh was last to approach Inco for healing.

"Wow, this is bad." He looked at the wound carefully. The center had turned black, and the edges were riddled with pus and green spots.

"The name's John Sampson. Your wife wouldn't heal me. I've been in a lot of pain and started fevering this morning."

"Dragons can only heal beings of the same sex, except for our own children. She would've done it if she could." He ignored the 'wife' title, feeling no need to explain their relationship to everyone.

"And that boy of yours—his scales popped out again."

Inco knew nothing about Jak having scales.

"His what?"

"His armor scales. They popped out just like they did in the forest. Or is that some kind of special armor shirt?"

"Yes, it's a shirt," Chance said. "I made it for him."

Inco turned to Chance, unsure if he was telling the truth or not. He smiled at Inco, and they both glanced awkwardly at John. Inco put five drops of xenum in John's wound and watched it close up. The injury left a visible deformity where skin and muscle were missing, but the scarring was minimal.

John sighed in relief. "Thank you so much."

Inco nodded. "Infections usually fade once the injury heals. See a healer if the fever doesn't lessen."

John nodded and leaned in. "Am I understanding correctly? I can't kill a honey badger unless it attacks me?"

"That's right, and the honey badgers around my house are off-limits. The one that bit you is my son's pet. She was only protecting him."

"Yes, sir," John said in a dismissive tone.

Inco stared with a firm expression.

John glared at first, then softened. "I'll leave it alone. I'm healed. No need to take it any further."

His response satisfied Inco. After spending time with the Roanoke people, he and Chance had built a minimal level of mutual respect and trust with them. They successfully gathered all advanced weaponry, leaving them with what they needed for hunting.

Hours after arriving, they finally finished up, answering questions, and shaking hands.

"I'd like to thank your wife again for healing my Eleanor," Ananias said as he shook Inco's hand.

"Wife? Oh, Gail? She isn't my wife; she's my… co-parent," Inco struggled to find the right word, hoping co-parent would suffice.

"My apologies. Whatever her title, please give her my thanks." He smiled, prolonging the handshake. He leaned in and whispered. "And thank your son. I truly owe him my life."

"Huh?"

"Oh, uh. I thought you knew. My apologies. I'll let you talk to him about it."

"I'll do that," Inco said.

"Your wife—I mean Gail, offered the use of your well. I'd like to take you up on the offer."

"Yes, of course. Until we help you build one of your own, help yourselves."

He wasn't comfortable with the idea of them being near the house, but there were no other wells for miles, and he didn't want to give the impression that they had anything to hide. He remembered Procerus's instructions on the royal boys.

"By the way," He said to Ananias. "Have you any knowledge of an Edward the Fifth and Richard of—"

"Shrewsbury? First Duke of York, Knight of the Garter, Earl of Nottingham?"

"Yes, yes, all of that. Do you wish to stake a claim on them?"

"I'm not sure what you mean. They disappeared over a hundred years ago, likely killed by King Richard the Third."

"They appeared here, alive and well."

Ananias choked with surprise. "The young princes are alive?"

"Yes. They're with an elven family and are doing well. We only ask because of your shared origin."

"We cannot stake a claim on them. Only they can do that. Inform them of our existence and let them know we'll honor them as King Edward the Fifth and Prince Richard, as they deserve," Ananias proclaimed.

"They may be your royalty, but only within the laws of Origo. Our laws take precedence."

"Absolutely," he agreed. "Please, keep us informed of the young princes' decision."

Inco nodded. He gathered as many weapons as he could carry and walked toward the forest. Chance and Mikey filled their arms with weapons and followed.

CHAPTER 31

Jak was outside when Inco, Chance, and Mikey reached the clearing with their arms full of weapons. He'd neither seen nor heard of Mikey, so he was suspicious and hesitant when he saw him approaching. Raisin felt Jak's apprehension and stretched to follow his gaze.

"Hide," Jak whispered.

Without question, Raisin scurried into a little custom pouch Gail had sewn into Jak's loose collar.

"I like this new pocket," he whispered. From inside, he could look out without being noticed and could stay in place without falling or slipping, making him easier to hide and carry.

"Oh, hey, they're here," Gray exclaimed. "Jak, Chance has a new, uh, brother, sort of. They're joining us for supper." He approached and put his arm over his brother's shoulders, admired his new height, then shook him playfully. "You're still short."

Jak playfully boxed with him. "Little package, big power."

"What's wrong with being short?" Raisin piped from the collar pocket.

"Maybe we should start some lessons," Gray suggested, still boxing with Jak. He glanced at Inco as he walked past, knowing he overheard.

Inco flashed a warning look but didn't outwardly object. He glanced at Jak with a double-take as his eyes widened in shock. He hadn't seen his son since they had heard the gunshot sounds from the sitting room. Since then, the boy had grown taller and doubled in weight. He looked back to Gray, who sighed with a raised brow of shared amazement. Inco couldn't ask about it in front of guests, so he and Chance continued into the house with the weapons.

"Lessons? Really?" Jak asked.

"Sure, why not? You can learn from the—" He jumped back and made a silly fighting pose. "Mastah of Disastah!"

"Aw, hey." Mikey put down the weapons and jumped into an equally silly fighting pose, waving his hands in the air. "You know that Bruce Lee stuff?"

Gray lowered his arms and looked confused. "Who's Bruce Lee?"

"Are you kiddin'? That guy that tore up Rome."

Mikey pulled off his backpack. He reached in and pulled out two sets of two sticks. Each pair of sticks was connected by silver metal links. He held one stick in each hand and skillfully swung them in, out, over, and around before catching the swinging sticks in his armpits.

"Waaaaoooooaaa," he howled in a low, warbling voice.

Gray scratched his head, unimpressed by the display of swinging sticks. His mind was stuck on Rome. "Rome gets torn up?"

"Oh yeah, Rome's done, dude, but Bruce Lee didn't really tear it up. He just beat up some bad guys there. Rome, like, fell apart, or something like that."

Jak stared at Mikey. He noted his strange clothing, odd smell, and inconsistent body language, but most of all, he noticed that Mikey was about the same height as him. Although Jak's height had recently caught up, size was still something that stayed in the forefront of his mind.

"The Byzantine Empire remains, right?" Gray asked.

"Nope. That's gone too. I ain't so good with history, though, so I can't tell you all the facts. But that Caesar dude's on salad dressings and pizza."

"Whoa!" Gray tried to absorb the enormity of Mikey's claims.

"Yeah, well, anyway. I got these nunchuks for Christmas a couple of years ago. I spent a lot of time copyin' people on TV. My ma got me in a few classes, too. I was pretty good 'til some fart-knocker got in my face, and I laid him out. The sensei freaked out and told my ma, and I couldn't go back. The place was bogus, anyway," he scoffed, again swinging the nunchuk around.

"I have no idea what he just said," Jak whispered to Gray.

Gray raised his brow and shrugged.

Mikey overheard. "Means I hit the dude for being an asshole. I'm over here if you got something to say," he teased at Jak.

He puffed his chest and held his arms out at his sides, letting the nunchuks hang loosely from his hands. Jak didn't understand the confrontational humor. He felt antagonized and responded with a glare.

"You wanna go there?" Mikey challenged.

Jak squared his shoulders and widened his footing.

"Jak, it's all right," Gray put a hand on Jak's shoulder. "He just talks different. He's from another time, remember?"

"I'm just messin' with you, home-skillet." Mikey smiled and draped his nunchuks over his shoulder to offer a handshake. "We cool?"

Jak balked for a moment before reluctantly accepting the handshake. His expression remained tense, however.

"Mind if I practice karate with you guys?"

"Karate?" Gray echoed.

"Yeah. Karate. You know, martial arts."

"They don't teach that to outsiders."

"They do in my time. It's popular. I'm not real good at it, but I'll show you what I know if you let me practice with you."

"I'll show him somethin'," Raisin piped from the collar pocket. He felt Jak's tension and shared his frustration with the stranger.

Mikey's face twisted in confusion. "What?"

"I'll polish your ass with my foot," Raisin threatened.

Mikey couldn't see Raisin, so he thought Jak was the one speaking.

"Oh, yeah? C'mon, I'll show you what a can of whoopass feels like." He took a step back and swung his nunchuk.

"Mikey," Chance barked from the doorway, having heard the last remark.

Without looking at Chance, he mumbled, "He started it."

He stopped swinging the nunchuks and let them hang from his hands again. Chance looked at Jak and Gray, their faces tight and sober.

"Let's all come inside. It's time to eat," Chance said.

Mikey huffed and rolled his eyes, then turned to put his nunchuks back into his backpack.

"Chicken!"

"Raisin, hush!" Jak exclaimed.

"Oh, that's it." Mikey whirled around and, in two steps, was in Jak's face with his fists clenched. Gray pulled Jak behind him with one hand and held his other hand palm against Mikey's chest.

Chance bolted from the doorway and grabbed Mikey from behind, picking him up off the ground. Mikey kicked, yelled, and struggled to break free.

"C'mon, dickweed, I'll knock your face in," he screamed at Jak.

Jak tensed, struggling to remain calm. He knew Mikey's anger was valid because of what Raisin had said, but he still didn't take the threats lightly.

"Stop it, fartknocker," Chance demanded.

"Ha!" Mikey instantly stopped struggling. It was as if he'd snapped out of a violent dream and was his cheery self again. He twisted his neck to look at Chance. "You *were* listening."

"Of course, I was." He loosened his grip. "You can't just go starting fights, though. Let people get to know you before you try to play rough. Agreed?"

"Yeah, I guess." He adjusted his shirt and pulled his pants up. He rubbed his nose on the back of his wrist and forearm. He looked at Jak mischievously. "Sorry, dude."

Jak's tension eased. He concluded to himself that Mikey was crazy, and that was that.

"Haha! Fartknocker! I'm going to use that one," Raisin squealed.

"Okay, I heard that." Mikey pointed. "Are you doing some ventriloquist stuff, or what?"

"What's a—" Jak couldn't remember the word well enough to repeat it.

Raisin peeked out, exposing his head down to his eyes, then ducked back into the pocket.

"What was that?" Mikey peered at Jak's collar. "Is that a rat?"

Raisin jumped out of the pocket. He held onto Jak's collar with one hand and waved a fist with the other.

"Who you callin' a rat, fartknocker?" he yelled. "Heh heh, fartknocker," he mumbled to himself, then looked at Jak with a grin. "That's a new one I just heard today."

"Whoa! That's tight. A talking gerbil," Mikey laughed as he pointed a finger at Jak. "I want one. Haha!" He tucked his chin against his neck and changed his voice to a deep mocking tone, "I've got a gerbil in my pocket."

"That's not a gerbil. It's a golem," Chance smiled.

"I've got a moron in my yard," Raisin mocked with the same tone and tune. He jumped to the ground and stepped toward Mikey.

"Shut up, you scab-pickin' fart-sniffer," Mikey replied.

"Butt-licker," Raisin shot back, trying to keep up.

"Vomit bag booger-eater."

"Shit-nose." He flashed a mischievous smile at Gray.

"Ass-munch."

"Uhmmmm, vomit, uh, eater."

"Yo mama."

"Huh?" Raisin's face twisted in confusion.

"Loser-says-what!"

"Wha—aw, man!"

Mikey squatted on the balls of his feet. "Haha, I like you, little dude."

"Little?" Raisin wagged his fist. "I resemble that remark."

Mikey leaned closer, putting one hand on the ground to support himself. He cupped the side of his mouth with his other hand and whispered, "I'll teach you everything I know."

"Yes," Raisin cheered in a whisper and strutted like he'd just won a battle. He climbed to Jak's shoulder and sat. "The new guy can stay."

Jak huffed and smiled at Raisin. "Very well."

"Let's eat." Gray slapped his hands together and rubbed them briskly in eager anticipation.

Everyone murmured in agreement as they made their way into the house.

***

That night was a new, exciting experience for Jak. Being around someone other than family was rare enough, but having them over for supper, laughing, chatting, and being able to be himself was something he never imagined possible. He didn't even notice what was going on between the parents. The others were so busy socializing they didn't seem to notice either.

Gail looked at Inco in a way she'd never looked at him before. She stared with a warm smile while her feet fidgeted under the table. She wore a dress Inco hadn't seen before. It was black with thick white trim around the neck, waist, wrists, and bottom. The fragrance of lemon and honey flowed from her and danced under Inco's nose.

Joss also wore a dress she hadn't worn before. It almost matched Gail's, but her dress was green, and the front was a low V-cut. She smelled of fresh-cut mint, complimenting Gail's lemon fragrance.

Inco kept his eyes on his plate. A strange kind of tension permeated the air and made him uncomfortable. He wasn't sure what was on their minds, and he didn't know how to respond or if he should respond at all. Although there had been a few tender moments over the years, he had managed not to cross any lines with either of them. The desire had always been there, but he had never quite understood the relationship between the women, nor found the courage to ask.

Gail sighed heavily, causing him to glance up without thinking. They both stared at him intently, but now their eyes had dragon pupils.

Inco snapped his eyes back to his plate. He suddenly looked forward to retiring to the solitude of his room for the evening.

CHAPTER 32

Gray shut the front door after showing their guests out, still smiling at the events of the evening. Inco wiped the table with a brown rag, brushing crumbs into his hand, then went into the kitchen and started moving things around. Gail and Joss were down the hall, putting Lilink to sleep. Jak sat in the middle of the sitting room floor, setting up the chaturanga game. He looked up at Gray, who joined him on the floor to play.

"I'm pretty tired," Inco mumbled as he left the kitchen, headed down the hallway. As he edged past the ladies' bedroom, he glanced at the dark gap between the floor and the bottom of their door. Anxiety rushed over him when the floor creaked loudly beneath his feet. He kept his eyes on their door, hoping they wouldn't hear him as he slipped into his room. Stepping into the darkness, he closed the door and put his back against it. His shoulders sagged as he let out a heavy sigh of relief at not disturbing the women.

A faint aroma of mint crept past his nose. The sound of fabric rubbing against fabric came from the far side of the room. His eyesight brightened with night vision, and he discovered Gail and Joss sitting on the padded chest at the foot of his bed. His heart jumped into his throat, and he jerked back, banging his head on the door.

Gray and Jak heard the thud from the sitting room. They looked at each other curiously, shrugged, and looked back at their game pieces.

"What's—?" Inco's voice cracked a high pitch. He cleared his throat and tried again, overcompensating for his high tone with an unusually deep one. "What's going on?"

"Sometimes you have to nearly lose someone," Gail started.

"To realize what they truly mean to you," Joss finished.

"What do you mean?" He pressed his back against the door.

"We almost lost you," Joss started.

"Without ever having you," Gail finished.

"Stop that," he whispered.

"Stop what?" Joss asked.

"Finishing each other's sentences. It's creepy."

Gail sauntered toward him. She pressed her body against his side, one hand on the small of his back, the other rested on his collarbone. She leaned her head against the crease between his arm and chest and sighed aloud.

"I'm sorry," she whispered.

The rigidity in his body eased with her touch. Her warmth melted away his anxiety. Lemon essence filled his lungs. Her hair brushed against his chin and lips. He turned his gaze toward her.

"Sorry? For what?"

"For waiting so long."

Joss joined them. "We're already a family, and now we're ready to be complete." She lifted his free arm and wrapped it around herself, pressing her body against his other side. She rested her head against him, slightly higher than Gail.

His hand rested at the bottom of her back, his wrist resting in the curve of her hip. He turned his face toward her, caressing her forehead with his chin.

"But, I thought you two… you know—" he fumbled for words.

In unison, they pressed their bodies against his and swayed as they shifted their weight from one foot to the other. He closed his eyes in ecstasy and took in a deep breath, letting it out through pursed lips while trying to control the urges he felt.

"We love each other with our whole hearts, but not in that way," Joss whispered.

"We occasionally help each other out," Gail said.

"But we prefer to focus on a husband," Joss added.

Blood rushed to his head, making his face feel hot. Joss's hand grazed low across his belly. Gail put her hand on his cheek and turned his face toward her. Her breath moistened his lips as she whispered.

"Sometimes together."

Joss pulled his face toward her in the same manner. She pressed her cheek against his and whispered.

"Sometimes apart."

"You mean, you both—"

He had feelings for both but never imagined they'd both have feelings for him. Of course, there was their kinship, but he'd never considered the odds of a dual relationship to be in his favor.

"We bonded in our first marriage, and that bond is forever," Joss said.

"We are, and always will be, a package deal," Gail added.

"Husband?" he pondered aloud. Inco had never married. All his intimate experiences had been among the fairladies of his youth. He had never thought much about marriage, but he often imagined growing old with Gail and Joss. In fact, he couldn't picture life without either of them now that they shared children and a home. It occurred to him he'd never considered marriage because he had already committed himself to his current relationship with Joss and Gail. Marriage was nothing more than a formality and a gateway to physical intimacy, which to this point, he assumed they didn't desire from him.

Joss sighed. "We've mourned long enough."

"We're ready if you'll have us." Gail offered.

Inco paused a moment to grasp what Gail had said. The words stung a bit. That they didn't know his feelings for them saddened him.

"I—of course, I will—er, would! But don't you want courtship and a wedding?"

He'd relaxed enough to embrace them and did so. He pressed his palms gently against their backs and caressed the curves of their hips, then grazed up to the center of their shoulder blades. They, in turn, pressed their bodies more firmly against him. He repeated his caress.

"Courtship would require parting ways at the end of the day," Gail said.

"How would that work in a shared home?" Joss added.

He smirked. "You have a point. Should we at least plan a wedding?"

Gail tugged the ties of his collar until they fell loose. "I've already been married the human way. I want this marriage to happen the dragon way."

"And I wouldn't have it any other way." Joss placed her index finger on his chin and ran it to the base of his neck, seductively exhaling through parted lips.

"Think you can handle it?" Gail teased.

His body language shifted from nervous to confident as he further straightened his back and huffed. He looked at Gail, then to Joss, then back to Gail. His brow twitched, briefly widening his eyes while a wry smirk pulled at his lips.

"Shall we find out?"

Without warning, they yanked him toward the bed for a night he would never forget.

CHAPTER 33

Morning light seeped through the dense curtains, giving the room a dim, warm glow. A thin beam of light came through a tiny hole in the curtain and landed on Inco's eye as he slept flat on his back in the center of his bed. His eyes fluttered as the brightness agitated his slumber. He tried to rub his eye but found his arm pinned from the shoulder down. Still half asleep, he attempted with his other arm but found it pinned as well.

As he became more aware, he opened his eyes to see Joss sleeping beside him, pinning his arm. He drew his head back in brief surprise, then eased back onto the pillow and smiled. Memories of the previous night flooded his mind.

He looked at Gail, sleeping in a similar position on his other shoulder, and realized he had no feeling in either arm. As much as he loved the closeness, he had to move. He lifted his head and looked back and forth between his two beautiful brides, trying to think of a way to move without waking them.

"We're not asleep," they said in sync.

Inco threw his head back onto the pillow. "That's so creepy!"

He pulled his arms from under them and stretched, admiring the new marking on the third finger of his left hand. Where a wedding band would be were three lines.

The line farthest from his finger tip looked like an S turned backward on its side, with two perfectly even parallel lines stacked on it. He took a deep breath, enjoying the lemon and mint aromas that still lingered, wondering if he was looking at the mark upside down or downside up. He interlaced his numb fingers over the top of his head and gazed at his brides. Their heads remained on the outer edges of his chest. As they stirred again, pulling in closer, he noticed the matching mark on Gail's left hand.

"Two dragon marriages in one night," he pondered aloud.

"Mmm-hmm, you did very well," Joss said in a teasing tone.

Gail put her hand on Joss's. "He did great. Don't knock him down just yet. Let him bask in his glory a moment longer."

Inco became curious. "Will things be different between you two now that there's no first or second wife?"

"Nope, that's how it's always been," Joss said.

"But, I thought—"

"The strongest shape is a triangle, no matter the angles. The strongest triangle is an equilateral."

"Yep," he sighed. "Now, I'm even more confused."

Joss chuckled. "So… a perfect triangle has three even sides. The weight, angle, and pull of each side perfectly balance the others. Give extra privilege, hierarchy, or energy to one, and you weaken them all."

"Hmm." He scratched his chin. "If I'm never *right*, I might feel… um, *obtuse*?"

"Ugh," Joss rubbed her brow.

"You're so *acute* when you're frustrated."

"He's going there," Gail grumbled.

"All right, all right, I'll stop," Inco chuckled. "No need to rise and run."

Joss looked at Gail, silently mouthing *one… two…* On three, they each grabbed one of his nipples and twisted.

"Ahh! I'm sorry!" He squirmed. "I'm just so glad to have you in my arms, and I never want to *foil* it."

"He makes one more pun, and I'm killing him. Plain and simple," Joss said.

Gail nodded. "We'll plant prickle bushes over his body."

A terrible and frightening thought crept into Inco's mind. He took in a deep breath and held it, pondering a new thought while staring at the ceiling. His body's stiffness was obvious to Gail and Joss, so they both propped on an elbow to face him. He let out his breath and cleared his throat.

"Don't dragon wives have the option to eat their husband if they're unfulfilled?"

The women burst into hearty laughter.

"No one's done that in centuries," Joss managed to speak through her convulsions.

"What would be the odds of you being the first after so long?" Gail added.

His eyes widened. "Double the chances of most!" His lips quivered into a smile, losing his inner battle to remain serious.

Gail and Joss's laughter increased before fading to smiles as they sat up on their opposite sides of the bed. The white bedsheets fell from their shoulders and crimped onto the bed. Inco leaned back against the headboard and watched in peaceful delight as they twisted and stretched their naked bodies.

"Oh, my!" Joss groaned.

"What is it?" Gail whipped her head around to see.

Joss slipped into her dress and turned around. "This will be an interesting conversation with the boys."

Inco stretched and sat up. "Yes, well, I have to talk to everyone about a few things. I'm not sure what happened, but Jak's a lot taller, doubled in muscle, and I'm hearing stories of him having scales and fighting with someone named Roger."

The ladies glanced at each other, silently agreeing not to continue the course of this conversation. As a distraction, Joss tossed Inco's pants onto his lap.

She turned away and said, "Lilink should wake soon."

Gail reached for the door and looked back to make sure everyone was presentable. Inco had both legs in his pants and stood to fasten them while Joss tossed his shirt onto his head.

***

Their playful happiness filled Gail with joy, and thoughts of how their lives had changed in just one evening circled in her head. Her smile broadened as she thought about standing close to Inco, embracing him as they watched their children play. She imagined the three of them snuggling in the evening, gazing at the stars. Her thoughts ventured into the future, sitting together as their grandchildren opened gifts. She imagined them jumping with their new toys, the words "Thank you, Grandmas and Grandpa," echoing in their sweet innocent voices. She'd spent nearly three-quarters of a century mourning Tibbel, but now her life felt complete once again.

***

When they entered the hallway, they heard Lilink cooing in the sitting room. Gray paced the room, holding her in his arms.

"There they are," he mumbled to Lilink, smiling as they approached. He handed Lilink to Gail, who sat down and began breastfeeding her. Joss patted his shoulder as she passed him.

"Was she fussy?"

"A little. I heard her from your room, and I knew from the, uh, *noises* I heard last night," he raised his eyebrows, "that you three were a *little* busy, so I brought her out here. We've been having a *very* important conversation this morning."

Inco caught Gray's glance and looked away. The idea of Gray hearing anything that happened the night before was embarrassing. He picked up a pillow and threw it at him.

"Go wake Jak. We need to talk to you both."

"I bet you do," he jeered as he dodged the pillow.

The parents sat comfortably together on a long seat when Jak and Gray came into the room. Jak yawned and stretched. His half-open eyes stayed on his feet as he shuffled to a seat next to Gray, facing the parents.

"What's going on?" Jak asked.

"We have news." Gail wore a big smile.

"This early?"

"Yes." Joss smiled. "We want you to know something."

She looked to Inco to finish the announcement. He smiled and put his hand on hers.

"Your mothers and I had a dragon wedding last night," he proudly announced. "We're married."

"Really?" Jak smiled. "That sounds… good, I guess."

"Yes. We're a complete family now." Gail's eyes sparkled.

Gray grinned. "I knew it! Congratulations!"

Jak shrugged his shoulders. "Great. Can I go back to bed now?" He was happy for them, but in his mind, nothing had changed, and he didn't understand the word or significance of 'dragon wedding.' He did understand marriage, but they'd already been living and parenting together for years. From Jak's perspective, the benefits of being married only affected them.

"Not yet. We have other things to talk about." Inco's tone became serious and firm.

He let go of Joss's hand and leaned forward with his elbows on his knees, rubbing his thumb over his chin stubble.

"I've been sick for a few days, and yesterday was pretty busy, but now I want to know what happened in the forest. You're taller and stronger than you were a few days ago, Jak. And what's this I hear about scales and killing?" He interlaced his fingers and let them fall together in front of him.

"I—"

Jak was nervous. He felt reprimanded by Inco's tone and lowered his head in shame. Regret and fear made him nauseous. Gray saw Jak's shame. He scooted his chair closer and put an arm across his shoulders to console him.

"He uhm…" Gray uttered, his voice cracking as he struggled to form the words. "He killed the man that hurt you."

Inco's face lit with shock. "After what we had just told you about the prophecy? Jak, how could you?"

"I'm sorry," he mumbled.

"What about the scales? What's that about?" Inco tried not to sound angry.

Gail resorted to a soothing tone. "They only seem to come out when he feels threatened or protective."

Inco whipped his gaze to her, "You knew about this? And you didn't tell me?"

"When you came home, we had guests. I haven't had a chance."

"I'm sorry, Pa," Jak repeated, still hanging his head.

"Sorry? 'Sorry' won't save you if the council hears of this. I'm learning that people already know. Fortunately, they have said nothing." He shot a snide look at Gray for telling Chance. "You must keep your abilities hidden, Jak."

Gray cut in. "But his Qi can heal the dead. Without it, you'd be dead. That has to count for something."

"And it can cure the ill," Gail spoke just above a whisper.

"Cure the ill?" Inco flashed a confused look at Jak. "Who did you cure?"

"The colony leader's baby," he mumbled.

"You did what?" Inco boomed as he stood. Joss and Gail both grabbed at his arms, attempting to calm him, but he pulled away. "You used your Qi around strangers?"

"I'm sorry," Jak's voice trembled as tears welled in his eyes.

Gray rose from his seat, his eyes sharp and expression firm. He widened his footing and spoke calm yet assertive.

"Calm down, Inco."

His head tilted, and his vision narrowed. "Excuse me?"

"Calm... down!" Gray repeated in a firmer tone.

"Don't you tell me to calm down, Gray," he grew louder. *"He's my son."*

"And my brother," Gray shouted, stepping forward.

Jak looked up to see Inco and Gray standing toe-to-toe, posturing and clenching their fists. He touched Gray's hand, but there was no reaction. Jak had seen Gray upset a few times in his life, but never to this degree, nor had he ever seen Inco and Gray square off, and the sight was frightening.

Inco fumed. "This isn't about you. This is about Jak keeping his abilities and temper under control."

"Where's he supposed to learn that? From *you*?" Gray shot back.

Inco grabbed Gray's shirt collar into his fists, yanking him in to where their noses almost touched. He drew in a deep breath, glaring into Gray's eyes.

Joss grabbed Lilink, breaking the latch from her breast. Gail started toward Inco and Gray, but Joss caught her arm. She mouthed *no* while shaking her head and then signaled for her to follow. The two went to their room.

Gray's face soured with anger. He brought his palms together in front of his belly.

Inco growled. "You'd better watch how you talk to me in my own—"

Gray's hands shot up together like a spear between Inco's arms, breaking his grip and forcing his arms apart, then struck him in the chest with both palms. Inco fell back against the wall with a grunt.

Jak jumped between them. Inco shoved him back to his seat and lunged at Gray. Gray pivoted and ducked to one side, stepping behind him. Inco turned around and lunged at him again.

"Stop," Jak yelled, jumping between them again. He held one palm out at each of them, glancing back and forth.

"He's my son!" Inco asserted.

"I heard you the first time. You keep saying he's your son, but you're treating him like a criminal." Gray snapped.

"Stop! Stop!" Jak cried. "It's all my fault. I *am* a criminal. I'm evil." His cries turned to sobs. "I'm evil. I'm sorry. I'm so sorry." He fell to his knees and leaned forward until his forehead met the floor. He balled his hands into fistfuls of hair at the back of his head.

Gray shot a condemning look at Inco and knelt at Jak's side. He pulled the boy to his chest and embraced him. Jak continued to sob and blubber his shame. When Gray looked up at Inco again, his expression had turned to sadness.

Inco's anger faded. He reflected Gray's expression and joined them on the floor, putting his hand on Jak's shoulder.

"I'm sorry, son."

Inco looked at Gray as if to echo the apology to him as well. He stared for a moment, shifting his apologetic look to one of contemplation.

He then leaned in closer to Jak. "Maybe if you learned some techniques, you'll gain a better grip on your abilities."

Gray showed mild surprise as Inco looked back at him.

"Your big brother spent years learning many forms of combat and defense," he spoke softly to Jak but maintained eye contact with Gray. "You'd be learning from the best."

Gray smirked. "The Mastah of Disastah."

Inco realized that he'd let his anger get the best of him. He felt shame and regret having treated Gray the way he did. He felt even worse when he thought of how he'd pushed Jak. His guilt and regret peaked when he thought of how he could've hurt Lilink. He slumped, holding a palm across his brow, silently scorning himself.

Jak felt his father's emotions but didn't react. His own feelings were overwhelming enough.

Gray leaned over to talk directly into Jak's ear. "Training will help. I promise. You won't even feel like the same person after a while."

Jak kept his face to the floor with his hands over his head but gestured through his fading sobs with a grunt.

"I'll take that as a yes." Gray smiled. "Come on. It's time for you to see a marketplace in Origo. We need supplies, and we can get you outfitted at the same time."

Jak sat up, his face still strained from crying, and gave Gray a look of surprise. "I'm going somewhere?"

"Yep. Your ass is mine for at least the next four years. I'm your sensei now. What I say goes. Now go put on a high-collar shirt. Let's go."

Inco dropped his hands into his lap and sat up. He glanced at Gray, then gave Jak a forced smile and hesitant nod. "Go on. Do as your sensei says."

Jak's sad face twisted with excitement. He rushed to his room to change.

Gray called out a taunt as Jak ran off. "You won't ask to play ball with other boys when we get there, will you?"

"Ha! Ha!" Jak yelled back.

Inco headed toward the door. "I have to get to the Roanoke people. They're expecting me to help them drill a well and teach them to make adobe."

Gray reached without looking and snagged Inco's arm. He stopped, staring at the door and clenching his jaw to hold back his emotions.

"This is the right thing for him," Gray whispered, still not making eye contact.

"I know," Inco said, "I know."

CHAPTER 34

Jak jumped off Gray's back at the edge of a small town. It bustled with creatures going in and out of a strip of adobe buildings. Each building looked the same—small, square, and muddy-red. They had slanted flat roofs made of the same material, with tall windows and doors made of wood from trees that had fallen naturally, each crossed with a flat iron X.

"Is this Gabril City?" Jak awed at the commotion.

"No way. Gabril City is five hundred times as big. This is a little place called Gamma, but they have the best blacksmiths and armor dealers in all of Salus."

A dozen shops lined each side of the busy wagonway. The streets were full of humans, elves, trolls, and many creatures Jak had neither seen nor heard of. They all scurried in and out of shops and up and down the wagonway. A small humanoid creature bumped into Jak.

"Excuse me," the stranger said politely.

Jak stared curiously. The waist-high creature scurried away. He had large pointy ears, and thick spiky hair brushed back but didn't lie flat. He wore a dressy black tailcoat suit trimmed with white ruffles around the neck, wrists, and ankles. A glistening glow flickered from his shoes, where a narrow slit held a golden coin. He looked back, revealing his greyish-blue face with round bulging eyes, nostrils but no nose, and thick, dark-blue lips. He had no eyebrows or facial hair except for the thick golden lashes.

"So many buttons," Jak mumbled, squinting at the sun's reflection.

"Forty-nine, to be exact. Seven rows of seven. It's standard for them."

"Them who?"

"He's a Tellem, from the north. They're very wealthy and keep their riches in the northwest mountains of Tellurica."

Jak remembered mention of such creatures in Gray's stories but couldn't remember specifics. "So, they're like dwarves?"

"No way. Dwarves try not to spend a dime of their riches. Sometimes not even to eat. That's why they're so skinny. Tellems can make gold from straw, so they spend it lavishly."

Jak grew excited as he remembered one of the many stories Gray had told him long ago. "From straw? Like Rumpelstiltskin?"

"Sh," Gray hushed while stifling a chuckle. "They hate being called that and don't ever mess with a Tellem. They follow all the Origo laws but find loopholes like mice find grain. They'll trick you. Never make a bet or ask a favor of a Tellem. You'll pay much more than you ever wanted. They're notorious for negotiating you to a higher price that you can't pay."

"Like when Rumple—I mean—that one guy made the queen agree to give him her firstborn because she didn't have jewelry to pay with?"

"Exactly. If you lose a wager and don't have a payment on you, they'll settle for something much more valuable to be delivered at a later date."

"What did he want with that baby, anyway? Was he going to eat it?"

"No. He would've brought the baby to Origo, and the Tellems would've raised him to be a guardian or slave. But that was many centuries ago, and slavery has since been abandoned."

"What do dwarves look like?" Jak asked.

Gray looked around and pointed to where three men, hardly taller than the Tellem, stood in a circle. "Over there."

Two had their backs to Jak. All he could see was the long brown hooded cloaks they wore. The fabric was old and worn and looked like a stiff material one would use to hold onions or potatoes.

As the dwarves chatted, the two parted, and Jak could see the third facing them. His skin was greyish-red, similar to the greyish-blue of the Tellem. His nose had very little bridge at the top, but the bottom was long and pointy. He had dark beady eyes that peered through narrow eyelids. His mouth was so small he looked as if he was talking through pursed lips, and his hair was long, oily, and matted. The dwarves' clothes, a beige tunic, and brown pants, were riddled with moth holes.

"Wow!" Jak whispered.

"If one ever asks you to guess their name, don't. They'll never leave you alone until you guess correctly. They can be quite the nuisance."

"But wasn't it the Tellem that makes you guess their name?"

"He only did that in the story because a dwarf had done it to him once. He never guessed correctly, and after three days, he killed the dwarf to silence him. That's why he gave the queen three days."

"He was real? I thought it was just a story."

"He was as real as you and me. He lived over seven hundred years, wreaking havoc for nearly six hundred, and died almost a thousand years ago. We still see Tellems as trouble-makers because they are, but it took them many centuries to prove they aren't dangerous or evil."

"Where do dwarves live?"

"They live in the northeast mountains. Tellems build tiny houses into the mountain walls. Dwarves live in natural caves and tunnels. They're both very tricky, crafty creatures." He looked around as they continued to stroll along the wagonway. "Looks like a lot of the northern creatures are in the market today. They must expect foul weather."

"How do they know?"

"The abatwa. They're the third dominant creature of the north. There are others, but the main three are natives of the north and make for most of the population. Oh, look."

Gray strode briskly to the far left of the wagonway, where he squatted to talk with someone. Jak joined him and saw a tiny woman, about as tall as his thumb, carrying an infant that was so teeny he couldn't make out its face.

"Where did you first see me?" the tiny woman shouted, which was still somewhat difficult to hear.

Gray pointed high to his left, "I saw your great height from the mountains over there."

The tiny woman laughed. "Good job, Gray. Now, if you happen to run into any primitive abatwa, you might just live through the encounter."

"You never know." Gray smiled.

"What're you talking about?" Jak looked at them both, his expression curious.

"The abatwa have been around since the beginning of Origo. If a larger creature ever spotted one or spoke to one, the abatwa would ask, 'Where did you first see me.' The answer must be, 'I saw you from the mountains over there, because of your great height' or they'd shoot the offender with poisonous arrows and kill them. If anyone called them small or tiny or cute, they'd be killed. If anyone ignored their questions, they'd be killed, unless the offender was a child under ten or a pregnant woman."

Jak stared intently at the woman. She wore a plain blue dress with trim so thin he couldn't make out the color. Her black hair was drawn into a tight bun on her head. She might've been pretty, but it was hard to tell.

"What're you staring at, young man?" the tiny woman yelled.

"Uh—" he hesitated, embarrassed that he'd been called out.

"Tell her you're marveling at her enormous size and would like to flee in fear," Gray whispered in his ear.

"I'm marveling at your size—"

"*Enormous* size," Gray nudged with a whisper.

"Uh, I mean, enormous size, and, uh, I want to run away?" he said with uncertainty.

The woman laughed. "Very good, young man. You, too, shall live."

"Do they still—"

"Oh, no. They follow the laws like all intelligible creatures. But if you step on one, you'll die within five days. It's a natural phenomenon, and they have no control over it.

Never step on an abatwa unless you want to wake up dead one day."

Jak looked at the tiny lady again. She put her index finger to one side of her neck and slid it across to the other side, then laughed again and walked away.

"Bye, boys."

The brothers visited a few shops. Jak was weighed and measured, turned and measured, twisted and measured, and even laid down and measured. He held and swung weighted sticks of different sizes and lengths. They took no items from the stores. Gray paid, and they left empty-handed.

"Why did they have to measure me so much? Will I train in full body armor?"

"You'll get an outfit for training, but I bought you a new some new clothes as well."

"Why? I have plenty of clothes."

Gray adjusted the cuff of his sleeve and chuckled. "You can wear that stuff at home, but when we go out, I want my brother looking nice at my side. I'll come back and pick everything up next week."

"Can I come?"

"Of course. You'll carry it all home."

CHAPTER 35

Jak and Gray returned from Gamma exhausted and hoping for a long nap. It wasn't to be, however. Before they had dropped their bags, they were invited to join the rest of the family at the dining room table.

"What's going on?" Jak asked as he pulled out a chair and sat.

Gail sighed, forcing a somber smile. "This meeting is long overdue. So much has happened in the past week."

Joss nodded. "From Inco's wound, illness, and final healing, to our dragon wedding—"

"Directly followed by a violent fight between Gray and Inco," Gail cut in, her tone more serious. "You have no idea how frightening that was. And Lilink... she could've been hurt."

Gray and Inco both clenched their jaws and stared down at their hands on the table.

Joss put her hand on Gail's and sighed, breaking the awkward silence. "The tensions between us all are too much to be left unsettled. We must be careful not to let this family drift apart." Her eyes rested on Jak. "More than anything, you need to know that everything your father has done was for you. He has always wanted nothing but the best for you, Jak."

As Joss went on, Jak listened but already knew these things without being told. He had more insight into how Inco thought than Joss and Gail combined. Jak was fully aware of the stress, anxiety, and pressure Inco felt, and he realized that his father, trying to be strong and independent, kept his emotions bottled.

Jak spoke to Inco. "I remember playing in the yard when I was little. We'd laugh and joke without a care, and when it was time to go in, you'd carry me at your side. I was invincible at your side. I could've ruled the world."

"You were such a happy little guy."

"I was until I started showing abilities. I lost you. Not in a day or a week, but over time, I lost you. You stopped playing, and then you stopped joking. The time came when you hardly spoke at all."

Inco looked at his hands. He swallowed hard before responding. "I tried to erase my fears with denial. I thought if I could just convince myself there was nothing to fear, I could will it to be the truth. But I lost touch with reality instead."

Gray spoke up. "And while Inco pushed too hard to keep you safe, I pushed too hard to give you freedom. I was so focused on getting you out in the real world, I became blind to the dangers."

Jak hmphed. "Then, the village incident happened. For years, I knew you were worried and afraid, but there in the cave, I felt it for the first time. I felt yours, Ma's, Gray's, and…" Jack broke off and reflected on the mental image he still carried of Æmma, trying to remember the feelings he absorbed from her. A chill ran down his spine, and he changed course. "I thought things would get better when we came here."

"They did, at first, but then…" Gail faltered.

Jak continued as if she hadn't interrupted. "As soon as I realized I could feel the emotions of others, I focused on Pa's. His concern festered into anger, and I was too young to separate his emotions from mine, so I slipped as well."

Gray cut in. "The martial arts will help you find your center. It's not just learning to kick and punch—you'll be fine-tuning your mind and body from the inside out. Most people live their entire life in their head, using their body as a tool. You will learn to live everywhere in your body and even expand past it."

"You are still our son," Inco asserted in an unexpected and heavy tone. His expression softened to a faint smile. "But you are now in Gray's care. Make us proud."

"Yes, Pa."

With that, the meeting ended. Jak went to bed but couldn't sleep. He was too excited. Training would start in the morning.

CHAPTER 36

As a member of the council, Chance's role in Gray's childhood was to provide martial arts training. He had taught Gray everything he knew. They considered themselves to be equals in the field, but Gray knew Chance still had the advantage of nearly a hundred years of experience. He accepted an invitation from Gray, and to make things interesting, he brought Mikey along.

"I thought you were my sensei," Jak complained to Gray.

"I am, but you need a sparring partner, and I could use help with teaching. Chance has quite the list of credentials. The dragon who trained him, Xùnsù, was a whole bucket of badass. He sparred with Spartacus, trained with Lu Bu, practiced with the samurais, and learned several hand-to-hand combat styles from various Chinese masters."

"You told me a story about Lu Bu, but it was a long time ago. Didn't he make something explode on Earth?"

"Ha. No, he had an explosive temper. But yes, he lived on Earth. He was a great warrior and an asshole."

Mikey crossed his arms. "When I said I knew some karate, you said they don't teach outsiders in your time."

"Yes, but the people in that area love dragons and don't consider us outsiders."

Jak furrowed his brow. "Then why didn't we live there?"

"Are you kidding? They'd love us to death. We wanted a normal life for you."

"I'll never be normal."

"Yes, Jak, you will. We're going fishing, camping, hiking, and with any luck, you'll make a few new friends, but first, we train. Now come on over here, we'll start with posture."

***

Two and a half years later, Jak stood in the same place, showing Lilink proper posture. Her petite size was average for a two-year-old. Her straight, medium brown hair parted just to the left of center and veiled her cheeks, flipping at the ends and trailing to her waistline. Though her mothers made her many fine dresses, she preferred to wear pants like Jak.

She enjoyed the daily hour set aside solely for her to learn to 'pite,' as she called it. At first, it was just a silly excuse to get her to burn off some energy before naptime, but within a few days, she proved to be a true student with budding skills. Pride swelled in Gray's heart as he watched his improved little brother pass on his knowledge to their little sister.

"You show me five times, e'ry day. I know how to stand. I want to kick." She displayed a perfect forward kick to Jak's crotch, then stepped back into a ready posture. Her button nose flared and crinkled behind her tiny fists while Jak held his groin and seethed.

Gray guffawed at the irony of Jak's interactions with Lilink. It rang echoes of his own memories with Jak. He didn't feel bad for Jak at all since his temporary pain was nothing compared to when Jak was four and snapped Gray's leg in two with a kick. Lilink, however, didn't panic or cry the way Jak did. She hadn't learned empathy as yet.

"I'mma kill your face," she declared and leapt onto Jak before he'd caught his breath.

Gray moved back as they rolled toward him, wrestling on the ground. Gray's laugh went into a full cackle. Jak's laugh was laced with a little pain, while Lilink was determined to deliver her full wrath.

"Stop reminiscing, Gray. It's distracting."

"What are you, a mind reader now?"

"You don't have to be a mind reader to know what that look on your face means."

Gray smiled. "She has your temper."

"That's because she has my childhood," he replied in grunts as she continued to tackle him, focusing on one arm. "They keep her locked up where no one can see her."

"Hmm. Maybe she needs a big brother to speak up for her as you had." Gray said, kneeling closer to the pair. A glimmer twinkled in one eye. He glimpsed Lilink struggling with Jak's arm, seeming to put him in position for an armbar, but dismissed the notion that she might actually know what she was doing.

Jak let her wrestle his arm while catching his breath.

"Do you think they'll listen?"

"You must be persistent, but…" he noticed that Lilink had gotten Jak's arm in a perfect armbar. "Whoa, Li—"

She thrust her hips while pulling Jak's wrist into her chest and popped the joint in his elbow.

"Argh!"

"Oh, shit! She just did a perfect armbar."

"I don't care what it's called. It hurt!"

"Hahaha, what goes around, comes around, little brother. She popped it like a knuckle. Not like she, oh, I don't know, broke your leg or anything like that."

Jak sat up and rotated his arm while the pain subsided. "When did you teach her that?"

"Huh? I thought you did."

"Kate taught me." Lilink smiled, her chest puffed with pride.

"Ugh, I must talk to the mothers. This imaginary friend stuff is getting old." He rubbed his healed elbow and brushed the dirt off his pants with sharp, hasty movements.

"Are you mad at me?" She looked at him with a pitiful, pouty expression.

"No, Li. I just think you need real friends." He picked her up. She nestled under his chin and put her first two fingers in her mouth.

"Imaginary or not, that armbar was pretty amazing," Gray gloated.

"Stop acting so proud. You didn't teach her."

"I'm the Mastah of Disastah." He smiled. "I taught her without showing her. I'm just that good."

Jak looked to Gray, sensing the doubt and caution that had radiated from him since they had begun training. These feelings almost always came with jokes of pride and superiority, which he came to understand was Gray's way of self-soothing, the same as Lilink sucking her fingers. He smirked at Gray's silliness as it was about to end abruptly. Chance came from behind and wrapped his arm around Gray's neck.

"Mastah, my ass-tah!"

Gray tried to laugh through the pressure on his neck, then grabbed at Chance and did a forward flip to the ground. Jak stepped back to avoid being kicked and then realized Lilink was dozing off in his arms.

"I'll be right back. She's ready for her nap."

Gray sat up and watched Jak cradle Lilink close to his heart, stroking her hair as he took her into the house.

"He's doing so well."

"He has an outstanding teacher," Chance sat up behind him.

"I mean, with everything. He hasn't had an outburst in two years, he's learning the arts faster than I ever did, and Lilink couldn't ask for a better brother."

"He's getting every bit of that from you. Like I said, an outstanding teacher." Chance shoved him and jumped to his feet. "Now stop being such a sentimental bitch and bring it!"

***

Lilink stirred and woke as Jak laid her in her bed.

"Wally."

"Who's Wally?"

"My blanky."

Jak realized that she was asking for the blanket he gave her—the same one that enveloped him as a newborn.

"You named it Wally?"

"No, it's just his name."

"Ok," Jak chuckled. "I'll look for Wally. Where did you leave it?"

She put her first two fingers in her mouth and stared at the corner of the room, reaching out her free hand. A strange breeze swirled within the room. Jak's hair danced around his head, blocking his view as strong winds rushed toward the corner. Lilink smiled with her fingers still in her mouth. Her tiny teeth pressed into her knuckles, and she let out a giggle. Jak held his hair back and watched. The gusts grew stronger as the blanket fluttered toward her. When it reached her hand, and she grasped it, the winds came to an abrupt stop.

"What just happened?"

"Thank you, Kate," she murmured with her fingers still in her mouth.

"Kate?" He looked around the room, wondering if there truly was someone else in there. He sensed nothing out of the ordinary. If there were another person in the room, he would pick up their emotions.

As he focused on his empathy, a faint feeling of adoration came from the space beside the bed. It turned to surprise and then vanished. The feelings were so slight he didn't know what to make of them. He looked at his sister, who had drifted to sleep, and wondered if it could have been the mixed emotions of twilight.

"Lilink." He shook her arm to wake her.

"Hmm."

"Never do that around anyone. Do you hear me?"

"Hmm."

"Lilink, look at me." He put his hand behind her head to get her attention. "Never do that around anyone. Do you want to make new friends?"

"Friends?"

"Yes. Do you want to play with other little girls and boys?"

"There are other little girls?"

"Yes, and if you want to play with them, you can't do things like that. All right? It's scary?" Jak couldn't think of any other way to explain.

"Okay," Lilink used the phrase she had learned from Mikey while drifting to sleep again.

Jak pulled his hand from behind her head and brushed the hair from her face, then whispered, "Don't give them a reason to keep you locked up."

CHAPTER 37

After a month of debate, followed by Gray's secret encouragements, Gail agreed to take Lilink along on her visits to heal the Roanoke people. Excited to see their daughter in a new environment, Joss joined them. Inco spent much of his time helping the Roanoke people build homes, so he was already there.

Jak would hear nothing of his baby sister socializing without him. He allowed his parents to think it was the excitement that drove him, partially because it was true, but he was more concerned with what Lilink might do while there. He hadn't told anyone about the winds causing Wally to float, and after several talks with Lilink, he hoped he would never have to.

Gray, of course, was responsible for Jak, and the visit would give him the perfect opportunity to gauge his progress. And so, Lilink's first visit to the growing colony became a full family affair.

"Jak, come give me a hand over here," Inco called from a rooftop.

Jak nodded at his mothers and rushed off with enthusiasm. He had never helped his father build anything larger than a table and, even then, he only handed him tools.

Lilink bubbled with joy when she saw a group of children playing. She immediately ran to join them. Gail wanted to follow but resisted. Instead, she watched her play with another girl her size. When a woman approached the little girl to check on her, Gail recognized her as Eleanor Dare. Her gaze trailed off in thought until Gray lightly bumped her shoulder with his.

"This is your chance to make a few friends as well," he said.

"Oh, I'm perfectly content with just my family."

"You've given them the use of half your lands, and your daughter will grow with their daughters and sons. It's not about you anymore."

"Watch your tongue, young man," Joss warned.

"Hey!" He stepped back with his hands up. "The truth hurts."

"So does a swift kick to the—"

"He's right," Gail reached for Joss's hand. "This is the start of a new chapter—Lilink's chapter."

Gray smiled as he stretched his arms, one over Gail's shoulders, and the other over Joss's. The three watched Eleanor approach, her daughter and Lilink leading the way. Anxiety flared in Gail's gut.

"I healed her once," she said quietly.

Gray grinned at her. "Well, that's a good start."

"And Jak healed her daughter."

"Does she know Jak is different?"

"If she hasn't caught on, she will eventually," she said in hushed tones as Eleanor came within speaking distance with the girls.

"Is this precious little one your daughter?" She brushed her hand over Lilink's shoulder.

Gail and Joss responded simultaneously, "Yes."

"Oh." She looked back and forth between Joss and Gail, her face strained with confusion. "I, uhm. I…"

"Women on Origo can have babies without the help of men," Gray said.

She gasped, pulling her hand to her chest. "Really?"

"No," he stifled a chuckle.

"Oh, get out of here, you." Joss smacked him in the chest.

He laughed and jumped back, then headed toward Inco and Jak. "You don't have to tell me twice."

"Eleanor, isn't it?"

"Yes." She relaxed. "And this is my daughter, Virginia, but we call her Ginny."

"My name is Gail, this is Joss, my sister-wife, and that's our little girl, Lilink. That man over there on the roof is our husband, Inco."

"Oh, sister-wife. That makes perfect sense. I thought, well…" she trailed off, looking toward Gray.

Joss gave a soft grin. "No, women can't reproduce without men."

"Unless they're a troll," Gail added.

"If they're a troll, they're not a woman," Joss said.

"Oh, right."

"So many things to learn and remember. I never know what to expect in this world." Eleanor sounded tentative. "Even saying 'this world' feels strange to me."

"I'm not very sharp with it all either, so don't feel bad," Gail said.

Eleanor smiled and edged her way next to Gail to watch as the girls returned to play. A little boy around the same age as the girls joined in.

"Oh, here comes little DJ Harvie. Such a sweet boy."

***

From that point on, the tot trio met to play several times every week, and as the winds of autumn cooled the air, a friendship warmed between Joss, Gail, and Eleanor.

"How will these little darlings play through the winter?" Eleanor sighed.

Joss shrugged. "We'll just let them play indoors."

"If we ever have time. I've decided to start schooling Ginny this year. I want her to catch up to Lilink."

Gail raised an eyebrow. "How so?"

"She's so smart. I've never heard a two-or-three-year-old with such a vocabulary. You did well to start her lessons early."

"We only read to her. She hasn't started lessons."

"Really? You just read to her and…"

"Yes, it expands their vocabulary early on."

"I'll start reading to my Ginny tonight."

"We could school them together," Joss suggested. "It's time for Lilink to start, and the den is large enough for more than three students. Do you think DJ's mother will let you bring him?"

"Oh, I'm sure she will. Poor darling, the stress of being brought to this world has made her lame. She hardly rises from the bed. A lot of mothers stopped giving lessons when we arrived here. There are far more pressing things to worry about."

Gail looked out at the other children playing in the field. Some were barely older than the tots, while others were near Jak's age.

"It's a shame we can't teach more of them."

Joss looked at the openness of the west side of the meadow and pondered.

"Maybe we can."

CHAPTER 38

Joss stood at the dining table, cleared her voice, and made brief eye contact with each family member.

"In a few weeks, Jak will be sixteen years old, and fifteen days later, Lilink will be three."

Inco put his arm around Jak and smiled at Joss as she continued.

"Jak, you are becoming a fine young man. And Gray, you've really come through for this family in the way you've helped Jak over the past three years. We've seen your hard work, and we're so proud of you both."

Jak elbowed Gray in the ribs and grinned. Gray ignored the jab and accepted the compliment with a smile.

"Now that things have settled down with Jak, it's time to focus on Lilink. We thought that socializing would rid her of the need for this imaginary friend, but it hasn't. She's mentioning parts of the prophecy around other children and adults. She claims to be learning it from Kate, but she must hear these things from us, so we need to watch what we say around her. Let's avoid making the same mistakes we made with Jak. Gail and I believe that early exposure will give her an advantage Jak didn't have, but the information must be provided in small increments."

"I agree," Jak blurted, then bit his lip for having interrupted.

"So do I," Gray said.

Everyone's attention shifted to Inco, who gazed at Joss without expression. A wave of serenity flowed from him, catching Jak off guard. He noticed Jak's surprise and smirked at him.

"We should've told you sooner," he said.

Joss continued, "We've put together a storybook for Lilink. It tells the prophecy in a way that she can understand, and as she gets older, we can adjust it."

"Great! I'll read it to her tonight," Jak said.

"You might as well. We put her in her own bed every night, and yet she wakes with you every morning," Gail said with a smile.

"She does it on her own. I get to bed, count back from twenty, and before I reach ten, she's pushing the door open. It's adorable. I figure she'll grow out of it, eventually."

"Speaking of growth," Joss said. "Jak, you have outgrown the lessons we can give."

"I'm done?"

"Not quite," Gail chuckled. "We've arranged a new teacher for you. His name is Lex, and you'll start the day after your birthday. Enjoy the brief vacation."

"Oh, hey, I had Lex as a teacher for a while. He's great." Gray said. "You'll like him."

"Someone outside the family?" Jak perked with a mixture of excitement and disbelief.

Inco grinned and winked. "We all learn from trolls around your age."

"Trolls?" He glanced at each of the parents. "I've never seen a live troll."

"Well, you're going to be seeing a lot of them next year," Joss said.

"Yes, yes, yes, yes," Gail chanted in a whisper, then stopped and pressed her lips when everyone looked at her; everyone except Joss, who smirked and tried to maintain composure.

"What's happening next year?" Jak looked around, "And why am I the only one surprised by any of this? Did you all already talk without me?"

Gail smiled. "No, Jak, not all of us, but things have been changing over the past year. You pushed for Lilink to have friends, which led to us having friends. We're part of a community now, and we plan to enrich it as much as we can."

"Put more than two hens in the same pen, and they'll plot to take over the world." Inco sat back and braced for one of the women to throw something at him, but neither did. Instead, Joss gave him *the look*, which was just as frightening.

"The foundation is being set this fall," Joss continued. "Construction will begin in the spring, and we hope to open the doors by the fall of next year."

"Doors to what?" Gray wanted to know.

Gail shook both hands at either side of her face and squealed with excitement. "Gabrinoke University!"

"Gabrinoke?" Jak echoed. "I thought that was just a nickname for the Gabril meadow because the Roanoke people live there now."

Breathless with excitement, Gail continued. "They like the nickname. I sent a request through your father to have the meadow renamed 'Gabrinoke.' Isn't it exciting?"

Gray chuckled at Gail's enthusiasm and nodded in agreement. "But why are they building a university?"

"They're not. We are." Joss put a hand on Gail's shoulder. "Lilink's friends are so far behind, and the older ones have nowhere to go once their parents teach them all they know."

Jak humphed. "I'm surprised the trolls would trust them."

"It took some talking, but they agreed to teach at the university. Some even agreed to pull their hair back to avoid scaring the children."

"Hey," Gray chimed. "Can I have a classroom?"

Joss tilted her head in surprise. "What for?"

"For to have more students, of course. I can teach a crowd way much gooder than just one person."

He smirked, giving Joss a wry wink. He knew she would cringe at the poor grammar he faked, and she did. She leaned toward him, glaring into his eyes.

"Do that again, and I'll throat-punch you in the nuts with my foot. How's that for grammar, karate boy?"

They stared into each other's eyes for a moment, then burst into laughter.

"I suppose you can use one of the great rooms, but you must stick to a schedule," Joss said.

Gray gave a big smile while looking at Jak, wiggling his eyebrows several times.

Jak returned the smile but couldn't focus on the gesture. Joss's voice faded to background noise as he drifted in thought. So many things were changing, all in one conversation, and he wasn't sure what to think of it all. He sensed elation from Gail, Joss, and Gray but continued to feel serenity flowing from Inco. He glanced at his father, wondering what was going through his mind to create such a level of comfort and peace when a sudden wave of tension took over. Inco's body language shifted just as quickly as his emotions, and Jak felt nauseous from the sudden change.

"Jak, did you hear me?" Joss's voice broke through the white noise in his head.

"Huh?"

"DúKrue camping. You'll be starting in March."

"Aw, come on. DúKrue camping? Is this another new thing I have to learn?"

"No, it is precisely as it sounds. You camp while waiting for your DúKrue."

"Why?"

She laughed through her words, "Because we don't want you to damage our house, is that all right with you?"

"It's a dragon and migma tradition that goes back longer than any living memory can say," Inco said.

"He won't damage the house. Look at him." Gray put one hand in front of his face and pretended to hold Jak between his thumb and index finger. "He's going to be a tiny dragon."

Jak tossed a rag at Gray while Inco stifled a chuckle. Gray threw the rag back, and Jak tossed it at his father instead. Inco laughed but didn't respond. His body language showed humor, but the emotions flowing from him remained tense.

"I'll be fine, Pa. You don't have to worry." Jak turned his attention back to Joss. "How long do I have to camp?"

"Until you have your DúKrue."

"That can happen any time... as much as six months after my seventeenth birthday."

"Yep."

"So, I have to sleep outside for a year?"

"Not just you," Gray spoke up. "I'll be there, and Chance and Mikey will join us from time to time. Oh, and Raisin."

"That won't make the nights any warmer."

"You can sleep in the center of the den on frosty nights, but if you have your DúKrue in there, you could still damage the house, so don't get used to it."

"What if I don't have a DúKrue? It's possible, right?"

Joss sighed. "The word 'possible' has very little meaning with you, Jak. We have no idea what to expect, but if you don't have your DúKrue by the following March, then it would be safe to assume you never will."

"I told you we're going camping, didn't I?" Gray winked.

Jak scoffed. "Three years ago! I figured it was an empty promise."

"Would you like to go now? Make up for lost time?"

"No. Not if I already have to camp a year."

"Then stop your crying." Gray winked again. "It'll be fun."

CHAPTER 39

Large orange furry feet shuffled across the bare soil in short, choppy strides as Lex approached the front door of Jak's home. His long, florescent orange hair covered his body like a child standing under a sheet, save for the bottom, which stopped at ankle length. Underneath, he juggled several items. A heavy book fell from his grasp, and the corner crunched into his foot. As he hobbled on the other foot, a well of ink fell from his hand. In an attempt to catch it with his foot, he kicked. The glass shattered, and ink splashed across the door, creating back spatter that gave him a new, speckled look.

He lowered his bruised foot, let out a heavy sigh, and then knocked just below the ink blob.

"‿**‿*‿*," he grumbled under his breath.

Inco swung the door open and offered an enthusiastic handshake.

"Hey, Lex, how have you been?"

"‿*‿**‿‿‿*."

"Oh," Inco recoiled. "I'm not sure how squids urinate, but I'd imagine it's not too far off. I'll get you a moist towel."

Lex picked up the book and shuffled through the door.

"‿*‿.***‿?"

"He's in his room." Inco turned and yelled, "Jak, Lex is here."

The only time Jak had ever seen a troll was when he jumped over them in the forest, but Gray described them in his stories. However, nothing could have made it any less shocking to see one up close and alive for the first time. He stopped at the mouth of the hall and stared, unable to speak, and then felt a wave of cuddly feelings come from Lex.

"_*_~_**_~_."

Jak blinked hard to break his stare and turned to Inco. "What did he say? Is he even talking to me? I can't tell which way he's facing."

"_*_~_**_~_?"

Inco responded to Lex's question. "No, sorry, we forgot to tell him." He turned to Jak. "Trolls don't speak the common tongue."

"So, I have to learn a new language before we can start lessons? Great!"

"No, Jak. Just listen."

Jak waited for him to continue until Inco gestured toward Lex. "Not me. Listen to him."

Jak turned to Lex and let out a heavy sigh. The long veil of hair parted ever so slightly. Four stubby furry orange fingers reached from within the split and pulled it open, revealing a tiny sliver of a face. As Jak leaned in, the hand pulled back, and the gap closed.

"Trolls are very shy about their appearance," Inco said.

"So, he speaks a foreign language, hides his face, and his emotions are as fuzzy as his fingers. How am I supposed to learn anything?"

"Just listen."

Lex said, "_*_~_~_*_~_*_."

Jak stared at Lex, unsure if he should be replying.

" ¸*¸¸*¸***¸*¸**¸¸**¸*¸*¸,,,*."

He glanced at Inco, then back to Lex, furrowing his brow in frustration.

" ¸*¸¸*¸**¸*¸¸*¸**¸*¸*?"

The heightened tone at the end made Jak feel an uneasy pressure to answer an unknown question. He shifted his weight, scratched an itch inside his ear, and tried again to focus.

"What's the point of this?"

"Sh."

" ¸*¸¸**¸*¸¸**¸*?"

"Whoa, I heard that." He looked to Inco. "Pa, did you hear that?"

Inco smiled and nodded.

" ¸*¸¸*¸*¸**¸?"

"Yes, I can hear your words," Jak spoke slowly while amazement bulged in his eyes.

" ¸*."

"Wha—?"

Lex wrapped his arms around Jak's waist and purred.

"Everyone loves Trolls," Inco said. "Even mermaids are fond of them. They're affectionate, passive, and peaceful creatures… emphasis on the affectionate part."

Lex let go of Jak, handed him the book, and then pivoted to head toward the door.

" ¸*¸¸*¸*."

"What? The whole thing by tomorrow?" He bounced the book in his hand, gauging its weight. "This'll take at least a month."

" ¸**¸*¸!"

Lex shuffled out the door, pulling it shut behind him. Jak grunted, slouched, and looked at the book. *Honourable*

Houses of Origo, A Complete Record of Viceroys, Tribes, Marks, and Truths.

Gray leaned over Jak's shoulder. "It's mostly pictures."

Jak ducked and spun around, startled by his brother's sudden appearance.

"Too late, if I were hunting, you'd be dead." Gray laughed. He took a bite from an apple and pointed with the hand that held it. "That was my favorite book when I was a student. I think I still have a copy somewhere in my room back at Misty's." He swallowed and smirked. "Except mine has all the fool's challenges in it."

"Ahem." Inco cleared his throat and offered Gray a downward stare.

Jak furrowed his brow. "All the what?"

"Uh, the cool languages," Gray stammered with a chuckling undertone after catching Inco's death stare. "There are *so* many languages besides the common tongue."

"So I've learned. That troll came in here, making weird noises that turned into words, hugged me, gave me homework, and then left. What kind of joke is this?"

"All right, I'll give you the condensed version of what you need to know about trolls."

Gray put his arm around Jak and walked him outside. When they reached the firepit, he took the book and opened it to the middle, and then sifted through pages. He sat on the pearled adobe bench, put one ankle over the opposite knee, and laid the book open across his legs.

"Here we go. House Troll. You know, it never occurred to me how biased this information might be."

"Why?"

"Because trolls wrote the book. Look, here we have the mark, which looks like a troll standing in the center of a flaming, five-point star."

"Oh, wow, there's Lex." Jak pointed at the picture.

"That's not Lex, but it's a troll. They all look alike, other than the shades of orange. The older they get, the brighter their fur becomes."

Jak pointed at the page. "The viceroy section is blank."

"Trolls function in harmony without a leader, see here, their House Truth is 'Good is known,' meaning they don't need someone to keep them in line. They're not capable of doing wrong. It's not in them. Trolls aren't like any other creature on Origo. They never truly die since they pass on parts of their consciousness to their offspring. We know that trolls pair to have offspring, but the rest is fuzzy. No pun intended."

"Hilarious."

"They don't have any sex organs. There are no males, no females, and no babies."

"No babies?"

"DúTrolls hatch as baby trolls, but regular trolls don't. They reproduce fully grown offspring, possibly the same way they reproduce physical items of any kind. It's their most cherished secret."

Jak rubbed his denim pants. "Like these jeans are a reproduction of the ones Mikey wore when he first arrived. So, they can reproduce anything?"

"That's right. Let's see," Gray scanned through the paragraphs, "You've heard their language."

"Yes! It was bizarre. He was beeping and growling one minute, and speaking the next, except he was still beeping and... I don't know. It was weird."

"An old fable claims that the first troll ever created poked his head through a portal when Babel hit Earth, but was so smart, he found a way around it."

"Does it tell you what they look like under all that hair?"

"No, but I can tell you. They grow that super long hair from their entire head, including their chins, cheeks, and foreheads, making their faces look tiny. Their face and body have the same short fur you saw on his feet and fingers. Once he gets used to you and warms up—"

"He seemed pretty warmed up to me. He hugged me."

"That's just their nature. Once he gets comfortable around you, he'll start tying his hair back and braiding his beard."

"You keep saying 'he,' but I thought you said they don't have sex organs."

"Lex identifies with men, and he's ok with the term 'he.' Some trolls identify with women and are ok with 'she.' If you don't know, just ask."

"So, each creature has a house?"

"Trolls have one house, but most creatures have three: one for each of the old Qingdoms that remain. Wolves have one ruler but six houses." Gray flipped several pages until he reached the wolves' section. "They're all houses with individual viceroys, but they have a leader named Wingren. She rules over them all and barely acknowledges Salus's government."

"She doesn't look like a wolf."

"She's human, but she was born from the womb of a wolf. One is born every fifty years. In their youth, they go by the name June, the female version of Junior."

"How can she be a junior if she isn't named after her own parent?"

"They make their own rules, I suppose. Anyway, as June grows, Mother Wolf and Wingren teach her everything she needs to know by the age of thirteen. That's when Wingren becomes Elder Wingren. She retires with a few wolves, and June becomes the new Wingren."

"That's so weird."

"You won't think so after you read the rest of these. They're all strange in their own ways."

"Which house is ours?"

Gray flipped through the pages again and stopped. "Gabril used to be House DúHuman East but has reverted to council authority since the viceroy's death."

Jak pointed at a photo on the House DúHuman East page. "The previous viceroy was someone named Tibbel. Isn't that Joss and Gail's first husband's name?"

"One and the same," Gray said. "See here, it says Gail and Joss could have taken over at the time of his death, but they declined. I'd imagine they were too grief-stricken."

"So, Pa's in charge?"

"Not exactly. He's the one deciding, but it's all at the discretion of the council."

"But he's married to them now. Can't he take over?"

"No, a council member cannot be a viceroy. It presents a conflict of interest. You're reading this to understand the beginnings of politics and society, Jak. It's a delicate study and will shape you as you grow into adulthood. I'll be including it in your training from here on as well." He handed the book to Jak, its pages still open to House DúHuman East.

"I guess I can read it through by morning. It's kind of interesting."

"There you go. I'll give you the day off to study. You'll like Lex. He's a fun teacher."

"Thanks," Jak meandered toward the house, his eyes locked on the book. There on the page, next to 'previous viceroy,' was a well-drawn sketch of Tibbel... Lilink's blood father.

Jak wasn't sure why he felt such distaste for a man he'd never met, but he found himself unable to look at the picture. He gazed at the words on the page, but he wasn't reading them. Waves of hatred, anger, remorse, fear, and confusion flooded his head and blurred his vision. He laid his hand over Tibbel's face and balled his fist, crumpling the paper and ripping it from the binding, then slipped it into his pocket before going into the house.

CHAPTER 40

Jak's self-control and discipline improved dramatically as his academic and physical training achievements increased. Everyone, but especially Inco, profited from Jak's emotional stability. Inco's smile returned. He made random jokes, which seemed funnier than they should because of the shock value. He'd been melancholy for so long, the moments of joy and humor had magnified effects. But like most good things, it didn't last. As the month of March approached, the family's attention focused on Jak. He would soon reach the age of DúKrue—from sixteen-and-a-half to seventeen-and-a-half years old for DúHuman and DúHuman migma alike.

Inco stood at the edge of the clearing and stared into the forest, his mind a numb hum under spinning thoughts. Gray approached from behind and kicked a small pebble toward him.

"We're literally going to be in shouting distance. You know that, right?"

"It's not the distance that worries me. It's the DúKrue. This is it, Gray. This is when we find out how we've done."

Inside the house, Jak snuggled with Lilink. Every night since she was two, she'd climb out of bed after her parents left the room and wait by the crack of her door for Jak to go to bed. When he would enter his room, his path would interrupt the light flowing in from the hall, and she would run in and join him. Every night, without fail, but now it would come to an end.

She breathed in gasping shudders after a hard cry, overwhelmed with grief that Jak had to spend an entire year outside the house.

"I'll see you every day, Li," Jak spoke in a soft, melodic tone. "And I'll be close enough to hear you if you call out."

Her emotional waves lessened, as did her voice. She responded with a soft moan, put her fingers in her mouth, and drifted off to sleep. Jak stared at her, not wanting to leave. He wondered if he might get away with falling asleep and leaving in the morning but then realized Lilink might go through the emotions all over again. It was best just to go now. He would see her for her daily lessons, which would still take place in the clearing at the house since they would be nearby.

He slid to the edge of the bed and crept into the hallway. When he reached the sitting room, he found his and Gray's camping gear was propping the front door open. Gray's voice traveled from outside.

"No, we won't be drinking or smoking, Inco. Jak's training demands a pure body."

"Fairladies?"

"Definitely no fairladies. The boy wouldn't even know where to put it."

Jak stepped out and saw Inco and Gray, standing side by side in the middle of the yard, looking out at the forest. "I'm ready."

"Oh, good." Gray patted Inco on the shoulder and jogged toward Jak. "Come on, grab your bag, let's go."

Jak put his camping pack over one shoulder and tried to reach back with the opposite arm.

"What's the rush?"

"Marshmallows. The newest and greatest portal replica ever!"

Gray helped get the backpack onto Jak's back, then handed him the chest clasp and slapped his shoulder.

Inco flashed a wry smirk. "Sometimes, a good scare can spark your DúKrue."

"Thanks for the warning," Jak smirked and rolled his eyes toward Gray. His gaze drifted back to his father, who appeared in deep thought, staring straight through Jak.

"I'll be fine, Pa."

"Just be careful out there."

"We're going to be—"

"Within shouting distance, I know."

Inco headed into the house while Gray headed in the opposite direction. Jak watched the door shut behind his solemn father, then jogged to catch up with his brother.

"What were you guys talking about when I came outside?"

"You know, calming his concern, lying to him. Come on, we have a party to get to."

"I thought we were going camping."

Gray laughed, "Oh, we are."

Jak could see the faint firelight from the yard as they were leaving but didn't expect to find a crowd of people surrounding it when they arrived. A man with the lower body of an equine sat at the edge of the campsite. He melodically tapped one hoof against a boulder while blowing on a one-sided kuvytsi. Next to him, a female counterpart plucked at a gittern while dancing in place. Many other people and creatures laughed and danced around the fire. Some had cups of ale while others puffed from pipes.

"What's going on here?"

Before Gray could answer, a choir of giggles approached from the far edge of the campsite. He perked with excitement.

"The fairladies are here."

"Fairladies?"

"Fairladies—lady fairies. They're bridge guards by day, party animals by night." Gray strutted toward the ladies as they stepped into the camp clearing. Their large translucent wings sparkled with orange and yellow reflections of the campfire.

"Lumen Bridge is falling down," Gray sang as he approached one of the ladies. He wrapped his arms around her lower waist and picked her up, flashing a wry grin as she caressed his face. "My fairlady."

Jak stood still when he noticed another fairlady gliding toward him. He felt a flutter in his chest that slowly climbed his throat, making it hard to breathe. She folded her wings back and swayed as she moved closer. Her long black hair draped over one breast while the other was almost visible through her thin sleeveless shirt.

"I'm Sareen." She pressed her body into Jak, put one hand on his hip, and ran her the other through his long hair. "What's your name, handsome?"

"Ja… Ja…" he tried to speak, but the words lodged in his throat.

275

As she pressed into him, he gave way and stepped back. She followed, keeping her body pressed against his. He continued to step back until his heels struck something hard, then she gave him a light shove, causing him to sit on a large log.

"Just relax, Jaja." She leaned in and kissed his neck, then whispered in his ear, "Let me take care of you."

"Mmm, these are nice," a small voice uttered.

She leaned back and smiled, caressing her hands along the sides of her breasts

"These? You can touch them."

Raisin popped his head from Jak's collar pocket. "Bring 'em back over here, and I will!"

Sareen shrieked and jumped back.

"I—" Jak gave a frozen stare, still unable to speak.

Raisin stood on the brim of Jak's collar, smiling seductively back at her, and winked.

"Don't be deceived by looks, darling. I come in *all* sizes."

Sareen gasped and looked to Jak's blank expression, then made a high-toned hmph as she smacked him across the face.

"Loosen up, Jak," Gray yelled from a nearby log where a fairlady danced on his lap. "Someone bring my brother some ale."

Something soft and furry snuggled against Jak's arm. His heart skipped a beat, and he whipped his head around to see a troll snuggling his arm while holding out a cup of ale. Jak had felt awkward on the many occasions when Lex leaned his head on his shoulder while explaining a math question or errors on an astrology paper, but he'd grown accustomed to it. He even found ironic humor in Lex's pet-like behavior.

"Hey, Lex. What are you doing here?"

"*_**_?"

"Well, it's a party with alcohol and sticky-puffs. I thought trolls couldn't do anything bad."

"*_**_~*_*_~*_*_*."

"I never thought of it that way. I wonder if intent can determine fate as well."

He took the cup and stared into it, watching the bubbles drift across the ale. His thoughts drifted as the bubbles thinned and disappeared. When he looked up, Lex had left.

"Jak," Gray hollered. "Come here. I have something for you."

He looked at Gray but didn't move. He brought the cup to his face and smelled the pungent aroma of the ale.

"You drink this?" Jak groused.

"Sure do."

"It smells like shit."

"Tastes like shit, too, but you stop noticing after the first few."

He sipped at the ale on his way toward Gray.

"Relax, little brother. It's your DúKrue celebration."

"Do all these creatures know about me?"

"No. They all think you're my human brother who's keeping family tradition. A lot of humans do it. You're not the first."

"Oh, I'm pretty sure I'm the first." He tipped his head back and drank the last drop of ale.

"Ha, you have me there, I suppose you are. Now stop talking. I have something for you."

"What is it?"

"A gift."

"Well, no shit." Jak rolled his eyes.

Gray pulled a long, braided rope from his satchel and handed it to Jak.

"She slapped me, hard, and stormed off. I hardly think she'll let me use this on her," Jak scoffed.

"No, it's a..." Gray paused. He noticed Jak straining to keep a sober face. "That's a sling, and you're an ass."

Jak's mouth stopped twitching, giving way to an enormous grin.

"I'll show you how to use it in the morning. They're pretty badass. Now go get yourself another ale, but I'm cutting you off at five."

"Why five?"

"Because I have to stay sober enough to supervise, and I'm not being outdone by my little brother."

As the night went on, Jak continued to drink. Raisin wandered off with Sareen. The rest of the creatures went home. Jak and Gray sat near the remnants of the fire, poking at the embers with long sticks.

Jak nudged his brother. "You never told me the family phrase was a House Truth."

"What?"

"You know," Jak groaned. "*We all have darkness in us. It's—*"

"*It's what we do with it that matters—House DúHuman North*," Gray cut him off with a mumble as he stared into the fire. "It became a family saying for you when you were little."

"Which house is Pa from?"

"DúHuman West."

"What about you?"

"Let's just enjoy the fire, Jak."

"Are you from the north?"

Gray sighed and walked to the barrel of ale to pour another cup. He drank, then chugged until the cup was empty again. Jak could tell he'd upset him before he felt the waves of sadness.

"What's wrong?

"I'm just not in the mood to talk about Houses."

"You're lying. Something's making you sad. What is it?"

"I'm sad…" he paused to ponder. "Because my little brother isn't so little anymore."

He filled his cup and took a drink before returning to his seat on the log. Jak looked at him, his lip curled in disgust.

"Another lie."

Gray huffed and turned to Jak. "What do you want from me?"

"I want to have a normal conversation with my brother without it turning to taboos and mysterious silence. Is that so hard?"

"Then pick another topic."

"No. I choose this topic because now I'm curious. What does the north have to do with the prophecy? Is it because it's Bakúnuh's Qingdom?"

"Not everything is about the prophecy, Jak."

"Then what is it?"

Gray closed his eyes, lowered his head, and let out a long sigh.

"I'll tell you this once, but you have to promise you'll never mention it again."

The waves of sadness intensified, and Jak found himself overwhelmed with a grief that wasn't his own. Tears welled in his eyes, and he wondered if he really wanted to know what Gray was about to tell him. Before he could reply, Gray started.

"Her name was Constance."

He fumbled through his satchel and handed Jak a small portrait of a beautiful woman with dark hair. As Jak studied her face, he realized he saw Gray in her image.

"Was she—"

"She was my mother." He took back the photo and gazed at it. "Her father was, I mean, is the Viceroy Durus of House DúHuman North. He was never a friendly man, but he's always been successful in keeping the House in order. The Houses of DúHuman West and North have never gotten along. They've never gone to war, but they've been rivals as long as anyone can remember.

"To make peace, my mother was betrothed to Simeon, the son of Viceroy Amory of House DúHuman West. The problem was, though she loved her people and had nothing bad to say about Simeon, she loved another. On the night before the wedding, she ran off with her lover, and they married in secret. Dragons, creatures, and humans from all the lands came to the north to help search for her, but no one found her until she came back on her own."

"So, she was all right?"

"Upon arrival, yes. Durus locked her in her room with her handmaiden, and before nightfall, the marriage mark on her hand disappeared."

"How does that happen?"

"It only disappears with the loss of love or life."

"Durus killed him?"

"Probably, but there's no proof." Gray rubbed his brow, visibly upset. He clenched his jaw to ease the anger, but it still showed.

"What about Constance?"

"She remained locked in her room and conceived during the night. The egg grew inside her until her Dú could no longer hold it, and she had no choice but to take dragon form. She tried to—" He lost composure and held his face in his hands, taking deep, gulping breaths to calm himself.

"We can talk about it another time," Jak said.

"No. I said I'd tell you once, and this is it." He wiped his face, took a deep breath, and then continued. "She couldn't hold back the screams. When Durus came to her room and found her in labor, he became furious at her defiance. He ripped her Qi from her chest and locked her in the room again. For hours, she screamed in agony as her body shrank around the fully developed egg. By the time she was back in her Dú, the egg had destroyed her insides. The handmaiden had to cut her open to remove the egg."

"You?"

"Yes. I was in that egg. I crushed my mother's heart before my own began to beat." He couldn't hold back the tears any longer. He leaned forward, pressed his forehead into the portrait, and wept quietly.

"No, your grandfather did."

"Don't call him that. He's nothing to me," Gray scoffed. "If it weren't for the handmaiden, he would have killed me too. She hid me in my mother's secret compartment under the floor planks, then smuggled me out and took me to the authorities."

"He murdered two people, and he's still the viceroy?"

"No one ever found the bodies. Durus claimed that they ran off again and accused the handmaiden of helping. He admitted that the egg was Constance's but said that she abandoned me to be his burden. He called me a spawn of defiance and exiled me along with the handmaiden. The government raises all orphaned dragons, so she took me to the Nesting House and Orphanage in Yekka."

"How do you know she didn't just run away?"

"Durus never looked for her."

"Maybe he—"

"It just doesn't feel true, you know? It doesn't feel like she ran away. I think that—I mean, I'd know, brother. I'd know if she was alive."

"Well, if his story is the official story, how'd you find out this version? The handmaiden?"

"No, she was a human and died long before I hatched. Misty told me when I was seven years old."

"Seven? Why so young?"

"She was preparing me."

"For what?"

"She used to think I was the Son of Darkness, Jak. She never said it, but it all makes sense. My father was rumored to be human, which would have made me a migma, and by the time my egg was cut from my mother's body, she was in full human form. Her womb had somehow stretched around the entire egg, so it had to be cut open as well. I would have been a migma born of the womb. That, along with the House Truth being about darkness and my lineage of brutal men, she thought… well, I can't blame her. But Misty never told me about the Son of Darkness, even after I had my DúKrue, and she could see that I was a full-blooded dragon. I didn't put it all together until you came along, and Inco told me the prophecy."

"How did she prepare you without telling you?"

"By teaching me love, forgiveness, mercy, and devotion. Misty also taught me my lineage, so I would have something to model against."

"What did Pa think?"

"He said I was just *special,* but he meant I was *damaged* by the family magic... or karma. He never talked to me about it. I just overheard him and Misty from time to time."

A long pause brought in the sounds of nature. Jak went to the barrel and filled his cup. He stood there and watched his brother sigh over the tiny portrait. The sadness that emanated from Gray made him regret asking, not only for Gray's sake but for his own as well. It wasn't a story he wanted to remember.

The face on the portrait mixed with images in his head, creating gruesome scenes of blood and death. He reached for his Qi as he pictured an evil man rip Constance's Qi from her chest, removing all her dragon abilities in a single moment.

"Without a Qi," he whispered to himself.

"What?"

Jak held his hand over his Qi while staring back at Gray with an expression of realization.

"Has anyone ever been able to take dragon form without their Qi?"

"No."

"No one?"

"No, not even the elementals. Jak, the story's over. There's nothing more, all right?"

"I can control my DúKruc."

"What? No, you—" he suddenly realized what Jak was thinking.

"Without my Qi."

"Oh, for shit's sake! Why didn't we think of it sooner?"

"Do you think the parents will let me come home?"

"I don't see why not, as long as you keep your Qi off while you're in the house, but we can't go tonight."

"Tomorrow?"

"No, we have to stay three nights."

"Why?"

"Raisin bet you wouldn't last three nights. If he wins, he gets my room for a month."

"And if you win?"

"I get to teach you to use that sling with him as the rock."

"Ha. That sounds like a win for you and me both."

He noticed Gray's strained smile and knew sadness still flowed through his heart.

"Hey, Gray?"

"Hmm?"

"I'm sorry. I'll never mention it again."

CHAPTER 41

Though Jak had only camped for three days, Lilink developed a severe case of separation anxiety. It started with simple whining and crying whenever he left the house, but as time moved on and summer breezes cooled with hints of autumn, her anxiety changed. She no longer cried out with her voice. Instead, she now had a pull. Jak could absorb a multitude of emotions and would instantly recognize the unique feel of his sister's pull. He could feel it only in his heart while he felt other emotions all over his body and through his psyche. Still, life went on as usual.

Exhausted after a full day of training, Jak headed to bed but knew it would be a while before he could get some rest. He sat on the edge of his bed, took off his shoes, and counted down.

"Twenty, nineteen, eighteen."

Lilink pushed the door open and peeked inside. Jak smiled and gestured for her to enter the room. Without hesitation, she ran and jumped onto the bed, giggling as she bounced.

"All right, silly girl, calm down. I need to talk to you."

She jumped up, brought her knees to her chest, and landed butt-first on the bed. Jak crawled onto the bed and lay beside her.

"We need to talk about the pull feeling."

"The 'come home' feeling?"

"Yes, Lilink. You need to be careful with it."

"Why?"

"Because if I come running home every time I leave the house, Mamas and Papa will figure it out. You know what happens then?"

"They keep me home?"

"Yes, which means you won't be able to go to school with your friends. It opens in a few days. You want to go, don't you?"

She put her fingers in her mouth, gave him sad eyes, and nodded.

"Then you have to be careful, just like your wind ability."

"That's Kate! I tell you e'ry day, that's Kate."

"All right, all right, it's Kate," Jak rolled his eyes and smiled at her exaggerations. "Either way, you have to be careful. Only pull me when it's truly important."

"What if I can't find Wally? Is that important?"

"Only if you ask Mamas and Papa to help you find him first."

"What if a big monster comes in?"

Jak saw genuine fear in her eyes. "What monster?"

"A… a reewee big one, up to the sky."

"Then you can pull me, but that kind of monster doesn't exist, Li."

"Yeah-huh. He's Kúnuh, and he's reewee dirty and reewee big."

"Bakúnuh?" Jak was startled by the mention of his name. "Is he in your book?"

"My book says he's a bad guy, but Kate told me what he looks like."

"Li, what does Kate look like?"

"She's imbizible."

Jak pondered the potential reality of Kate. Lilink had gained knowledge that had to have come from somewhere, but she was also showing abilities, and the knowledge could be one of them. Perhaps she had absorbed it the way Jak absorbed emotions and gave it a name as a way to explain it. He remembered the first time he felt the emotions of someone else and had no idea what to make of it. It was impossible to even describe at the time, and it hadn't gotten any easier with time.

"I think Kate is part of you, and you have to control that too. Don't get too far ahead of Mamas on the book. Let them teach you."

"Then maybe you won't be bad?"

"Huh?"

"Kate said you will be bad. Can Mamas change it?"

"I will not be bad, Li."

"Promise?"

"I promise."

He pulled the blankets to her shoulder and snuggled her. As he listened to her breathing, he closed his eyes and pondered. Vague images flashed inside his eyelids—Images of fire, soil, and water crashing and bursting against one another. Sleep pulled at his consciousness. He felt a lightening of thought. A vision appeared of Lilink standing over him, her arms extended at either side, her head tilted toward the sky. Wind and water swirled behind her. She looked down and, without warning, threw both arms toward him. The water and wind swelled in view, crashing down on him.

Jak sat up, startled, gasping for air. He felt as if he had only slept a wink, yet the sun poured early morning light over the windows. Lilink squirmed and reached for him, so he lay back down, breathed in her scent, and gazed at her. His eyes could see nothing but innocence and purity, yet the image of her standing over him was seared into his mind. He had little time to dwell on the visions.

***

Over the next few days, he and the rest of the family worked day and night to get Gabrinoke University ready in time for its grand opening. The university buzzed with trolls all that week as they prepared curriculum and stocked classrooms with replicated supplies. They gave the trolls a space inside the university to sell their inventions and duplications in exchange for teaching.

The school sat at the eastern edge of Gabrinoke. They plowed the soil around the school and sowed grass seed that produced a soft yellow grass for a playground with swings, a seesaw, and a cluster of small adobe domes and tunnels.

It had been several months since Gail had presented Inco with a written request to rename and map the meadow as Gabrinoke. The council initially declined the request. She was quite despondent until three weeks later when Inco presented a revised map. On it, the Gabril meadow and the rest of Gail and Joss's property was clearly titled 'Gabrinoke.' She and the residents were overjoyed.

Joss and Gail focused on running and organizing the school. They became the official headmistresses of the university, with the Gabrinoke people calling them Lady Gail and Lady Joss. They humbly accepted the titles, but Inco wasn't humble about it at all. He reminded them that being Ladies made their husband a Lord and would jokingly display lordly behavior by puffing his chest, deepening his tone, and mocking snobby, overconfident lords. Everyone enjoyed his performances and soundly applauded each time he acted the Lord.

***

As Jak passed his seventeenth birthday, Inco was in the best mental state he'd been in since Jak was three. Chance and Mikey spent so much time with them they'd become family. The school drew everyone together, and the family connected with the Gabrinoke people. For the first time in Jak's life, he was a part of a community.

Though his DúKrue could still happen, the parents let him remain at home as long as he didn't wear his Qi in the house. They wanted to believe the boy wasn't a migma because that would finally discredit the prophecy. Having him home allowed them to act as if he was nothing more than human, but anxiety returned as he reached seventeen years and three months. The crucial age of seventeen and a half, an age no DúHuman had ever reached before having their DúKrue, was fast approaching. If Jak could make it three more months without having his DúKrue, they could put the prophecy behind them. The problem was that it was common for late bloomers to have their DúKrue in those last few months. Because he'd been small throughout life, he was definitely a late bloomer.

To get his mind off the passage of time, Inco joined in the daily training. It became a pivotal point in their relationship. Jak felt more comfortable being himself around Inco as they grew closer through sparring.

The bond between them blossomed, creating an atmosphere Jak hadn't felt since he was very young. Being older now, Inco treated him with respect rather than focusing on structure and discipline. Their conversations were interactive rather than one-sided lessons or lectures. He fervently hoped that this time, his father would remain happy and sociable.

Gray didn't think about Jak's age at all during training. He put all his focus on the training at hand while increasing the intensity. Having always been a jolly, fun-loving, and youthful-minded spirit, taking him seriously during practice was something Jak struggled with, even after four years. Inco became his regular sparring partner as Gray and Chance coached.

The only downside was that his father was considerably less skilled. During his stressed-out phases, this might've angered him, but with his worries down and the increased bond he felt with Jak, he took the defeats quite well.

Lilink continued to communicate with Kate. The imaginary friend was always around, and Lilink adored her. The family started worrying when they noticed her knowledge of the prophecy surpassed what they'd taught her. Just as she had done with Jak, she claimed that Kate talked to her about the story.

Inco, being optimistic, said that Lilink might have overheard more than she should and gave Kate credit for the information because she was too young to explain it otherwise. Gail's instincts told her that Kate was real, and if she wanted Lilink to have accurate information, she had to be the first to teach her. Joss had a similar feeling and was also the one who had pushed the hardest for their children to be informed. Together, they rewrote Lilink's bedtime story to include more detail and updated it more often.

By the time Lilink was four and a half, she knew a simplified version of the entire prophecy up to the starting of the war. The family left out the predicted end.

***

Jak reached the six-month point since his seventeenth birthday and the family no longer expected a DúKrue. Because of his training, they were confident in his ability to control himself. The boundaries and restrictions set by the parents loosened with the lessening of fears and concerns.

With Jak being past the age of DúKrue, Lilink's understanding of the prophecy became unnecessary. The parents stopped reading the book and talked about the prophecy less and less. They even tried telling her other stories to distract her, but she continually insisted that the prophecy story was her and Kate's favorite. She wanted nothing to do with any other stories. Jak convinced them to ease up, and when they stopped trying to steer Lilink away from the prophecy, she stopped clinging to it. Within a few weeks, she stopped talking about it, and the prophecy became a part of the past.

Although they had celebrated freedom from the prophecy when Jak turned seventeen-and-a-half, everyone became completely convinced when he passed his eighteenth birthday. The last bit of hesitation and concern that had lingered since spring was laid to rest. They couldn't explain his Qi or abilities, but not being a migma meant he couldn't be the prophesied Son of Darkness.

***

By Lilink's fifth birthday, she'd sprouted into a little lady. Her hair had grown longer but still parted slightly to the left and veiled her cheeks. Four faint freckles flecked her button nose. Her bluish-grey eyes had grown brighter since she was born, and the dark grey ring had grown darker.

The portals had continued to be unpredictable since the Roanoke people had come to Origo. It didn't take long for everyone to realize there was a direct correlation between the ground tremors and the portals. Every time the ground shook, the portals flickered. Every time a portal opened, the ground shook. One didn't happen without the other.

Many more people had come through portals. Everyone was checked in, given official citizenship, and helped to settle wherever they chose. Origo experienced significant advances during this time. Many came from the future and had items from their time. A handful of newcomers presented medical knowledge and advanced treatments. They introduced transportation devices called bicycles. A history book with dates far into the future was discovered among one person's belongings, but the council locked it away with the weapons in a vault, claiming it could be devastating to know or alter Earth's history.

New foods were brought in, along with agricultural advances and alternative uses for various plants. New instruments and musical abilities spread throughout the lands. Origo grew, peacefully advancing and developing at a rapid rate.

Life was wonderful for all. Lilink was five, a beautiful, brilliant young lady. Jak was eighteen, well-rounded, disciplined, and excelled in his studies. Mikey was also eighteen, less disciplined, and a *lot* more obnoxious, but a loyal friend. Chance had more freedom now that Mikey, Jak, and Gray didn't need him for training, but he still visited often. Raisin learned a new vocabulary of insults and slang from Mikey. Inco was happy and fulfilled. Gail and Joss had found a new calling with their university. Gray was Gray, his same jolly self. The only worry still on anyone's mind was Æmma.

Æmma was still in the cave on Earth, or at least she was the last time they had used the portal. It had been over five years since they had been to see her, but Jak and Gray hoped that she was still there.

Every time the ground shook, Gray or Inco would rush as fast as they could to the Airland portal, but it was always closed by the time they arrived. They never stopped trying, though, and promised Jak they never would.

CHAPTER 42

Jak lay on his back with Inco's arm secured between his legs and wrist held firmly against his sternum. Jak's legs crossed at the ankles, and his legs rested across Inco's chest. As he lifted his pelvis, Inco's elbow was painfully torqued backward.

"Just tap out, and it'll be all over."

"Don't tell me what to do, you little shit. I'll figure a way... ah!"

"I'm just trying to save you some pain, old man. You're not getting out of this, so you might as well give up."

"It's 'Lord Old Man' to you."

"Oh, right. Lord Old Man, Sir, Your Majesty of Excellence and Wisdom. Haha, you can be Qing if you want, but you're still not getting out of this arm-bar," Jak teased, flexing his butt muscles to put pressure on Inco's elbow.

"Do you know the best part about getting old?" Inco pushed Jak's legs a bit, allowing him to raise his back from the ground. He flexed and yanked his trapped arm, allowing him to bend his elbow and dig it harshly into Jak's groin.

Jak groaned in pain and let go of his wrist.

"When situations get sticky, you learn to... roll with it."

He rolled toward Jak, pushing his legs up as he went, pinning Jak's knees to his shoulders. He laughed as he slapped Jak's butt and let go.

"Way to go," Gray clapped his hands. "It's about time you won a match."

Jak lay on the ground still, holding his groin and laughing through the pain. Inco stood tall and smiled down at him.

"Jak, do you know where you went wrong?"

"Yes, I—"

The ground shook beneath them. Gray burst into dragon form without hesitation and soared over the trees toward the Airland Portal. Jak jumped to his feet, and he and Inco watched Gray soar up until their gaze met the sun, and they looked away.

***

Gray flew fast, reaching the portal quicker than he ever had before. He was so determined to get there in time he didn't slow down or land before taking his Dú. He changed as he landed, causing him to fall and tumble across the stone surface. His half-dragon half-human body continued to transform as it scraped, bumped, and flipped through the portal wall, coming to rest face-down, in human form, in the center of the cave.

"I made it!" Gray stretched his arms and yelled at the top of his lungs, but his nose and mouth pressed against the hard ground and muffled the sound. His entire body hurt from the rigorous tumbling. He had dirt in his eyes and felt impact sites all over his body as he struggled to his feet.

His left leg throbbed, but the excitement of finally making it through the portal overshadowed the discomfort. On his feet, he looked around, but dust and darkness hampered his sight.

"Æmma, I made it. I'm here," he called out louder than necessary. Tears flooded his eyes and cleared away the dirt just as he reached the stone slab that had been Æmma's bed for so long.

"I'm here. It's time to get you out of this cave. Jak wants to—"

He stopped talking as he tried to understand what he was feeling. His vision was still a blur, but he was at the slab and could feel nothing there. He slapped the stone in various places, mumbling unintelligibly.

After rubbing his eyes for a few more minutes, he could finally see. Æmma was gone. Nothing remained.

She must've woken up, but where did she go? There's no way she made it down the mountain. Could she have found the portal? Gray thought to himself. *The portal. Maybe it's still open.* He started toward the portal wall. *What if I go through and can't get back? Would Æmma and Jak be separated forever? But she isn't here, and I definitely don't want to stay on Earth.*

He stared at the portal wall. *I have to go back. Jak needs me.*

He lifted his foot to the wall, but it bounced off. The portal had closed. He held his forehead in his palm as he slumped to the ground. He sat with his eyes pressed against his knees and balled his hands into fists, pulling at his shaggy grey hair.

Why did I hesitate? Ugh, I'm so stupid. Where did you go, Æmma? Did you wake up? Aw, man, you must've been so scared and confused. And you couldn't escape, the mountain's far too high. You would've died trying. You would've died.

These thoughts echoed in his mind before he scrambled to his feet and ran to the cave entrance. He looked down the mountain at nothing but snow and ice. He took dragon form again and circled the mountain's bottom in a tight spiral toward the top. When he reached the snow cap, he flew to the top and spiraled down. As he went, he blew the snow from the mountain surface to expose anything that might be unveiled under the drifts. For several hours, he searched the mountain but found nothing—no clue to explain the disappearance of Jak's mother.

It's early fall here. It was near winter when I left. I must've gone through a time change. Dammit! What am I going to do now? I don't even know what year it is. Why's all this happening? How—

He lost his train of thought out of frustration. Hovering just outside the cave entrance, he stared into the distance, his mind a blank, without a single plan.

That's the way to your village. He addressed Æmma in his thoughts. *What if you woke and didn't remember the attack? What if you made it off the mountain and tried to go home?*

If she did, it was unlikely that she made it down, and even more unlikely that she would've made the long journey back to her village, but he flew toward it, anyway; what did he have to lose?

Maybe the villagers rebuilt. Humans are always rebuilding and destroying and rebuilding again. Maybe you found a new husband and had a few more children, and—

He tried to imagine a happy ending for Æmma. Nothing he could think of would put Jak back in her arms, though. His childhood was the one thing she'd never be able to rebuild or replace.

There it is. Gray approached the Dera Wudu, where he and Inco had napped that afternoon. *They've rebuilt. It looks the same, except the angle is different. I don't think this is where we were.* His eyes grazed the tops of the trees as he hovered. *I think we were over there,* he thought, looking at an area of the woods near the field. He headed that way when a noise caught his attention. A group of men approached the edge of the village.

It's… It's happening now? How can… I've traveled back to Jak's birth day? How can this be? What can I do? Can I stop the raid before it happens? But then, I'd lose Jak. And what if I see myself?

He remembered a theoretical conversation he'd had with Lex while smoking dried sticky-puffs. Lex theorized that one or both versions of a person would cease to exist if they came face to face in time and space.

Stopping the raid will save Jak from the Darkness curse. But it could be my suicide.

Overcome by a deep sadness, he nevertheless knew the answer. *I have to do it for Jak and Æmma. They deserve an authentic life. I'll stop the whole thing before it starts.*

He flew toward the village. As he reached the first house, he tumbled hard across the cave floor, landing face down with his mouth and nose against the ground just as he'd done before. He rubbed his dirt-filled eyes. And just like before, Æmma was gone. He raced out of the cave and back to the village. The attackers were approaching again. He rushed toward them, only to find himself face down on the cave floor again.

"Dammit!" Gray yelled, rubbing the dirt from his eyes again. He flew back to the village but took a different route. *I'll catch them before they reach the village. I must see myself from the woods, and that causes some kind of trigger to set me back. Maybe this way will work.*

It didn't, and once again, Gray rubbed cave dirt from his eyes. He didn't even remember making it to the village, and this time the tumble seemed more painful than before, almost as if the portal was throwing him harder each time—perhaps to emphasize the futility of his attempts to change fate.

Determined and stubborn, he swore to himself it wouldn't work. He rushed out again.

As soon as the woods came into view, he tumbled hard onto the cave floor again.

"Shit! Shit! Shit!" Gray screamed at the portal wall.

Frustrated, he angrily charged again, only to tumble and land face down again. He screamed his failure into the ground and punched the rock-hard surface.

"Why," punch, "Can't," punch, "I," punch, "Save," punch, "Them?" punch.

Blood trickled from his throbbing knuckles. As he pushed his chest from the ground, a strong wind carried the smell of ash and soot past his face. Gray realized he wasn't in the cave anymore. He turned around, and the smoke cleared to reveal the landscape of Origo blazing with fire as far as the eye could see.

"No," he muttered as he sat up. "No." He kicked himself backward. "No!" He tried to yell, but it came out a whisper. He continued to push himself back until he reached the portal wall and rolled into the cave.

As before, Æmma was not there, but Gray barely noticed. The shock of seeing Origo on fire had broken his heart and thrown his mind into complete disarray.

It can't be real, he thought. *It just can't. Jak. Lilink. Inco. No. My mind's playing tricks on me.*

He touched the portal wall, pushing his hand through then retracting it.

It's still open, but… what will I find on the other side?

He bent down and rested his face against the cold stone of the wall, but only a second before pulling away. *What if it's real? I don't want to know, but I must.*

He poked his head through the portal. Sunlight struck his eyes like hot coals. He clenched them shut, took in a deep breath of fresh Origo air, and opened them again. Bright skies shone down on a paradise of nature, just as he'd left it.

It wasn't real, he thought as he stepped the rest of the way through the portal and cheered, "Woo-hoo!"

Gray rushed home just as quickly as he'd rushed to the portal. He wanted to make sure everyone was still there, and history hadn't changed. He wasn't sure whether he hoped for it or against it, though. The pros and cons of either circumstance were too overwhelming to consider, causing his mind to freeze and go blank. He only hoped that whatever happened, it would be in everyone's best interest.

Origo was just as he left it, but his appreciation of the scene heightened his senses. The air seemed sweeter, the trees were more vibrant in their fall colors, and the sun was brighter.

As he passed the Airland Mountains, just before crossing the Misbaden Straight, he looked down to see a group of people setting up a festival.

Weren't they already partying when I passed them before?

He looked at the sky to check the time with the sun, but this did him no good. He'd never truly understood the technique. As he continued over the strait, he noticed the same fishermen he'd seen before.

I guess I wasn't gone very long.

A short time later, Gray approached the eastern side of Gabrinoke. He descended with his sights set on the clearing where the house was. A dragon shot from the opening and headed straight for him. The dragon was himself!

"What the—"

The approaching version of himself didn't seem to see him. He didn't slow or sway out of the way. At maximum speed, and with no time to think, Gray brought his legs and arms out in front of him, preparing for impact.

"Ahh!"

His other self flew right through him, becoming transparent and vanishing like a smoke-ring. Gray looked back while still descending toward the forest clearing. He saw nothing in the sky behind him. The other version of himself had disappeared.

"What just ha—"

Swoosh! Crack! Snap! Bang!

While he was looking back, his angle altered, and he hit the tops of the trees before the clearing, then crashed sideways into the trunk of a tree that sat behind the house.

Gray groaned in pain. So did the tree.

CHAPTER 43

Jak and Inco looked up to see what had thrown Gray from the sky, but the sun made it impossible to see, so they ran back to where Gray leaned against a tree.

Inco knelt next to him. "What happened? Who did this?"

"Oh. I think I broke a few ribs."

"Well, that's what you get for messin' around," Jak yelled. "Hurry. Get to the portal before it closes,"

"I already went. I've been gone all day," he tried to yell back, but the pain in his ribs muted it. He changed to his Dú and sat up, propping himself against the tree he'd collided with.

"Stop playin' around. It's not funny. Hurry."

"I'm serious," he said, almost pleading as he pulled off his Qi. He put several drops along one side of his chest, held his breath for a few seconds, and then let out a heavy sigh of relief.

"But you just left."

"The portal twisted time. I already went, and I made it there in time, but she wasn't there. I'm so sorry, Jak."

Inco's brow furrowed. "She wasn't there?"

"Where is she?" Jak spoke louder than he meant to.

"I—" Gray faltered, unsure how to explain what happened. "I arrived there before her."

Jak brushed his hair from his face and stared into Gray's shifting eyes.

"You arrived… huh?"

"When I went into the cave, she was gone. I searched the entire mountain, and then I checked to see if she might've tried going back to her village."

"There's no way," Inco blurted.

"I know, but that's where she was. I—"

"Why didn't you get her?" Jak raised his voice again.

"I tried. She was running from the village."

"She's in trouble?"

"*Stop,*" Gray yelled, then lowered his tone, "just let me explain. When I went through the portal, she wasn't there. I searched the mountain, in case she tried to get down, but there was no trace of her. I thought maybe she tried to go home even though I knew how unlikely that was."

He glanced at Inco. "But the portal had closed, and I didn't know when it would open again, so I figured it wouldn't hurt to check. When I reached the Dera Wudu, I could see her village. It was as if nothing had ever happened. I realized the attack hadn't happened yet."

He rose to his feet and looked at Jak. Tears welled in his eyes, making them glisten in the filtered rays of sunlight. "The invasion was just beginning. I thought maybe I could stop it, but every time I tried, I found myself back in the cave."

Jak took in a deep breath as Gray's emotions mixed with his own.

"I tried Jak. I truly did. Every time I tried, I grew farther from reaching her. The last time I tried, I didn't even make it to the woods. Then…" He remembered the devastating sight of Origo in ruins but decided it was best to leave that part out. "Then I was back in the cave, and the portal had closed again."

***

Jak stared at Gray. His face reflected the same sorrow and disappointment, but he didn't flinch. They'd been trying to reach the portal for years with no success. It was the moment Jak had been waiting for, and it was a complete disappointment. Nothing could describe how he felt, so he didn't even try.

He felt Gray's genuine disappointment, and his sadness overwhelmed him so that he almost didn't notice the hint of omission. It made him curious, but he was already so upset, he decided it best to brush it off and move on. He went into the house without saying another word. Gray's story upset him, but he bottled it without realizing he was doing what Inco does when he goes into his 'strong and silent' phases.

Ever since he'd learned of his mother, he had felt a strong desire to meet her. It wasn't because of an emptiness he wanted to fill. Gail had done an excellent job of being a fulfilling mother figure, and when Joss joined the family, the two of them met all his mothering needs.

Meeting Æmma was about his origins. He wanted to know what type of people he belonged to, as well as trivial things such as whose eyes he had or what personality traits he might've gained through his lineage. He would now have to accept that he may never know these things while trying to reason with his feelings and excuse them away.

"Maybe it's for the best," he thought aloud, mumbling under his breath. "Ma pretends she wants me to meet Æmma, and so does Joss, but it's obvious they don't. Every time we bring her name up, Ma gets so upset, and Joss gets worried about Ma. If I don't meet Æmma, no one has to suffer."

He continued reasoning away his emotions on his way down the hall to his room. His arms and shoulders felt heavy under the burden of anger and sorrow.

"It doesn't matter where I'm from." He balled his fists without noticing. "It's not like I belong there anymore." His forehead rested against the wall next to his bedroom door. "I don't belong on Earth or Origo. I don't belong anywhere." He punched the wall without thinking.

The adobe cracked in three directions, shooting out from the impact site. Jak's anger dissipated in regret as he inspected the wall.

"Come in," a voice called from his room.

He opened the door to see Raisin sprawled out on his bed, resting his back against a pillow, his body stretched large and round, like an orange. One of his hands rested behind his head while the other held a piece of meat.

"What's up?" Raisin tore a piece of meat off with his teeth.

"Are you eating all my bacon?" Jak walked to the corner of his room, where strips of meat hung from a wooden rod fixed to the wall. "It took me fourteen days to cure this meat. I'd like it to last just as long."

Raisin belched. "You should've made more."

"Look at you. You've doubled in size from stuffin' your gut," he yanked the piece of bacon from Raisin's hand and ate it.

"Hey, my cooties were on that!"

"Extra flavor," he stuck out his tongue, displaying the chewed bacon.

"Bogart! I was done anyway." Raisin tried to stand but fell back onto the bed. "I'll just rest here." He patted his belly and closed his eyes with a content grin on his face.

"Worst pet ever," he mumbled on his way out of the room.

"I resemble that remark," Raisin yelled from the room.

Jak smirked as he continued toward the front door. He knew Gray had done all he could and felt terrible for being so harsh. When he went outside, Gray and Inco were talking to a couple of people. They looked like they could be from Gabrinoke, but he knew the Gabrinoke people pretty well, and he didn't recognize either of them.

Inco called from across the yard, "Jak, come over here."

He meandered toward him while still carrying Lilink. He poked and tickled her, not paying much attention until he stood next to Inco. As he looked up, he met a familiar face.

"Hello, Jak."

"Æmma?"

CHAPTER 44

Inco swallowed his emotion as he watched Jak talking to Æmma. He and Zebulan moved a few paces away to give them some privacy.

"I can't thank you enough, my friend."

"No thanks, necessary, but I hope they're able to build something between them. I know what it's like to be estranged," Zebulan said.

"Still, I'm surprised."

Zebulan shrugged. "It was nothing. I was near the portal when the tremors happened. It only took a moment of my time."

"I mean... I know your feelings about Earth humans coming to Origo."

"Yes, well I—" He rubbed the back of his head.

"Don't get me wrong," Inco added, "it takes both sides to create a balance. I respect your views, but—"

Zebulan waved him off. "At least *she* has family here. Jak is your family, and she's Jak's family, so she has a place here. This doesn't change how I feel about the others."

"Of course, I understand," Inco smiled.

Zebulan placed a hand on Inco's shoulder. "I must be going. You all enjoy the rest of your day."

"Of course. But I wanted to ask—was she awake when you—" Movement in his peripheral vision caught his attention. Lilink swung a wooden sword and galloping on a brown hobbyhorse from the Gabrinoke path. Anxiety rushed blood to his head. How would he explain Lilink if Zebulan asked? "I, uh, nevermind. It doesn't matter. I'll, uh, see you at the next meeting?"

"I'll be there."

Zebulan took dragon form. Larger than the average dragon, his body completely black, with broad and muscular shoulders, he was a sight to behold. He glanced at Jak before soaring into the sky.

***

Jak watched as Zebulan took dragon form. He felt deceit emanating from him, which seemed odd, but he wasn't sure why since he had no idea who he was. He brushed it off and turned his attention back to Æmma, but Lilink came galloping into the yard.

Her hair, braided into a bun, sat high on her head. She wore a light green tunic with shells woven into the fabric around her high collar. Most of her shirts and tunics had a tight collar to avoid slipping off her shoulder and exposing her mark. Her pants were denim, replicated by the trolls, and were loose down her legs. She wore moccasins, each with a shell fixed over the bridge of the foot.

Gail and Joss murmured through light laughter as they strolled up the Gabrinoke path. They each held a small bundle of flowers and were wrapping the stems in strips of cloth.

"Jak, I'm a knight," Lilink squealed as she turned about with her hobbyhorse and hugged its head. "This is my horse, Roodin."

Jak picked Lilink up, admiring her horse while trying to dodge, getting bumped in the face by her wooden sword. "Roodin, huh? That's as good a name for a horse if I ever heard one."

"I named him after Kate's baby. She said Roo means dragon. He's a dragon DúHorse."

"Is that so?" He turned to the horse. "Nice to meet you, Roodin."

Lilink wiggled the horse's head and spoke for him in a squeaky voice. "*Nice to meet you, too.*"

He chuckled and bent over to put Lilink down. She whispered in his ear. "Who's that lady, Jak?"

"She's—" He paused as Gail and Joss stepped into the yard. His heart rose into his throat as he braced for Gail's reaction.

"Who's this?" Gail smiled at Jak.

Æmma turned around. "I'm Æmma, daughter of King Æthelric, wife of Ætheling Ælwulf. I'm Jak's mother."

Gail froze. Her arms dropped to her sides, and the flowers she carried fell from her hand. She was shocked into silence. The wave of emotion between her and Æmma nearly knocked Jak off his feet. He put one hand over his eyes to stop the spinning feeling, shuffling his feet to maintain balance.

Lilink took the news in stride and asked, "We have three mamas?"

"No, no, honey. Jak does. You just have two." Joss lifted Lilink and placed her on her hip. She knelt down to pick up the flowers Gail had dropped.

"It's nice to meet you, Æmma," she lied. "I hope you're

hungry. The stew's been on all day." She wrapped her free arm around Gail and guided her away and toward the house.

Æmma turned to Jak with confusion on her face.

"That's my little sister, Lilink. And they're my mothers, Gail and Joscolyn, Joss for short. You've met my father, Inco, and my brother, Gray," he nodded toward each person as he spoke. He'd regained his balance but still felt a strange weakness in his body.

"I'm so sorry. I shouldn't have introduced myself as your—"

"It's all right. I'm sure she understands." Jak rubbed his head again.

"No, it's not. I see you have a full family and a full life. I should go." She headed toward the Gabrinoke path.

"Wait."

"It'll just cause pain if I stay." She stopped but didn't turn around.

"Ma- I mean, Gail shared me with Joss… she can share me with you. I'm not a child anymore, so you won't have to disagree on proper guidance or what I should eat."

"Yes," she agreed. Tears welled in her eyes and streamed down her cheeks. "I missed all that."

"Don't cry with sadness. We should cry for joy," Jak pled as he walked toward her.

She still had her back to him, so she wondered how he knew she was crying. She wiped the tears from her face before he reached her.

"I've been waiting eighteen years to meet you. The least you can give me is a day."

"Did you—"

"Did I what?"

"Oh, never mind. Just—"

"Tell me. Tell me all your thoughts. I want to know."

She turned to face him. "How did you know I was crying?"

He shifted his weight and looked away.

"You felt it, didn't you?" She strained a sad smile. "You have the cursed-gift."

"The what?" The reference to a curse puzzled but also alarmed him. He'd had enough 'lousy juju,' as Gray called it, in his life. The last thing he needed was a curse.

"The cursed-gift," she repeated. "Your great-grandfather Yffa had it. He inherited the gift from his father, Usfrey, and it goes all the way back to the God Woden and Goddess Frigg. Yffa passed it to Aethelric, who passed it to me. We feel what others feel. Sometimes it's powerful, sometimes faint, but always present."

"I gained that from *you*?"

"Of course. How else would you have gotten it?"

Jak smiled but didn't respond. He'd eventually have to tell Æmma about his abilities, his Qi, and the prophecy, but would have to wait until he established a more comfortable relationship with her.

"You have your father's eyes." She put her hands on his cheeks and studied his face as if she'd have to remember him forever from this one moment. She pushed his hair behind his ear, smoothed his eyebrows with her thumbs, and caressed the delicate beginnings of facial hair on his chin.

Flashes of the village raid flickered in her eyes. Her pulse quickened. She pictured Ælwulf's face as he lay dying in the field. Gray's kind dragon eyes flashed in her memory, the tear that wiggled its way down his scaly face, glistening in the scattered light breaking through the forest trees. Jak's infant cry echoed as an old melody played in her own weak, crackled voice.

She sang tremulously. *"Slæp slæp, Lýtla bera, þū eart ġesund mid mē."*

"I know that song," he said softly.

"I sang it to you every night while you were in my belly." Her breath quivered. "I've missed so much."

"We have time. You haven't aged but a few months in the time you were healing."

She smiled. "Yes. Zebulan told me that aging, while healing, was slower than normal. He said it was one-tenth the normal human aging."

"It's lucky he found you just as you woke. You could've died in that cave with no way down." his attention turned to her dark grey dress. "Did he give you a new dress? That's not the one you wore in the cave."

Her look of admiration turned to confusion. "He gave me this dress, yes, but I woke here. I've never even seen the cave."

"How long have you been here?"

"Only a few hours, I think. Zebulan says we had just arrived at his house moments before I woke. He made me some tea, dug this dress from his late mother's belongings, and helped me understand where I was and what had happened to me. He had very few details but told me enough to know I was going to be meeting my son as an adult, and we're not on Earth."

"Wow. He saved you just before waking from an eighteen-year sleep because he was near the portal at the time it opened. That's a lot of lucky coincidence." He tried not to mistrust but did, anyway.

"Woden was watching over me."

"Who?"

"Woden. He's the God of War. He would've been watching as our village was raided, and he watched over me to preserve our royal lineage. We're of the Gods, Jak."

"Royal? Gods?"

"There's so much to tell you. Oh, I don't know where to start."

Jak's mind spun with this news. He smiled as his mind raced with all the things he wanted to know.

"How about… when you met my father?"

"What a great place to start!" She smiled and looked into his eyes, and then her own eyes widened with awkward amazement.

"What is it?"

"You were born just days after my seventeenth birthday. If you just turned eighteen, we're almost the same age! I think you may even be older."

"That's pretty strange," he pondered aloud, then laughed to break the ice again. "You're jumping ahead. What about my father?"

"When I first met your father, he was a real arsecop. Oh!" She covered her mouth and smiled with her eyes, then lowered her hand, "Well, I suppose you're old enough for a curse word."

"Ha, I've said worse, but I've never heard of an arsecop," he laughed. "So I guess I'm still learning. So he was an arsecop, huh?"

"Yes, through and through."

***

She continued talking as they strolled down the path to Gabrinoke. They took several laps around Gabrinoke, talking and laughing.

"Rædwald, your grandfather, has always been a sight to behold. In his youth, he became quite popular amongst the servant girls, but he only took an interest in one of them. Her name was Edyt. They lost their good wits one day, and nine months later, Edyt died giving birth to a baby boy, your father, Ælwulf. His name was the last word spoken by her lips.

"Tytila, your great grandfather, learned of the birth and allowed Ælwulf to remain in the home as a 'cousin' of the family. He didn't have much choice—Rædwald was king far before he took the seat. However, he didn't have the power to make Ælwulf his heir. The only way Ælwulf would rule was to marry the only daughter of another king—me.

"Well, I suppose I wasn't the daughter of a king yet, but my father Æthelric was the eldest child and heir to king Ælla. Rædwald came to my father the day I was born. He offered protection and allegiance to the royal family of Deira in exchange for a union that would make his son ætheling to the throne. No one told your father or me, though. We didn't find out until the day King Ælla died, and my father became king. Can you imagine? My grandfather died, my father became king, and I lost my right to choose love all in a single day. I felt like I could die."

Jak stared at her, his eyes devouring her every glimpse, his ears devouring her every word. He didn't speak, but she knew he wanted more. Feeling her son's enthrallment pulled a joyful smile across her face.

"We were like day and night, Ælwulf and I. He was bold and vivacious, and I was not. I could barely stand it. The one and only thing Ælwulf and I agreed on from the start was that we did not want to get married. He was too wild for me, and I was too boring for him."

"But if the king arranges a marriage—"

"An Angle woman cannot be forced into marriage." Æmma pressed her lips and raised her brow. "But, an Angle father could also reject all other suitors to enforce the desired match. If we wanted to be free to marry who we chose, we would have to change their minds. So, we plotted together, but no matter how hard we tried, our pleas fell on deaf ears. My father is a stubborn man, but *Rædwald*—I could barely breathe in his presence. Nothing was going to change their minds. Kings, puh, they're mules with crowns."

"What did you do?" Jak's eyes radiated with curiosity.

"We spent so much time trying to find a way out of marriage, we fell in love. My father and Rædwald couldn't make it happen fast enough. They didn't want to risk either of us changing our minds, I suppose," Æmma laughed with her hand over her chest. When her arm fell to her side, it grazed Jak's, and he caught it on the return swing. They slowed their pace, eyes locked, hand in hand, and exchanged warm smiles. Æmma saw Ælwulf in the face of her son. The memory of his death still stung, and she tried to picture his face from memories before his death. In her heart and mind, it had only happened a day ago. The fact that those memories were eighteen years old was something she struggled to process.

"And then I was born?" Jak broke the silence.

Æmma snapped to attention and realized she had trailed

in thought. She flashed a wide smile and nodded. "More or less, yes. We conceived you almost immediat—"

A hissing sound made Æmma jump and turn, releasing Jak's hand and grabbing at her dress.

"What's wrong?" Jak followed her gaze but saw nothing to cause alarm.

"I thought I heard a snake."

"The snakes here—oh, you'd know it was coming a long time before it got that close. Their wings are *very* loud." Jak smiled.

Æmma looked at the trees, concern in her eyes.

"They've already migrated south. Relax, I won't let anything get you, I promise," Jak chuckled.

Æmma laughed along, and she and Jak continued their walk. She heard the hiss again but realized it was a distant voice. She glanced at people moving about Gabrinoke and shrugged it off.

"So you got married, and then you got pregnant," Jak said. "Did you live in a castle?"

"No. Our structures were nice in the heart of Deira, but your father and I lived in a little village by the Dera Wudu, as far away from the Gododdin people as we could get. We lived in a grubhouse. Our plan was to move back to the capitol after your birth, and Ælwulf will become king under the overlordship of my father—I mean—he would have. I keep forgetting…" She rubbed a burning tear from her eye.

"Did he get to hold me?"

"Yes, for a moment." Æmma pictured Ælwulf handing her the baby on the horse. She didn't want to tell Jak that the only time his father held him was in their escape. She pictured the moment before they ran out the door. "He kissed you, too." She grinned and touched his hairline. "Right there."

***

Jak smiled. He felt his mother's radiance, love, sorrow, and joy all at once. Another sensation caught his attention, but he couldn't place it. It felt similar to weakness but different. She'd also just awoken from an eighteen-year sleep. His uncertainty came and went, but the emotions between himself and his mother outweighed everything else.

"Jak, it's time for supper," Lilink's tiny voice called from the path just after Æmma and Jak had lapped past it.

She galloped toward them on her hobbyhorse with her blanket draped behind its head. Joss leaned against a tree at the mouth of the path and watched.

"I have her. We'll be right there," Jak hollered, gesturing a half-wave in her direction.

She smiled, returned the half-wave gesture, and disappeared back onto the path. Jak smiled as he watched Lilink continue toward him. Her expression kept switching between a radiant smile for him and a serious, dutiful look toward the horse. He chuckled at the cute nature of her acting skills until she lost her footing and fell to the ground.

"Ow!"

Jak and Æmma ran to her side. She whimpered a little but didn't cry.

"I hurt my finger," she whined, holding it up.

Her knuckle had a deep scrape, and a tiny trickle of blood crept from a crease in the skin. As soon as she saw the blood, she panicked.

"It's all right, Li."

Jak didn't want Æmma to see his Qi but needed to relieve Lilink of her pain. He subtly moved and adjusted his footing to have his back to Æmma as he pulled his Qi off his chest. Holding it concealed in his hand, like he did when he healed Ananias's daughter, he held it over the injured finger and squeezed. He pulled his hand away, and nothing was there except the scrape. Jak tried again, this time pressing a little harder. He felt the release from the Qi and was sure some had come out this time, but as he pulled his hand away, he saw that he'd squeezed out far too much and covered more than the one finger in xenum.

"What's that?" Æmma looked over his shoulder.

"Uh, ointment. Just a little something I keep on hand."

Lilink watched a trail of black xenum run down the side of her hand while another streak puddled in her palm.

"Just wipe it on Wally, Li. We'll wash it tomorrow."

He helped her rub the xenum off her hand with her blanket, then lifted her over his head. She giggled and kissed his forehead on the way to rest on his hip.

***

Æmma watched Jak. Her mind wandered into seeing him as Ælwulf and Lilink as the son he had looked forward to raising. She wondered if he would've smiled at their son in the same way. She imagined the scenes she dreamt while pregnant—Ælwulf tucking their child in, helping him walk, and teaching him to shoot a bow and arrow. These scenes shuffled through her mind as she admired Jak's love for Lilink.

Anger crept into her thoughts as she struggled to comprehend that the grown man in front of her was the baby she'd just given birth to. In her mind, he should only be a day old. She wasn't even used to having a flat abdomen. Her hand gravitated to her belly, just as it had for the last nine months of her memory.

Her eyes met Jak's curious gaze. She snapped out of her daze and smiled at him, then widened her smile when she met eyes with Lilink. Lilink didn't smile back. Her expression was serious but soft with concern.

Lilink whispered into Jak's ear, "You should give her some ninnum. Her blood is sick."

He didn't understand what she meant. He looked at her, puzzled, and she gazed back at him. Her brows lowered, and her eyes moistened as if she were going to cry.

"We'll talk about it later, Li," he whispered.

She rested her head on his shoulder and wrapped her arms around his neck. She stayed this way until they were home. When Jak put her down in the yard, she was her happy self again, galloping in a zigzag to the door.

Jak was anxious, and he knew that Æmma felt the same. For his part, Jak worried about Gail feeling replaced, Joss feeling threatened, Inco being caught in the middle, or Æmma feeling unwelcome. He wanted nothing more than for everyone to get along.

Chance and Mikey were there. They came over for supper often, so it was no surprise. Everyone introduced themselves and sat down to supper.

"Errmrrguness," Æmma exclaimed loudly with a mouth full of food. Her eyes fluttered high under closed eyelids, and she fanned at her chest as if she were calming her heart.

"What is this miracle in my mouth?"

"Crendala." Joss knew her cooking was exceptional but still enjoyed hearing it from others.

"I want to eat this every day. I've never had anything with so much flavor."

"Oh, but then you'd be missing out on all the other wonderful flavors of food here on Origo," Gail bubbled.

Considering her shock earlier in the day, Gail was amazingly composed and cheerful. This came much to Jak's delight. He beamed with joy as he looked around at everyone he loved and cared about—together, healthy, and happy. He sat back in his chair and interlaced his fingers behind his head, realizing that it was the best day of his life.

After supper, the parents took Lilink for her bath and to get ready for bed. Raisin, Mikey, Chance, and Gray all went back to Gray's room and played Chaturanga and cards. Gail brought out an extra pillow and blanket for Æmma to sleep in the sitting room. She settled in, as did Jak, and they stayed awake talking.

Lilink laid in bed and watched the light beam from the hallway, waiting for her brother to pass through it as he went to bed, but he had drifted off to sleep in the sitting room. Lilink fell asleep waiting.

CHAPTER 45

A dull ache woke Jak from his sleep. He sat up, disoriented, and took a moment to remember where he was. Æmma was gone. He looked around, but she was nowhere in sight. The dull ache intensified, demanding his attention. It was the pull, the same one he had felt in the past when Lilink missed him, only much stronger. It drew him toward the front door, but Lilink was in bed. He realized she was probably upset that he hadn't come to bed yet. He walked down the hallway toward her room, and the pull felt stronger, but from the opposite direction. It was as if he were pulling away from it.

He pushed Lilink's door open. She wasn't there. He patted the bed to be sure, then looked under it. She wasn't there.

"She's probably in my bed waiting for me," he muttered.

He left her room and crossed the hall to his. No one was there. The pull grew stronger, and he worried. He opened the door to his parents' bedroom and tried to see if he could spot Lilink, hoping she had wiggled into bed with them. He couldn't tell from the distance, so he crept closer. She wasn't there either. The pull wrenched at his chest, stronger than ever before. He pressed his palm against his Qi and seethed.

"What're you doing?" Joss slipped out of bed and tiptoed to Jak.

"I can't find Lilink," Jak whispered near her cheek.

Her face twisted with confusion as she snapped her gaze toward him. She nudged him toward the hallway and followed him out.

Joss rushed to Lilink's room. She came back out a moment later and went into Jak's room, then came back out. Next, she opened Gray's room and high-stepped over sleeping bodies to check for Lilink, then came back to the hallway. She hurried to the sitting room and looked around. No Lilink. No Æmma.

"Where's Æmma?"

"I don't know. She was gone when I woke up. I was too busy looking for Lilink to wonder where she went."

"We have to get your father!"

She scurried into her room and reemerged a few moments later with Inco and Gail behind her. They all wore the same clothes they'd worn the day before.

"Where's Æmma?" Inco asked, his eyes still puffy and tired.

"She's gone," Joss answered. "If she has my baby, so help me—"

Gail was as alert as if it were midday. She checked all the places Jak and Joss had already checked. Inco had awoken enough to appreciate the seriousness of the situation and tried to calm his wives and devise a plan.

"We'll go to Gabrinoke and get as many people searching as we can," he said to Jak. "Tell Gray and Chance to get out there now. I want you, Mikey, and Raisin to search the yard and campsite, but stay close. Make sure to check back here frequently in case she comes back."

"But—" Jak paused, his hand subconsciously reaching for the pull sensation in his chest. He caught himself wanting to tell his parents about the pull and run out and rescue Lilink, but exposing her gift would also mean bringing her back home to a life of restrictions and sheltering. However, if he let the parents leave for Gabrinoke, he could find Lilink before the searchers and keep the pull a secret for a little longer.

Inco glanced at Jak's hand covering his Qi. "What is it, Son. Can you feel her emotions?"

"No." Jak dropped his hands into his pockets. "She's too far."

Inco patted Jak's shoulder, visibly straining to keep a strong face. "Don't worry, Jak. We'll find her."

Jak nodded and watched his parents rush out the door. The sun teased the horizon, throwing a fine mist of red hues over the dark sky.

"We're right behind you," Gray called from the hallway. He and Chance ran out the door, leaving it wide open as they rushed to catch up.

"Missing?" Mikey asked from the hallway.

"I know where she is… I mean, not exactly, but I know which way to go," Jak said, holding his hand over his chest as the pull reached an overwhelming strength. Raisin strutted past him toward the front door.

"Well, what're we waiting for? Let's go."

"Pa wants us to stay close to the house," Jak said.

"Yeah? Well, your Pa ain't here." Raisin looked to Jak. "Your call, Mr. Boss Man. What're we doing? Hanging out here or finding Li?"

Jak hesitated only a second before he dropped his hand for Raisin to climb up.

"Let's go."

Raisin stood on his shoulder, and Mikey followed behind. They went out of the house, across the yard, and into the forest, following the pull. Matilda met them outside of her burrow.

"What is going on? What is wrong?"

"I can feel her," Jak answered without slowing down.

Matilda tilted her head and watched them continue without her, then returned to her burrow.

Mikey ran a few paces to catch up to Jak. "Where are we going?"

"I don't know. I'm just following Lilink's pull."

Raisin humphed. "You get that too, huh?"

Jak glanced at him. "What do you mean?"

"That's what I feel when you're mad or threatened."

"Really? Why have you never mentioned it?"

"I never thought much of it."

Mikey shook his head. "Man, y'all got some weird voodoo shit goin' on! I hope it helps."

CHAPTER 46

Gail, Joss, and Inco walked between the homes of Gabrinoke, yelling *"Emergency"* at the top of their lungs. People rushed out and gathered to hear what was going on.

"Have you seen Lilink? Did she come here?" Gail asked Eleanor.

"No. I haven't seen her since you had her here yesterday. Is she missing?"

"Everyone," Inco stepped out in front of the crowd and yelled. "Our daughter, Lilink, is missing. She may be with a woman."

"The one we saw with Jak yesterday?" someone yelled from the crowd.

"Yes. Her name is Æmma. She's also missing. We may find them together, or we may not. If we could form a line at the trees and begin sweeping the forest, we may find them before they wander too far."

Everyone ran back to their homes for proper shoes and lanterns before rushing to the tree line. Once everyone formed a line, they walked slowly into the trees while calling out Lilink's name.

"Gray," Inco called out. "I need you to search the edges of the path. Make sure she didn't come toward Gabrinoke and wander off the trail or hide along the way. I'm going to check Zebulan's house. It's the only other place Æmma knows."

Inco took dragon form and shot over the trees.

***

Gray searched the path back to the house, focusing on the edges where the shrubbery was big enough for Lilink to hide. He reached the house before the search party and found Matilda in the yard.

"Hey, have you seen Lilink?" he called out to her.

"No. I am about to catch up with Jak. He knows where she is."

"What? He left?"

"Yes. I would be with him, but it is difficult finding an intelligible babysitter in the middle of the forest."

"Didn't you wean them two weeks ago?"

"Yes, but the biggest one, he is special. I needed someone to watch over him in case I am gone more than a few hours. Are you coming?"

"Where?"

"Follow me. I will follow his signal."

"Jak has a signal?"

"When he has powerful emotions, I feel it. I follow the feeling, and it leads me to him. If you intend to come, come now."

She ran into the forest. Gray ran after her. They caught up to Jak as he approached the back of a house.

"Inco told you to stay near the house," Gray scolded.

"Shh," Jak hissed. "She's in here. I can hear someone."

He peeked around the corner of the house. Inco looked over his shoulder, and Jak jerked himself back out of view.

"It's Pa."

Gray peeked just in time to see Inco fly off in dragon form. "He's gone. Why do you think she's here? Where are we?"

"I don't know. I just feel her. She's here," Jak whispered.

He peeked again and crept around to the front of the house. It was shut but not locked. Jak walked in without a second thought. Mikey and Gray hesitated.

"Wait, we don't know whose house this is," Mikey whispered.

"We can't just walk in there," Gray added.

Jak ignored them and continued with Raisin on his shoulder and Matilda at his side. Gray and Mikey looked around and hurried in to join Jak.

The house was eerily quiet. Curtains draped over all the windows, producing pinhole beams scattered through dim lighting, illuminating tiny fibers floating through the stale air. The angle at which the light hit the mantelshelf threw enormous shadows of the miniature animals onto the walls. A slight breeze fluttered the shade, causing light to shift. The animal shadows appeared to come to life.

"Why am I suddenly in the mood for a Scooby Snack?" Mikey whispered.

Everyone ignored him and crept to the back of the house. Jak opened a heavy wooden door that led to a dark descending staircase.

"Make that *two* Scooby Snacks," Mikey whispered again.

As Jak stepped onto the first step, the ground shook. He leaned back and sat in the doorway to avoid falling. The tremors grew to a roar beneath them. Things fell off shelves in other rooms. A loud, scraping noise came from the cellar.

The tremors hadn't stopped, but Jak descended the shaky steps, anyway.

"Jak, wait," Gray yelled.

Jak didn't hear him over the bellowing rumbles. He wouldn't have stopped, anyway. The pull from Lilink became frantic, and he could feel her other emotions. She was nearby and scared of something.

Jak reached the bottom step at the same time the tremors stopped. He stepped from the dim light that fluttered down the staircase but failed to light up the room. His eyes gave off a pale-yellow glow as his night vision took over. He realized that Lilink's pull had vanished with the last vibration of the tremors, but he could smell her scent in the room. She had freshly bathed, and Joss had moisturized her skin with lavender and aloe before she climbed into bed. She always smelled of it at night, and the smell was powerfully present in the darkness. Another fainter aroma caught his attention. He followed it to a candle. The wax was still hot and soft, and a spiral of smoke trickled from the wick.

Gray reached the bottom step. "Find anything?"

"No. But she was just here. I can smell her."

As abruptly as it had ended, the pull returned.

"I feel her again." He turned in the darkness and stepped toward the pull. "She's farther away."

Gray rubbed his brow. "How could she have been here and then suddenly be somewhere else?"

"The tremors—"

"But there are no portals in this area."

"There're no portals in Gabrinoke either, and yet over a hundred people appeared there."

"I don't know, Jak. It seems a little far-fetched to me."

"Then go home. I know what I feel, and I'm going to get my sister." Jak sidestepped past Gray and headed back up the stairs.

Mikey and Matilda met Jak at the top of the stairs. Gray followed, and the group went back out the front door.

"Jak," Gray called out.

Jak looked back, his expression cold and forbidding. Gray mirrored the expression at first, but then he closed his eyes and shifted to a softer tone.

"I just don't understand what this thing is that you're following."

"When I camped out for my DúKrue, Lilink missed me. This is what I felt. It comes from her."

"And I feel it when Jak is angry or in danger," Matilda added.

"Same here," Raisin said from within Jak's collar pocket.

Jak patted his Qi. "If I follow this feeling, I'll find her. I have to go, with or without you."

"Very well, little brother," Gray sighed. "But let's fly. It'll be faster. Just steer the way."

He took dragon form and crouched down. He knew Jak hated flying but also knew Jak couldn't argue the logic.

"Whoa, wait." Matilda stepped back. "Honey badgers do not fly."

"Hang on." Mikey ran into the house and returned with a large black satchel. He opened it and knelt next to Matilda. "You won't even know we're flying."

"That's not ours," Gray scolded.

"Yeah, well, the dude can have it back when we're done. I don't think he'll miss it," Mikey muttered.

"You want me to ride in a bag?"

Mikey humphed with a smirk. "You do sleep in a hole in the ground. This'll be just as dark and probably more comfortable."

"You have a point." Matilda let out a heavy sigh and climbed into the bag. Mikey climbed onto Gray's back behind Jak.

"I ain't used to ridin' bitch," Mikey jested.

"But… you *are* a bitch," Raisin joked back.

"Shut up, dingleberry!"

"After you, ass munch!"

Jak took hold of the lower bone spikes behind Gray's head as they rose into the sky. He steered his brother along until Gray took over and ducked into a clearing in the forest.

CHAPTER 47

Inco arrived at Zebulan's house to find the front door ajar. He knocked, causing the door to creep open a bit farther. He could see inside, but not very well. Zebulan was an exceptionally awkward person, and the idea of getting caught creeping through his house sent chills up Inco's spine. He knocked harder, opening the door almost all the way. The lighting was dim, but it appeared no one was home.

"Hello?" he called out. "Zebulan?"

There was no answer. The house was quiet and dark.

"Dammit!"

He pulled the door shut. He knew what he had to do next. It would likely result in him being removed from the council and possibly fined, or worse. He needed to go to Procerus and report Lilink missing, but that meant also declaring that she existed. All intelligible Origins were mandated to report to the census. Inco's family didn't know how to do this. Lilink was the daughter of a migma. They couldn't let that be known, nor could they claim her to be Joss's natural child because of their contrasting features. They had considered registering her as a Roanoke child once they started building a community with them but worried about the repercussions. That would give the Roanoke people claim to Lilink, and there could be penalties for being caught falsifying a census.

Lilink was more important than any consequences that could come. Inco knew it wouldn't be easy, but he set out to do what was necessary to find his daughter alive.

***

Procerus's home was west of the Airland Mountains, a little over halfway to the Airland portal but closer than the council chambers. It was still morning when he arrived. Procerus, dressed in nightclothes and a robe, sipped his morning coffee and read a book. He dropped the book and responded to the knock at his door.

"Inco? It's early for a visit but welcome. Excuse my attire… I'm not yet fully awake." He stepped to the side and welcomed him in. "Would you like some coffee?"

"Uh, no. I'm afraid I don't have time. I'm here to request a JDSR alert."

Procerus's face snapped to full alert as he sipped his coffee. "What? We haven't had a Juvenile Dragon Search & Rescue in all the time I've been head of the council."

He walked to a bookshelf and scanned the bindings. "I'd have to refresh myself on the protocol. What's the child's age, sex, Dú, and where were they last seen?"

"It's my daughter, sir," he blurted.

Procerus's frantic body movements halted, and he turned toward Inco.

"I wasn't aware you had a daughter."

"Yes, well, I do, and she's missing. We need—"

"Is she registered with the census?"

"No." He pursed his lips, anticipating what he'd been dreading.

"How old is she?"

"Five."

"Five days?"

"Five—" Inco hesitated.

"Weeks?"

Inco cleared his throat. "Years."

"I see." Procerus stood tall. His bushy eyebrows rose high on his forehead, and his beard shifted over his hidden facial expression. "And why was this young lady not reported to the census?"

"I was jealous."

Procerus glared. "Jealous? Of what?"

He struggled to fabricate a lie based on truth. "If we registered her, we would've had to put down her actual father's name. He's long deceased. I couldn't bear having another man listed as her father, but I couldn't falsify the census either."

"Instead, you avoided it altogether."

"Yes."

"That's a petty reason to avoid something so important, Inco. I'm surprised at you… but then again, I'm not."

"What do you mean?"

"I've noticed a change in you. You're not the man you were before you found that boy."

"Since Gray had his DúKrue, I've been a single, childless man. I now have two wives and as many children, plus I still play a fatherly role to Gray even in his adult years. That's enough to change any man, I'd wager."

"Yes, but it doesn't explain everything. Instead of requesting a plus-one, or uh, two in your case, you chose not to attend any of the council festivities over the years." Procerus drifted toward him. "You raised a boy from infancy to adulthood, half of that in Salus, but few have ever seen him. Now you have a five-year-old, unregistered daughter."

Their eyes locked as Procerus came to stand close enough for Inco to smell his breath. "What is it you're hiding?"

Contempt flashed in the corners of Inco's eyes. His pupils constricted, and his nostrils flared. He stood silent, clenching his jaw. Anger and anxiety boiled in his gut and compressed his windpipe, causing him to clear his throat in a deep, gravelly tone.

"Well." Procerus's tone abruptly became casual as he moved back toward the bookshelves. "We mustn't dwell on what can be sorted out later. A five-year-old girl missing in the Gabril forest will require immediate action if there's any hope of finding the child ali—" he coughed to interrupt his own poor choice of words. "Safe," he concluded as he pulled a reference book from the shelf and tucked it under his arm.

"Thank you," Inco strained to remain polite. He still felt cornered but tried to focus on Lilink. He took out his wallet and removed a small piece of paper. On one side, the date 9/27/5782 was written across the bottom. On the front was a pencil sketch of Lilink. It had great detail and was a perfect image of her. "Brown hair, blue eyes, average weight, and height."

Procerus took the drawing and gazed at it. "Any birthmarks or scars?"

Inco hesitated with a slow blink. "No, just a few freckles."

"Very well. Perhaps a troll can duplicate this quickly since it's small. I'll have it sent to the other council members, except Misty and Roe. I still think it's best to keep him away from the search."

"Chance is helping us search. I stopped at a few council houses on the way here. Zebulan wasn't home. And why's Misty not being included?"

"The plague has come to Origo, I'm afraid. She may not make it."

"The plague? From Earth in the five-forties?"

"Yes. These portals have been bringing more than just newcomers. We now have flying bugs that glow green at night. They've spread throughout the Grayson and Airland lowlands by the mountains. We've swarms of locust in Clayton. A ship appeared in the Misbaden Ocean, leaking black oil into the waters. The Justinian Plague has spread throughout Hazu, Steam Joint, and lower Faye."

"This is terrible."

"It hasn't just been bad for us. Earth has suffered quite the impact as well. These portals have caused an earthquake and fire in Antioch in 526 that didn't happen in its original history, and one in Beirut 551. It's caused hundreds of minor earthquakes in Constantinople, with a significant one in 557. A tsunami at Lake Geneva in 563, and the return of the Justinian plague to Earth every few years when it had been vanquished after the first wave. The Western Roman Empire even reappeared, then disappeared again."

"My daughter," Inco muttered.

"Right. On my way. You get back to the search." His tone deepened, and he gave a stern gaze. "We'll have a talk after she's found."

"There's one more thing," Inco said. "Zebulan retrieved Æmma, Jak's mother, from the portal yesterday. He brought her to us just last night. She's also missing."

"Just one thing after another, isn't it?" He stared at Inco, who stared at his feet. "Very well, what are her features?"

"Light brown hair, blue eyes, pale skin." Inco took a deep breath, still staring down.

"Dismissed," Procerus grumbled.

Inco left without another word. He didn't want to think about what lay ahead with the council. Instead, he took relief in knowing that hundreds of dragons and kindreds would join the search. As soon as he was a few paces away from the doorway, he took dragon form and shot into the sky toward home.

CHAPTER 48

Jak and Mikey jumped off Gray's back. He took his Dú and approached a house at the edge of the clearing.

Jak looked around. "Why'd we stop here?"

"This is Misty's house. If Lilink came through, maybe she'll know something," Gray said over his shoulder. He didn't knock on the front door. Having lived much of his childhood with Misty, the house felt like home, but he hesitated at the threshold given the group he had with him.

"Misty?" He called out. "Misty? Are you home?"

A faint cry came from a distant room inside the home. Gray hurried toward the sound. Jak and Mikey stood just inside the front door and waited.

"Misty?" he called out again.

He went to her room. The door was open, but not enough to see inside.

"Misty?" He whispered as he pushed the door open.

Misty lay in her bed, shielding her face from something Gray couldn't see. Her legs moved like a swimming frog under the blankets.

"No," she moaned.

"Mama Misty, it's me, Gray."

He approached her bedside and put his hand on her arm, lowering it from her face.

"No!" Misty shrieked and sat up, slapping the surrounding air in a frantic effort to ward something off.

Gray caught her flailing arms and held them still.

"Misty!"

"Gray?" her weak, elderly voice trembled as she opened her eyes a sliver. "What're you doing here?"

"We're looking for a little girl. She's missing and might've come past here."

"There are no little girls here, baby," she said.

Her arms felt hot in Gray's hands. He looked at them as he let go, noticing that her fingers were black and swollen. Her arms were puffier than usual and didn't rest flat at her sides. She held them out over bulky swelling in her armpits. Her ears also stuck out because of swelling.

"You're ill," Gray said, half talking to her, half talking to himself.

"Yes, baby. Move back, so you don't catch it."

"What is it?"

"The Justinian Plague, from Earth. A man from Ankara in 542 came through a portal and infected several people in Hazu. It spread to Steam Joint and southern Faye. Many are dying."

"What can I do?"

"I'm so thirsty," she complained, rubbing her neck.

Gray pulled back the blankets to help her up. Her legs rested in a frog position because of swelling between them. Her feet were black to the ankles, and several toenails had fallen off. Gray pulled the blankets back to her waist and helped her lay back down.

"I'll get you some tea," he said, then rushed back to the front of the house.

"Jak, come to the kitchen."

As he waited for Jak, he pulled a kettle from a cabinet and filled it with water from a covered jug. He then shoved several dried tea leaves in a silver tea ball and hung it in the kettle. Jak arrived as Gray lit the wood stove and placed the kettle on top.

"I need a few drops of your xenum," he said over his shoulder.

Jak put his hand over his Qi. "Why?"

"Misty's horribly sick. If we don't do something, she'll die."

"We have to go. Lilink needs me."

"I know, and we will, but Misty—she's my mother. We can't just let her die."

"I didn't say I wouldn't help her. We just need to hurry."

Jak pulled his Qi off and squeezed three drops of his black xenum into the swirls of tea.

"That should be more than enough."

Gray poured the tea into a cup. It was a beige color, but to get a good strong tea, it would have to boil longer, then he'd have to wait for it to cool. This way, she could take a drink right away. He added a spoon of sugar, spilling most of it on the floor with his hurried movements. He rushed back to Misty.

"Take a sip," he breathed.

Misty groaned, "Gray? Don't get too close, baby. What're you doing here?"

"I'm making you better. Take a sip."

He sat at the edge of her bed. One hand lifted her head while the other held the cup to her cracked lips. She sipped a bit, then coughed.

"A little more," Gray encouraged, lifting her head higher.

She sipped again, this time taking more and swallowing without coughing. Gray lowered her head back to the pillow, held her hand, and watched.

The blackness faded from her fingers. Her armpits shrank, and her arms rested at her sides. The cracks in her lips disappeared, and she could moisten them with her tongue. While she continued to heal, Gray went back to Jak and Mikey.

"It worked," he beamed.

"Great." Jak clapped a single time. "Now, let's go."

"Hang on." Gray poured three more cups of tea. "We've been exposed. We have to drink, or we could get sick. I've read about this plague, and it's deadly." He handed one cup to Mikey and one to Jak.

"We'll have my Qi with us," Jak said. "We don't need this."

"Humor me." Gray sipped his tea. "Give some to Raisin. Mikey, have Matilda take a few drinks. You never know."

Misty walked into the kitchen. "Never know what?"

Gray spun around to look at her. She was healthy and bright. There were no signs of the illness on her hands or feet or anywhere else. She'd been healed and looked as if she'd never been sick.

"Now, I know I was on death's door. What did you give me?"

"Just tea."

"Do I look like I was born yesterday? Tell me the truth."

"I can't tell you, but there's more here in this kettle." Gray held it high, then set it on a table.

"I'll take a guess it has something to do with that." Misty pointed at Jak's Qi.

He'd left his shirt open when he returned it. He yanked the laces tight to close the gap. Gray lowered his head in dismay.

"I can explain."

"You don't have to. I figured something big was happening. If his black Qi can cure illness, maybe there's more to the prophecy than we know. Who am I to impede destiny?"

"You mean you won't stop us?" Gray smiled.

"No, baby, I will not stop the natural flow of the world, even if I could. Those damned portals do enough of that. I have to report this, though. It's my responsibility as a council member, but I have a few things to do first."

She paced and rambled aloud. "I have to share this tea with the others who are sick. And I haven't cleaned this place in days. I won't be done with that 'til morning. Then I must make myself presentable. That could take some time as well."

"So?"

"You have until noon tomorrow before anyone else knows."

Jak stared at Misty suspiciously. "Why are you helping us?"

"I've known who you are since I first saw you in the cave. Inco covered your chest, but I saw it and noticed that his was missing. It happened once before when I was a child. The boy was only a week old when he was put to rest. They killed that poor innocent child in the name of fear. He never had a chance to do the right thing. You still do, and I have a good feeling about what you might do with that chance. Don't blow it."

"Yes, ma'am." He nodded with sincere respect.

"Go on now, shoo!" She waved at them.

Jak pulled off his Qi and squeezed it, shooting a stream of xenum into the tea.

"That should be enough for half of Salus."

"Thank you, dear. Now go."

CHAPTER 49

Inco arrived at the Gabrinoke village just as the first sweep of searchers returned from the forest. Gail and Joss had several maps out on a table they'd borrowed from the academy. They'd already made several marks on the papers and were organizing the next sweep.

John Sampson approached the table, removed his brown floppy hat, and nodded politely. He'd achieved a normal gait, but it was still evident he favored one leg. He held out a piece of cloth that covered half his palm. It was pale green with a single grey stitch running the length, creating a hem along one side.

"I found this on the jagged splinters of a broken branch, m'lady."

Gail had moved past the incident of John grabbing her arm but still wasn't comfortable enough to take it from his hand.

"Wally," Joss whispered.

Inco came to stand between his wives as John set the piece of cloth on the table.

"Who is Wally?"

"That's what she calls her blanket," Joss said, offering a stick of charcoal. "Can you show us on the map where you found it?"

John took it and leaned in to study the map. After a few moments, he made a mark. Inco leaned closer to examine the area. The mark was right next to the small clearing where Zebulan's house sat. Inco pushed to map a little closer to John.

"Can you draw a line with your approximate route?"

He made a light charcoal line that ran a finger-width away from the dot, then curved back and ran over the mark as it continued back to the village. The mark was the closest he'd gotten to Zebulan's house.

Inco walked around the table in the direction of the forest. "I'll go scour the area."

"I can help. I mean…" John cleared his throat. "I started off on the wrong foot with your wife many years ago. I was a desperate, sick fool, and I'd do anything to make up for it, especially after all you've done for our commu—"

He jumped back as Inco took dragon form.

"Hop on."

"Fly?" his voice quivered.

"I don't have time to wait. Jump on or meet me there."

"Oh. Uhm, uh," John muttered as he nervously grabbed a horn.

Inco lowered a little more as John pulled himself up. He grabbed the middle horns, then bottoms, and then tried wrapping his arms around Inco's neck. As he went back to repeat the process, Inco stood.

"Grab the lower horns. Here we go."

John did as he was told. He tucked his head, closed his eyes, and held on as tight as he could. As Inco coasted at a casual speed, he peeked and realized it wasn't as frightening as he'd thought it would be. He looked around, smiling, and then they landed at Zebulan's house.

"That was incredible," he said as his feet met the solid ground.

"You handled it better than most first-timers." Inco stepped back, took Dú form, and then gestured for John to follow as he headed toward the house.

The door creaked as he pushed it open and stepped into the brighter but still empty house. He and John wandered to the furthest room, where they found the cellar door ajar.

"Keep watch," he whispered to John as he stepped down.

He descended the staircase, which was lit by a beam of light coming from a nearby window. The rest of the cellar was in complete darkness. His eyes shifted to night vision as he scanned the area, finding only a single candle on the ground. He picked it up and inspected it closer. He could see nothing significant, just a cold yellow candlestick, so he tossed it to the ground and went back to the main floor where John waited.

"Whose house is this?" John asked.

"A fellow council member. He brought the woman you saw with Jak to our house yesterday. She's missing with our daughter. I thought they might've come here."

"We should look around outside as well," John suggested.

"Agreed."

He slipped past John to lead the way. Outside, he noticed marks in the dirt nearby. They were dragon prints, but they weren't his. If they were Zebulan's, they would have been bigger. These prints were average, the size of Gray's. He stepped out and examined them closer, noting the other smaller prints around them. He recognized Mikey's shoe print and the edge of Jak's. A honey badger had made a pair of animal prints between them.

"Dammit!"

John took long strides to get to Inco. "What's wrong?"

"Jak was here. And Gray." He pivoted, putting his hand on John's shoulder. "Here's the plan, I'll fly home and walk back this way. You walk toward my home. Do you know which way that is?"

"Yes."

"Good. I'll meet you somewhere near the middle. Just keep going until you see me."

"All right."

Inco walked away but spun back mid-stride. It had just caught up with his racing thoughts that John had mentioned a negative interaction with one of his wives.

"Are you the one who grabbed my wife's arm?"

"I… uh…" he stammered.

"Redemption builds honor upon error." Inco gave him a wry smile, then took dragon form and soared over the trees.

CHAPTER 50

"Where do we go now?" Jak asked as he climbed onto Gray's back.

"Home. We need supplies, and we have to warn Inco. When Misty reports—"

"I don't get it," Mikey complained. "She says she won't interfere with destiny but still has to report us? What's this got to do with destiny? I thought we squashed the whole prophecy thing."

"She's a spiritual woman, but she also made an elven oath to the council. It can get complicated for her." Gray said. "And *we* know the prophecy is irrelevant, but others won't at first. They'll react with fear and ignorance; the most dangerous combination there is."

He rose into the sky with everyone on his back and flew home. As they arrived, Inco already stood in the yard, his fists on his hips.

"I told you to stay close to the house," he bellowed at Jak.

"Let me explain," Jak shouted back, ignoring his father's posture as he approached. "I can feel her. I don't know where she is, but I know which way. I didn't tell you because I thought you might overreact and try to hide her from the world as you did me." He held a hand to his chest and lowered his tone. "I'm sorry, Pa. I have to go, but not just to find Lilink. I have to leave to save the rest of you."

"What are you talking about?"

Mikey, Raisin, and Matilda stood by but didn't dare comment. Gray approached at Jak's side, his mouth a grim line, his eyes somber.

"We just came from Misty's."

"Misty? I thought she had the plague. Have you been near her?"

"I put Jak's xenum in her tea, and she figured it out. She's giving us a head start, but the council will know about Jak by noon tomorrow."

Normally Inco would have reacted angrily, but this was too big for anger. He'd always known a time would come when Jak's secret would be exposed. His anger was based on denial, but Jak's secret could no longer be denied. He stared into space as he strained to maintain composure. The muscles in his forehead contorted, and his eyes burned with welling tears. His lips pursed to hold his emotion back. He couldn't. He put one hand over his mouth while shaking his head.

"It was always going to come to this," he whispered.

Gray's face mirrored Inco's as his own emotions surfaced. He nodded his head in agreement, unable to think of a response.

"Pa, I'm a man," Jak cut in. "You did your job. My fate's what I make it, but Lilink needs us. Whatever happens to me, I must find her first."

"I know, son. I know."

His father's quick agreement surprised Jak. He watched as Inco embraced Gray, then leaned back and looked him in the eye.

"Take care of your brother."

"I will, Father."

Gray had never called Inco by anything but his name. Inco strained a sad smile and sighed. Pride and joy wrapped the pain in his heart. He turned to Jak, who watched silently.

"My boy."

"Pa, I have to go." Tears filled Jak's eyes as his emotions combined with Inco's.

"Jak, son, I'm so proud of you. You've become a finer man than I ever could have hoped. Whatever happens, I trust you to handle it."

Jak couldn't respond without losing his composure. He embraced his father, the side of his face pressing against Inco's chest, just over his heart. He could hear it race, calm, and then race again. Inco kissed his head as they parted to look at each other one more time. Jak wasn't usually formal, but he decided to follow Gray's example.

"Thank you, Father."

Jak and Gray both wiped their faces on their sleeves as they headed into the house to gather supplies. Inco packed food into an old satchel. Jak grabbed his and Gray's camping packs. He packed his sling and a few smooth stones, then grabbed a green drawstring Qi pouch that perfectly covered his Qi for extra disguise. Once broken in, he could tighten it around his Qi without removing it, making it look like he was wearing a coin-sack on his neck, but this one was new and not broken in—it could come in handy.

Raisin grabbed his own little satchel Lilink made him during her sewing lessons. He paused and stared at it, running his gravelly thumb over the crossing stitch lines that formed an uneven star on the fabric. He flipped over the flap of the satchel to admire the R stitched onto it. The round top of the letter was tiny, and the legs were long, but it was still recognizable.

"We'll find her," Jak said.

"I know." Raisin sniffled.

He grabbed a tiny sling he used for practice and handed Jak the larger one he used when he absorbed stones and became large. Jak added it to his satchel and went into Lilink's room. He stared at her bed for a moment, imagining her reaction to being taken from her bed. He wondered if she woke right away or after being outside. The previous night had gotten brisk with late autumn chills, and it didn't look like any blankets were missing from her room other than Wally. He grabbed an extra set of clothes from her dresser and put them in his satchel. He then pulled a blanket from her bed and shoved it into the folds of his sleep sack attached to his camping pack.

Everyone gathered outside again. They each had a full satchel and a backpack. There were plenty of camping supplies between Gray and Jak's camp packs, so Inco just hung an extra sleep sack from Mikey's backpack, then went into the house and came back with four swords in sheaths.

"These two have been in my family for generations."

He handed two swords to Jak. Their handles were the length the blades should be, and the blades were the length of average handles.

"What're these?"

"It's a scindo."

"I've never used one."

Inco handed the other two swords to Gray and Mikey, then came back to Jak. He lined the swords up with the handles end-to-end, and twisted, then held out a bo, perfectly balanced on the ridge of his hand, shiny short blades glistening at each end.

"Remember your training with the bo and escrima? You're more prepared than you know."

Jak admired his new weapon with awe, then grabbed the center handle and twisted it apart, swinging each sword with the swivel of his wrists.

"I fit all the nunchuks in my sleep sack," Gray said. He looked past Mikey and saw something stir in the forest. "Someone's coming."

"It's a searcher," Inco said. "You all go. Go now."

"Who'll stay at the house?" Gray glanced at Jak and back to Inco. "I mean, just in case she wanders home."

Jak felt his brother's doubts just as he had several times since the cellar but tried not to let it bother him.

"I'll have this guy watch the house," Inco said.

"Pa—"

"Jak, never forget what I taught you. We all have darkness in us."

"It's what we do with it that matters," Jak replied, tears running down his cheeks.

"I love you all. Now go before anyone else sees you."

Inco jogged east into the forest. Gray cleared his throat, wiped his face with his sleeve, then walked to the back of the house, headed west.

"She's pulling southwest," Jak protested as he followed.

"We have to go where we won't be seen. If we fly over the city, someone will recognize us and know which way we went."

"It'll take us weeks to walk past the city."

"The treetops are bare here. We'll head west to the evergreens and camp 'til nightfall, then fly low to the trees between Gabril and Gabrinoke until we pass the city. After that, we'll follow your pull, but we have to stay hidden. We'll have Feathergreen shelter as far as Illume Lake. We'll go as far as we can, then take shelter before dawn."

"Very well," Jak agreed. He would follow for now, but once they were clear of populated areas, he intended to take the lead.

***

Gray continued toward the evergreens and pondered what lay ahead. He knew nothing mattered more to Jak than finding Lilink, and while he shared the same desire, it wasn't quite so simple anymore. They weren't just running to save Lilink. They were running to save Jak as well. Eighteen years of guarding his secret, shredded in a single morning.

As Gray reflected on failure, Jak pondered his victory. He had spent his entire life chasing but one prize, the trust of his father. He had finally won it. His childhood was now a thing of the past. As they made their way through the dense forest, a new journey began.

End of Book One

GLOSSARY

(Words, names, and definitions as they are
applied in this book)

- **Ab urbe condita:** Timeline of the Roman calendar.
- **Æ; æ:** Old English phoneme with varied pronunciations, applied in this book to represent a short [a] as in hat, trap, or map.
- **Ætheling:** An Anglo-Saxon who is eligible for kingship.
- **Anno domini:** Timeline of the current calendar.
- **Arsecop:** Manipulation of 16th-century terms, Arse meaning ass, and Cop meaning head.
- **Blood bond:** When blood and xenum are mixed and applied to a wound. The recipient becomes permanently bonded to the dragon donor, with familial type fondness. This does not require a ritual.
- **Blood bind:** When blood and xenum are mixed, ritualistically blessed, and given orally to someone who may or may not have wounds. This binding forces the recipient to be obedient to the donor. Donors and recipients sometimes share some or all of the senses, making them able to see, smell, or feel what the other experiences up to, but not including death. This binding will wear off over time, anywhere between 6 and twenty years, and does not give the recipient any abilities.

¤ **Blood Beget:** When blood and xenum are mixed, ritu-alistically blessed, and applied to a dead or inanimate recipient. The recipient will animate or rise from death and become the dragon donor's Familiar. They will gain at least one, but as many as all of the dragon's abilities. They retain their free will and can argue or disagree with the donor, but when the donor's life or wellness is at stake, the recipient is unwaveringly loyal, even to the point of death. Though Blood Beget requires a ritual, Jak can do it without one.

¤ **Caligo: [kuh-lee-goh]:** The southern half of Origo, which is clouded by volcanic ashes and does not spin. Thought to be an empty, dead wasteland. From the Latin noun meaning darkness, gloom, fog, and the verb meaning to be wrapped in darkness.

¤ **Caliver: [kal'i-vėr]:** A standardized Arquebus long gun introduced in the latter half of the 16th century.

¤ **Chaturanga: [chat-tour-ANG-ah]:** Meaning four limbs, a parent game of Chess but with four sides in-stead of two. The pieces of Chaturanga closely resemble the pieces of chess, but with different names. The Raja is the King, Mantri is the Queen, Ratha is the Rook, Gaja is the Bishop, Ashtav is the Knight, and Bhata is the Pawn.

¤ **Cursed Gift: [kur-sid gift]:** The ability (gift) of empathy accompanied by the inability (curse) to stop feeling the emotions of others.

¤ **Deira: [dey-ruh]:** One of the original kingdoms of the Anglo-Saxon invasion of Britain, established in the sec-ond half of the sixth century.

¤ **Dera Wudu: [dey-ruh woo-doo]:** Woods of the Deirans.

- **Dú: [doo]:** Proper Noun- The form in which a dragon is born and remains until maturity. Once a dragon has had their DúKrue, their birth form becomes their Dú.
- **DúKrue: [doo-kroo]:** noun: First dragon form. This is the first time a dragon takes dragon form, initiating their ability to change back and forth at will. This cannot be predicted or controlled and will spontaneously happen when a dragon's Dú body is fully mature. Timing varies based on Dú, as a DúFeathergreen (tree dragon) may have their DúKrue at 250 years whereas a DúHuman will have theirs at around 17 years of age and a DúFalcon may have theirs as early as one to five years old.
- **Galley: [gal-ee]:** A low, flat ship powered by as many as three rows of oars. One or more sails are usually attached to be used in favorable conditions, though the rows are used more often. Best known as warships, but also used for trades and piracy.
- **Gestation: [je-stey-sh*uh*n]:** Development of an unborn creature before birth or hatching.
- **Intelligible:** Able to understand, learn, and/or respond. Intelligible creatures are generally those who can speak the common tongue. However, creatures who do not speak the common tongue are considered intelligible if they are a kindred with an active dragon representative to translate and represent their needs while also explaining laws and limits in the creature's native language. Kindreds without an active dragon representative are considered unintelligible or partially intelligible and are not held strictly to laws. First offenses are waived, and they are usually paired with a dragon representative afterward.

- **Kindred:** These creatures are not dragons, but there are dragons who are born in their form. A human without dragon heritage is a kindred because there are dragons who take human form. Not all creatures are kindreds.
- **Kuvytsi:** An ancient Ukrainian and Russian version of Pan Pipes.
- **Migma: [mig-m*uh*]:** The result of a female dragon mating with a non-dragon male of their Dú. This creates a Migma, who is mostly the same as a dragon, except they only have xenum in their Qi, the surrounding scales are the same as the rest of their scales, and they cannot produce viable offspring. They are born and have their DúKrue the same as dragons.
- **Magma Heart:** The life-giving magma core of Origo.
- **Origo: [oh-ree-goh]:** Home planet of the dragons and many other creatures.
- **Origin: [awr-i-jin]:** A native or officially registered resident of Origo.
- **Qi: [kee]:** The center scale (or only scale in Migmas) that contains the dragon's xenum and abilities, including the ability to take dragon form at will. Without the Qi, the dragon is stuck in their Dú but maintains their dragon lifespan and any Dú flaws they may have, such as scaly skin or dragon eyes.
- **Qingdom: [kiNGdəm]:** An Origo territory ruled by a Qing. Origo's version of Earth's Kingdom.
- **Qing: [kiNG]:** A dragon ruler of an Origo Qingdom. Origo's version of Earth's King.
- **Rima: [Ree-m *uh*]:** The gap that separates Caligo from Salus. It has a strong wind vortex that will pull in nearby objects and creatures, causing death.

¤ **Salus: [sah-l*oo*s]:** The northern half of Origo, which has clear skies and still spins as it rotates around the sun.

¤ **Scindo: [SHēn-doh]:** A weapon consisting of a long handle with a blade at each end that can be separated into two shorter sticks, much like escrima sticks, each with a short blade at the end.

¤ **Slǣp slǣp, Lȳtla bera, þū eart ġesund mid mē:** Old Anglian lullaby, meaning "Sleep sleep little bear, you are safe with me."

¤ **Tether: [te*th*-er]:** A bond felt by fairies, similar to a blood bond, but without shared attributes or the use of xenum, blood, or any ritual. Onset is involuntary and permanent. If the subject of the bond dies, the tether is broken and can happen again with another subject.

¤ **Teulu: [Tay-lee]:** A Welsh word meaning 'family,' which was also used to describe a group of personal bodyguards and knights that followed individual princes and kings. Teulu men were local men over the age of 14 who considered themselves privileged to be part of the Teulu as opposed to the obligation felt by militias and other military groups. This book implies that the kingdom of Elmet was a Welsh kingdom and the Teulu set out to reclaim lands overtaken by the Angles to become part of the kingdom of Deira.

¤ **Xenum: [zen-*uh*m]** A healing liquid from within the Qi, as well as the surrounding scales of purebred dragons. Highly sought after by humans for its age-freezing, nutritive, and healing abilities. Deadly to recipients of the opposite sex. May cause xenum sleep if given after the recipient loses consciousness unless the recipient is being given his own xenum.

- **Xenum Coma:** Sometimes called xenum sleep, xenum coma is when xenum is given to an unconscious non-dragon, and their body lays in an unresponsive sleep until the xenum wears off. The xenum usually nourishes the recipient until they wake, but in some cases, it will wear off before the recipient wakes, and they will require more xenum to avoid starving. This can create a loop, as more xenum can also prolong the coma.
- **Xenum Poisoning:** When xenum is given to a recipient of the opposite sex who is not a biological offspring. Whether given orally or absorbed, the recipient will slowly become ill as the xenum flows through their blood, and will lead to death. The only cure for xenum poisoning is elemental xenum, or xenum from an elemental dragon, which has not been in known existence since the Rima was formed. The speed at which the recipient dies is dependent on how much xenum was given but doesn't normally take longer than a month.
- **Xenum Sleep:** When xenum is given to a recipient after they lose consciousness, and their body sleeps to heal. If the recipient is not a dragon, this can last years to decades and is called xenum coma.

ACKNOWLEDGMENTS

First, I would like to thank my seven children.
You made it real.

Jim, thank you for the infinite support.
You made it possible.

Holly Wingren, thank you for your help with
early developmental stages.

L. A. Stephenson, thank you for the fabulous revisions

Tim Eagling, thank you for letting me pick
your historical brain.

Jason Carnes, thank you for your
developmental support.

And to all my beta readers, I am forever grateful.

I would also like to thank all the artists and performers of
the 20th-century movies and music referenced throughout
this book & series. Your talents are legendary.

Printed in Great Britain
by Amazon